# QUINTANA MCCONNELL

# Where Light Stays

# Gilded Horizon Books

https://gildedhorizonbooks.com

# Beneath Whiskey Waves

**BOOK TWO**

*For anyone whose default superpower is invisibility*

*and those who mourn things they've never had:*

*May you find your happily ever after when you least expect it.*

In the end,
we all
just want
someone
who feels
like home
in a world
of strangers.

— Anonymous

# Prologue

## May 2004

The barn light flickered again.

Fletcher stayed still beneath the rafters, perched on the edge of the hayloft where the breeze slipped through the slats and smelled like dust, oil, and the faint scent of something sweet—molasses maybe. A crumpled paperback rested in his lap, dog-eared and sun-soft. The spine was cracked down the middle, the cover curled like it had lost its will to stay sharp. *Huckleberry Finn.*

But he wasn't reading anymore.

He was counting.

Not numbers—he never did that the way his classmates did, crisp and simple—but things. Details. Things that didn't go away, even if he wished they would. The moth-eaten holes in his shirt that he got bullied for at school. The way his mother's voice pitched when she talked to his father, like it was choosing between fight or retreat. The way he felt when he walked into the room and they didn't even look up.

Twelve years old and already good at disappearing.

A horse kicked softly in the stall below, unsettling the quiet. Fletcher didn't flinch. He liked reading and thinking. They didn't ask him to be loud. Books and thoughts could sit all around you in complete silence. It was what made no one suspect him of much, other than being dumb or mute. But things were blooming inside him, regardless of what boys like Billy Nelson thought.

Shearvale didn't bloom much. Not unless you counted soybean fields or the dandelions that got flattened by tractors.

"Fletcher!" someone called from outside. His father. Sharp, impatient.

He didn't answer.

The sunlight sliced through the barn slats, catching the edge of a pair of cracked work boots Fletcher hadn't grown into yet.

He'd tried wearing them last week. Lasted twenty-seven minutes before his heels blistered and he gave up.

Down below, the feed bins clattered. A door slammed.

Fletcher closed the book and stared at his knuckles. Dirt embedded under the nails. A scab across the top of his left hand where he'd scratched too hard last night thinking about the way the class had laughed when he answered that he wanted to be an archeologist during career day.

"C'mon now. Boys like you just…aren't cut out for jobs like that," Mr. Larkin had said. "Maybe a mechanic, or a trash man… or a farmer? That'd suit you."

Fletcher had pretended not to care.

He slid the paperback under a stack of burlap sacks near the wall. It wasn't safe to leave things out in the open—books got mistaken for clutter, or kindling.

Climbing down the loft ladder, Fletcher moved like someone practiced in disappearing. His feet found familiar rungs, each scuffed from years of other bodies climbing up to grab tools or hide from the rain. At the bottom, he paused.

A pitchfork rested against the stall gate. He lifted it, not because he needed to—just to move, to look busy. His father didn't like when people stood still.

In the back pocket of his jeans, pressed between a gum wrapper and a grocery receipt, was a slip of paper he'd torn from the end pages of a library discard. A quote, circled in fading pencil:

"Life can only be understood backwards; but it must be lived forwards."

# 1

# Gracie

Waiting for the snowdrops to peek through the frost-covered ground felt like a lifetime stretched thin. Gracie walked gingerly, examining the frozen topsoil and sleeping blades of grass, just as her mother had taught her as a child.

The ache of grief slipped past the warm wool of her buttoned-up coat, leaving an icy grip on her heart. Seven years she had been trying to grasp the concept of existing without living. Of needing connection yet feeling better off alone. Of life without Mam.

Pushing the thoughts away, she raised her eyes to the stone croft house that stood in the distance. Its limewashed outer shell and the smoke rising from the chimney soothed her as she exhaled deeply. Getting away from the city had its benefits and revisiting her childhood home was something she didn't do often enough.

The gardens here had always felt sacred to Gracie, a quiet sanctuary nestled within the vast embrace of the glen. Little white clouds rose from her lips as she headed in the direction of the charming home. The air was crisp and cleansing. It reddened her cheeks, and the wind whipped her long scarf around her, tangling it in the strands of her thick, vibrant hair.

Gingerbread red—that's what Da had always called it. The thought warmed her as much as his voice did, rough but kind. Their dependence on one another had increased with the passing of Gracie's mother, Lileas. It was a quiet bond, a shared weight against the sorrow. Though, Gracie knew that she stayed away, in Edinburgh, more than necessary.

*It's normal,* she reassured herself. *Everyone has to fly the coop eventually, don't they?*

Still, the guilt she felt for leaving Da to tend to the small estate alone seemed to linger longer than usual.

The emotions stayed heavy in her chest as she stomped up to the front door, arms full of marsh thistles. Her boots noisily grated against the mat that had long since lost its cheerful welcome.

Swinging the door open, the rustic charm and warmth of the hearth embraced her. Met with the earthy scent of peat from the fire and the soft ticking of the mantelpiece clock, she instinctively removed her layers and began to prepare the thistle to be hung for drying from the wooden beams of the ceiling. Daylight trickled in through small-paned windows and the room was aglow with strategically placed table lamps.

The space was calm and intimate. Functional, and homey. Soft woolen throw blankets were cast over the backs of chairs, and the sturdy pine table, built by Gracie's great-grandfather, served as the ideal workspace for her botanical needs. In fact, she wished she had a table like this one back in the city. Instead, her florist shop was furnished with cold stainless steel and modern finishes.

It had taken two long years of planning and saving money, finding the perfect business partner, and moving away from the Highland home she'd always known to pursue the dream of becoming a florist. In Gracie's estimation a florist didn't just sell flowers. They sold joy, comfort, and love. They were an accomplice to all of life's most important moments, both happy and solemn.

Da hadn't tried to dissuade her from going to Edinburgh, though the glint of loneliness in his eyes was almost enough to make her abandon the plan on her own. He'd hired an estate manager to keep things going and ease the burden on himself. But there was so much about the place that cried out for more attention, more money, and Gracie felt it crumble a bit more each time she came back to check on things.

She always tried to make sure and invite Da to come and see her. Offered to take him out and buy him a fancy cuppa or a new wax jacket, her treat. But he would always just smile and shake his head, saying he didn't belong in the big city.

After those conversations, Gracie always left wondering, *Do I?*

Nevertheless, tomorrow she would be headed back to her flat, the familiarity of her own bed, and to more orders for floral arrangements that would need to be fulfilled. Life continued its relentless march, indifferent to Gracie Buchanan. It was the only way she didn't lose herself in the otherwise solitary life she'd made.

In a city of over 500,000 people, she felt sure that she was the most isolated thirty-year-old woman amongst them.

She brooded over this as she carefully washed the sharp pruning shears she'd used to trim the thistles in the large farmhouse sink and nursed the minute cuts she had on her fingers from the thorny stems. Then she gathered the snipped blooms into small bundles of eight, tying them with twine near the base. Carefully, she finished by hanging each group upside down from evenly spaced nails in the beam over the table. The way her mother had done with various plants and herbs in her severed life.

As the last bundle found its place on the beam, she stepped back to admire her work. The dangling thistles leaves swayed gently in the draft, casting soft, spindly shadows below. It was a small, quiet act of preservation, not just of the stems but of a memory—of Mam moving through this very room, humming a tune Gracie could no longer fully recall. The ache of remembrance was sharp but fleeting, like the thorn-pricks on her fingers. This house held too many echoes, too much of a life that felt fractured beyond repair.

Suddenly, Da walked in. A towering man with wide shoulders and long, measured steps. His gruff exterior gave way to a teddy bear interior as he took in the sight of Gracie following in her mother's footsteps. Her movements gentle and meticulous.

"Ye've not lost your touch, lass," he said, his voice roughened by years of Highland winds but softened by pride. The corners of his mouth twitched into a faint smile as he stepped further into the room. His gaze lingered on the thistles, then traveled back to Gracie. "Your Mam would've loved to see you here, doin' this."

Gracie's chest tightened at his words, a warmth spreading beneath the ache. She wiped her hands on her skirt and offered a small smile in return, though her eyes stayed fixed on the bundles above.

"It's...it's not much," she murmured, brushing a strand of hair from her cheek. "But it feels right being here. At least for a little while."

"Sure ye can't stay a day or two longer?" Da pressed.

"No, Da. Keira's been holdin' down the shop for me long enough. If I don't get back, she'll think I've gone off."

His lips formed a line, and his bushy brows furrowed at her response. Though Gracie was positive he knew the answer before he had asked. As was the usual custom, she had gathered the cuttings she wanted from the land, managed a bit of time with her father, and would inevitably return to city life and wait for the housekeeper to send her the package of thoroughly dried thistles.

This was the routine. The cycle. The pattern by which they coexisted.

But every time the package arrived at her flat, carefully tied with twine and smelling faintly of the glen, a weight settled in her chest. The thistles dried perfectly, just as they always did, but they came with a reminder—that pieces of home could be sent to her, but she couldn't truly send herself back there. Not entirely.

Gracie poured each of them a cup of tea with milk and sugar. Sliding one across the table to her father, she changed the subject.

"Ye've got a wee lamb out there in the tall grass. Might bring her in before she catches cold. Fair bit of rain we've had this week."

"Ah, ye can take the lass away from the Highlands, but ne'er the Highlands away from the lass," he chuckled.

"Not this one, so long as ye've babes about, anyway. Ne'er could stay out o' that pen after school," she reminded him.

"Ye've got that right. But don't ye go worryin' 'bout the lamb. I'll be sure she gets in 'fore the night's up," he smiled.

Gracie gave a small nod of acknowledgement and quietly sipped the rest of her tea. She had always been an observant child and could often be found hanging around the livestock pens or by the stream, tucking cuckoo flowers behind the ears of the lamb.

She longed for the purity of times such as that. For the long days to eventually melt into evening with a molten sky above. To come home from adventures in the forest with muddy knees and a tear in the skirt of her school uniform. Mam would cluck and pretend to make a fuss, while unsuccessfully hiding a smile as she dabbed at her face with her apron.

Now, in contrast to the freedom of her childhood, she was tied down to adulthood with an iron chain that seemed to clank with every anonymous step she took forward. Regardless, she always painted on the brightest smile and the cheeriest outlook. Exaggerated positivity was Gracie at her peak. And if she couldn't be at her peak, she didn't know what to be.

As she contemplated the few chores that she was determined to see through before getting to sleep early, in anticipation of the long drive back to Edinburgh, she felt a sense of continuity. The intrinsic truth that life goes on regardless of where you plant your two feet… or don't. But a creak in the floorboard, slicing through the silence, as she rocked back on the chair was enough to jar her from her intrusive thoughts.

A thunderous pounding on the front door erupted into the small kitchen as Gracie rose to her feet. Letting out a sigh of exasperation, she shuffled, unhurried, to answer the persistent, muffled calls of a man's voice through the thick wood. Passing by the window, she realized that large lacey snowflakes were falling, but this didn't hasten her steps.

Through the tiny peephole, she recognized the jawline of Daniel Grant. Hair mussed from the wind and his long arm bracing against the door frame, there was no mistaking her ex for someone else. Daniel was the last person she expected to see. She hadn't told anyone she was in town, and given how their relationship had ended, his presence on her doorstep was far from welcome. A tepid annoyance bubbled up inside of her, but she swung the door open wide, in a way that mimicked her forced smile.

"Danny! What are ye doin' here? Ye're the last soul I'd have expected to see on an eve such as this," she managed.

Daniel stepped inside, uninvited, and moved closer to Gracie. So close, in fact, that she could smell the smoke from the wood stove and the combination of tobacco and vanilla from his faded cologne. His dark hazel eyes, though weary, sparkled with affection that she knew hadn't dimmed regardless of the distance between them. Her heart leaped into her throat and she swallowed hard to steady her nerves.

He tilted his head slightly and looked down at her. A small grin played on his lips as the wind whistled behind him; the door left open. As Gracie moved to shut it, he brushed against her shoulder, and she felt his familiar warmth. Nevertheless, she shuddered and muttered about the cold, hoping he wouldn't notice.

"Me Mam said ye were in town, visitin' ye'er Da. Were ye gonna tell me yerself?" he asked, his voice lowering softly. "Or slip off to Edinburgh unnoticed?" he went on, fidgeting with a small parcel in his hands.

"I'm not sure how to take that, Danny. I didn't tell anyone I was back home. How'd ye're Mam know?" Gracie replied warily, though her smile wore on.

Daniel's eyes narrowed slightly, as if weighing her question before answering. Then, as quickly as the tension in his demeanor had come on, he shrugged it off again.

"Eh, ye'er Da met her at the market this mornin'. Said ye're 'round for a bit. I just thought we were friends s'all," he said dishearteningly.

A flicker of guilt and frustration flashed inside of Gracie. Her hackles were up now. This was why she never told anyone when she was making a trip to the homestead. This is why she and Daniel could never work. There had been much need for control in their relationship, on his part. The Grants always needed to know everyone's business and wanted to decide what was best on behalf of the many. Gracie knew Daniel meant well, but the manipulation of his quote about their friendship was enough to involuntarily make her eyes roll back.

Daniel was too focused on continuing to pull at the string on the package he held as he awaited her response to notice her irritation. Of this she was thankful.

"Of course we're friends, Danny. But I've my own life and I've only been here a couple o' days. Between Da an' helpin' out, I've had no time for social calls. Ye know how it is 'round here," she explained, hopeful he would let it end at that.

With that, he looked deep into her eyes, as if drawing up the truth from a well. She couldn't tell if he didn't believe her or didn't want to accept that friends was all they would ever be. After a long moment, he gave a quick nod and held out the wrapped gift to her.

"Mam made ye'er favorite… Dundee cake," he blurted. "Told me I'd better high tail it o'er here and make sure ye had some for the trip back."

Gracie delicately took the package in one hand and placed the other on Daniel's shoulder.

"Tell her thank ye for me. I never could resist ye'er Mam's cookin'. Prob'ly saved our skins the last few years. Lord knows Da would've starved," she said with a chuckle. Then, more seriously, she added, "I know I hurt ye, Danny—leavin' the way I did. But it was so long ago now."

Daniel melted under her touch but didn't move away. Instead, he took a step closer and placed a sweet, knowing peck on her cheek. Then grinned mischievously.

"Don't ye worry 'bout me, Grace Mairi Buchanan. I've got a lot o' life left in me yet. Won't catch me swoonin' like a school girl 'cause ye'er out there somewhere minin' for gold," he said with a wink.

A weight lifted from Gracie's shoulders as she exhaled softly. Worry that Daniel would battle for her to, once again, reciprocate his feelings for her would've done her in. That conversation between the two of them had been had one too many times. And, despite his mother's generosity, Gracie knew that Mrs. Grant was just as disappointed that they weren't married with babies on the way as Daniel was.

Stalling in the entry, Daniel ran his hand over his face and shifted on his feet. But, Gracie, although an ever gracious host, didn't trust herself to ask him to sit down and put on a fresh pot of water for tea. It would all just lead down the same road she traveled three years ago and she couldn't afford setbacks and repercussions right now.

"Well, I should get to packin'. I've gotta head out early t'morrow," she stated, finally breaking their silence.

"Yeah, I get it. Next time, we'll have to catch up. Ye know, what *friends* do," Daniel said teasingly, but there was a hint of sadness in his tone. His shoulders slumped an inch or two more and he turned toward the door. Stopping midway, he put his arm around her and pulled her in for a sideways hug. Then, letting go, and without looking back, he disappeared into the snow.

Gracie, leaning her back against the closed door, bit the inside of her cheek and kicked at the worn stone flooring. The one area of the house that didn't have worn wood planks beneath her feet. It trapped all the cold from the outside and, as she stood reliving the chaotic romance she and Daniel had shared, a shiver ran up her spine.

Staring down at the carefully wrapped Dundee cake, she wanted to cry. To scream. To throw it across the room.

*Why couldn't I be like the other girls?* she thought. *Why couldn't marriage to the boy next door have been enough for me?*

But it wasn't enough.

She slowly peeled back the wrapping from the edge of the cake and tore off a small section, revealing the treasures inside. Plopping the piece into her mouth, the rush of orange, almond, and raisin flooded her mouth the way that memories of Daniel's proposal came back to her mind.

She had wanted to say yes to him, for a few glorious seconds. Then, reality set in. The inevitability of their unhappiness, the regret of letting the charade go on so long, and the bitterness of remorse for the part she'd played in it all.

As the sweetness of the cake dwindled, Gracie collected herself and began to make her way to the barn. She would double check that the lamb she'd seen in the meadow was brought inside, smell its fluffy fur, and hold it close—like she was holding on for the last time. Then, she would go up to her old room and neatly pack her bag for the journey back to Edinburgh.

Saying goodbye to Da was always the toughest part. But, to Gracie, every goodbye was like pruning a cherry tree. It doesn't bloom without first losing some part of itself.

# 2

# Fletcher

"Why Fletcher McCullough…I don't know that I've ever seen you look worse," Tate confessed. His tone was a mix of playfulness and honesty.

"Yeah, yeah, I know. That's only the millionth time you've said it," Fletcher responded, putting his head in his hands. "Cut me some slack, Tate. It's been a rough week."

"Rough or not, mate, you're still a fearsome sight."

Fletcher slumped forward and leaned his weight into the bar top, eyeing the dram before him between the gaps in his fingers.

He wanted to drown the day, the week, the month but, he didn't want to feel the loathing that would come afterward.

The smoky aroma of the whiskey curled upward, teasing him with the promise of oblivion, but the cold press of the bar against his arms kept him tethered to the moment.

Tate rested his hand on his own glass and swirled around the amber liquid inside it. He was nothing if not a friend that kept things blunt. The English blood running through him gave him the frankness of a quill dipped in truth—sharp and unflinching. However, he was never cruel. Fletcher wondered if it was the humor he used to mask his problems or the good nature of his immaturity that kept him high on life.

"C'mon, man. Lighten up. Things aren't that bad. You just focus too much on what's going wrong," Tate jabbed, clapping Fletcher on the back.

Fletcher sighed, exhaling a thousand troubled thoughts all at once.

"If it's so easy, what's your secret?" he asked.

Tate grinned, tipping his glass toward Fletcher as though about to deliver some profound wisdom. "Ah, the secret, my burdened friend, is blissful ignorance and an impeccable talent for dodging responsibilities," he said with a wink.

Fletcher huffed a laugh, low and tired, but it was a laugh nonetheless. Good ole Tate. He had all the whimsy and energy of the young man he was when they'd met at university in Cambridge. His rugby prowess and cricket skills, not to mention his boyish good looks, were enough to woo any girl on campus. The only thing they had had in common back then was their involvement in the school's literary society.

He smiled at the recollection of them side by side at their desks. Fletcher analyzing historical texts and Tate pursuing his secret poetry obsession, had been all the circumstances needed to throw them into an unlikely friendship. They had spent hours in that dimly lit, basement room breathing in the musty smell of damp stone walls; the boy from America becoming a man in England.

Tate was the brother Fletcher never had. Growing up in rural Pennsylvania, an only child on a vast farm, had been lonely. He craved the noise of people as if it were the soundtrack to peace, instead of the rumble of his father's tractor or the distant caw of crows in the cornfield. He would often spend his time poring over books in the hayloft and watching the horizon, wondering if there was anywhere out there where he truly belonged.

The way the evening light was filtering in through the window of the storefront, casting strange shadows on the floor, reminded Fletcher of the way the sun found cracks in the wooden walls of the barn and fell in patterns that he would pretend were the blueprints of ancient cities, waiting to be discovered. But the faint hum of traffic outside and the buzzing conversations of patrons near the entrance were all the reminder he needed that he was no longer twelve, and not at all in Pennsylvania.

"Dude, you'd just have to be me to understand, I guess," he said, turning back to Tate. "The lead to this research project just completely vanished. And Sophia dumping me kind of took me back… I don't know. I just feel like I'm going in circles."

"Nah, mate. You've got it all wrong. That project just turned into a mystery. Where's your inner *Sherlock Holmes*?" Tate grinned, using his best Benedict Cumberbatch impression. "And Sophia dumping you? She did you a favor. We both know that was going nowhere, and fast."

*Was it really that hopeless from the outside in?* Fletcher considered.

He and Sophia had dated for a few months. It was never anything serious. In fact, with his long work hours, they would often go for days without seeing each other. And Fletcher was notorious for not checking his messages. Maybe he came off inattentive, but he knew that wasn't the only thing that sent the relationship south.

A memory of him half-listening to Sophia complain about how he was more focused on his work than on their future during an overpriced dinner came rushing back to him. Fletcher was dedicated to history more than anything else, but didn't everyone have their passions? Sophia was also only twenty-three years old and was pursuing a career in event planning. It wasn't as if they were a complete package from the beginning, and Fletcher guessed he hadn't tried very hard to make it work.

In fact, it wasn't even a surprise that Sophia had broken things off. More of a source of frustration than anything else. Just another thing to deal with; another person's emotions to navigate. Fletcher adored being lost in a city; throngs of people to weave through. But he thrived on never being obligated to speak to them, to fix them, or to worry about them.

"Okay, it was going nowhere," he admitted to Tate. "But I'm just not good at relationships. You know that. I'm too busy and cynical for all that."

"Busy, maybe. Cynical? Definitely. But hopeless? Never. You just need a girl who loves old libraries as much as you do," Tate laughed. "Seriously, though, I'm a bachelor and I'm loving it. Who needs to be tied down at thirty-four anyway?"

Fletcher pushed his drink away, still untouched. It wasn't like him to leave a dram of whiskey alone on a night like this, but maybe there had been too many nights that began and ended the same way. Perhaps he really was spinning around and around, dizzy with the same thing day in and day out.

"Maybe you're right," he said, as he tugged on his coat. "Either way, tomorrow's another day and I have to get back to the grindstone. Feel free to stay and help Alicia lock up though," he added as he tossed a key in Tate's direction.

Stepping outside into the wintry air, he glanced behind him and up at the sign above the door. The Caladonian Cuppa was Fletcher's hobby. Something personal he could clutch onto when work got too foreboding, or he needed a place to unwind. He didn't like trying to detangle his thoughts in his quiet apartment, so the shop served as an escape.

He'd put almost all of his personal savings into starting it up. A coffee and tea shop was the initial vision, but something about that seemed too cliché so he'd added on a small whiskey tasting room with a bar in the back. That section was open in the evenings, for adults only, and it had become a second home to both he and Tate. The warmth of the polished wood and the subtle, yet stylish, armchairs gave it more sophistication than a pub, but it was decidedly less intimate than an upscale cocktail lounge.

His life as a historian was something of a solace. But, even still, he found that owning The Caladonian Cuppa gave him the freedom to develop both his creative side that often got left behind, and the need for company without getting too close. Even standing outside, he could hear the gentle clicking of glasses and the muted laughter of a couple seated in the window.

Without warning, he felt an ache growing inside him. Edinburgh was home. He'd talked Tate into going up there as an experiment. But, when he got offered a full-time position by Historic Environment Scotland, the impulse of living in the city turned into a need. But, that night, even with all of the lamplight and glowing, damp cobblestones ahead, the walk back to his flat felt oppressive.

Five minutes passed. Then ten. And by the time fifteen minutes was up, Fletcher was unlocking his door and patting Chantilly, his silky Irish Setter, on the head. She nosed her way through his pockets as he made his way to the bedroom, searching for treats or leftovers she could sneak away with. But, finding none, she curled up at the foot of the bed and eyed him, as if to say she was displeased.

"Don't look at me like that," Fletcher groaned, spying her expression from the closet. "I don't need two unhappy women on my mind."

Chantilly resorted to biting at her tail and ignoring him, as he finished getting ready for bed. His series of yawns put the late hour on full display, just as the moon was in the cloudless sky. The eerie light filled his uncurtained room. Three years he'd lived at this address and never bothered to put up window dressings. And, now, lying in bed, he could see the face of a man carved into the surface of the moon as clear as when he was a child.

Wind rattled the windows and the rush of a few cars passing by created a lullaby that even the most determined toddler couldn't resist. And so, with the moonlight spilling across his bed, and Chantilly at his feet, Fletcher fell into a deep, dreamless sleep.

# 3

# Conundrum

Driving down the A9 on a Monday morning, Gracie expected to run into steady traffic and road construction. But, on this particular Monday, the flow of cars was light, and the sky was delightfully clear after the previous night's snowfall. The evergreens that flanked each side of the highway looked positively enchanted under the heavy dusting of sparkling flakes. Each one twinkled in the daylight as she passed by.

She'd delayed her departure a couple of hours later than she wanted, but the run-in she'd had with Daniel, Da's concern about the weather, and her own desire to stop in Ballindalloch for a bottle of *Glenlevit 18* made it nearly impossible to resist a third cup of coffee and warming herself in front of the fire for an extra few minutes.

Keira would be thrilled to see the special occasion bottle of whiskey when Gracie returned. They'd likely have a drink together after they closed the shop on Tuesday and, by then, maybe Gracie would have wrapped her mind around the emotions the visit home had stirred up. The scent of Daniel's warmth lingered on her cardigan, and she found it simultaneously rousing and melancholic. A lump formed in her throat and she found herself turning up the radio, singing along, to clear the sensation.

BBC Radio Scotland was playing Adele's *When We Were Young* and, as she belted out the chorus, the atmosphere suddenly felt too hot, the seatbelt too tight, and the looming drive before her seemed too long. She rolled down the window, letting in a blast of frigid air, and slowed down, taking an exit towards Cairngorm National Park. This was the long way back to Edinburgh, but the winding roads and majestic scenery were a needed distraction.

The road signs became fewer and farther between, the hills rose and rolled into the distance, and the puffy clouds were crowded closely in the pale blue sky. The greens and browns of the landscape lasted for a few blissful hours and Gracie's thoughts mellowed in such a relaxing setting. She passed by shallow creek

beds and abandoned homes surrounded by aimless sheep,
bridges into the wilderness, and groves of trees layered with
thick snow. Immersed in the surroundings and accompanied by
a soundtrack of 2015 love songs, Gracie made her way, mile by
mile, closer to the history of a city made new by its inhabitants.
People like her, in pursuit of happiness.

Eventually, the sweeping panorama of the countryside gave way
to more congested roadways and roundabouts, streamlining not
only the traffic itself, but also Gracie's thoughts. She realized, as
she drew ever nearer to her flat on Lauriston Street, that she
wasn't quite ready to spend the rest of the afternoon alone
staring at the four walls and twiddling her thumbs until work
the next morning. For a few minutes she contemplated going
into the shop for a couple of hours and taking the load off
Keira. But she didn't want to look like she was checking up on
her or doubting her abilities.

Pulling into her parking space and turning the key, the engine of
the car became silent. She leaned back on the headrest and
closed her eyes.

*Anywhere but here. Everything but this,* she mused quietly.

Edinburgh was a part of her story now. It was like a tattoo,
immovable. A permanent brand on her soul. It was freeing, in a
way, to feel the obscurity in a city filled with people. To walk

down alleys and paths fraught with tourists without a single person knowing your name. It had its own secret kind of charm. But, other times, it was lonesome.

Today, it felt impersonal, and she needed something to drive that feeling away. She wanted friendly faces and warm hands around giant mugs, and to read a book with the gentle whisper of strangers' gossip enveloping her. Though it was dangerously close to work, Gracie heaved herself out of the driver's seat, ignoring the luggage in the trunk. Then she started in the direction of the aroma of freshly ground coffee beans, tea leaves, and whiskey.

Not ten minutes later, she stumbled over the threshold of The Caledonian Cuppa.

A newer shop in town and one that Gracie had frequented the last few weeks. It was growing on her. Its proximity to both her business, Thistle and Tulip, and her flat, made it extremely convenient and exceedingly tempting. The calm and sense of community that surrounded her there made Edinburgh feel like a small town. Standing amongst the other customers, it was if she'd stepped back in time, hiding behind her mother's skirt as they ordered a pot of tea at Scone and Petal. It always came out piping hot and Gracie, always praised for her good behavior, was given extra cream for her scone.

Initially, she thought about settling with her kettle and tassie at a table facing the window so that she could observe passersby. But ultimately, she nestled into the corner with her back to the street. In doing so, she had a clear view of the quote which hung on the wall opposite her in large scrolling letters.

*"Life can only be understood backwards; but it must be lived forwards."—Søren Kierkegaard*

*Why must we understand anything at all? Can't we all just be blissfully oblivious? Seems so much more romantic,* Gracie contemplated.

"No, girl. You know better," came a voice, a few feet away.

Looking over, she observed a large Irish Setter, appearing to want to play the role of a lap dog. The animal was practically leaping into the lap of a man who was already cramped for space by the large coffee, club sandwich, and laptop that occupied his table. The dog apparently had an affinity for the bacon falling out from between the layers of bread on the man's plate and was eagerly awaiting its affection to be rewarded.

Gracie couldn't help but giggle. She was overcome with amusement at the scene. The man, round tortoise shell glasses sliding down his nose, the dog with its paws planted firmly on his thigh, tongue lolling about, and the tinkling of glass plates being shoved together was meant for a photo.

At the sound of her laugh, though she'd thought it barely audible, the man looked up and caught her gaze. For a moment, the seriousness of his face felt alarming, and Gracie wondered if she had offended him by being entertained at his expense. But ever so briefly, his solemnity shattered into a devastatingly handsome smile.

His hands, which hovered above the keyboard of his computer, now grabbed the dog's legs and, gently, he guided them back down to the floor and smoothed its coat.

"You're an actress," he whispered loudly. "You know exactly what you're doing."

Gracie couldn't seem to tear her eyes away from the sight of this man interacting with his pet. Something about it was captivating and innocent. It reminded her of the many days she'd spent with the lambs as a young girl and all their mischievous ways.

"Sorry if she disturbed you, miss," the man spoke again. This time his words were directed at Gracie, and she felt her cheeks flush. She realized that he was American and that his voice was tender and deep. The blush deepened, though she knew he was only being polite.

"S'alright. The wee thing's adorable and gave me a laugh. What's her name?" she replied.

"Oh, um, her name's Chantilly. But Tilly for short."

"Hm. Lovely to meet ye, Chantilly," Gracie said with a nod toward the dog. Chantilly panted and wagged her tail at the sound of her name.

Coming back to her kettle of tea, she poured herself another cup and added milk, listening to the sound of the man now shuffling papers in the awkward silence that hung between their tables. He hadn't introduced himself, and Gracie didn't want to pry. But something about this man was intriguing. Was it because he was foreign? Or because she had nothing better to do than sit in a coffee shop and stare at a strange man and his dog?

The sound of pages scattering across the floor came next. To the man's obvious dismay, it seemed that whatever he had been working on was now strewn all over the tiled doorway, waiting to be trampled by the next bloke to waltz through. Without hesitation, Gracie knelt beside this curious man and began helping him gather his belongings. She noticed custom letterheads and fancy stationery amongst the lot but was careful not to give the appearance of snooping.

"Thanks," he said as she stood and handed over the pile she'd collected. "I guess I've got butter fingers. Serves me right for thinking I could escape the office early today without consequences."

"Ye'er office should rent ye a mule to lug all this 'round. It's criminal they'd have ye carry such a load."

"It's my own fault. The life of a historian means having a bad back from the binders you collect," he confessed.

"So, ye'er into history? Scottish history?"

"Not much of America is historic in the same way as Europe. Scotland is something special, and not just on paper. Or so I've read," he said with a chuckle.

"I'm not one to brag," she began, "but Scotland is more than just special. It's a phenomenon most folks miss out on."

The man cocked his head to the side and his blue-gray eyes shone behind the lenses of his glasses. He stared at her that way for a beat, and then, as if remembering his manners, shifted the papers to the crook of his arm and stuck his hand out for her to shake.

"I'm Fletcher," he announced. "Fletcher McCullough. And, if you don't mind, I'd love to pick your brain a little more about why Scotland is such a gem. From your perspective."

"I don't know what I've got to offer, but I s'pose that's alright," she replied with a shrug. "My name's Grace Buchanan, by the way. Ev'ryone calls me Gracie."

Fletcher grinned, but it was unreadable. "Gracie…" his words trailed off as the barista called to him from behind the counter.

"Hey, boss. We're outta oatmilk and the shipment says it's gonna take at least a week."

"No worries, Fi. I'll take care of it," Fletcher sighed.

"Boss?" Gracie asked, one eyebrow raised.

"Eh, yeah. I started this place as an outlet. An escape from my real job. Now, it turns out that I just have two jobs."

"So, you're an American, livin' in Scotland, with an Irish dog who has a French name, and a Danish quote on your wall?"

Fletcher held his hands up in surrender. "I'm nothing if not a conundrum."

She let out a stifled snort and threw her head back with glee. It was as if Fletcher didn't know who he was because he wanted to be so many things. But, instead of filling her with distrust, she felt empathy toward his disconnection.

As she meditated on this, Fletcher's phone rang, and he excused himself to answer it. Chantilly, all the while, lay fast asleep under his abandoned chair. By the time he came back, he seemed flustered and annoyed.

"I'm sorry, Gracie. I know we were going to have a chat, but something important has come up regarding a research project I'm working on, and I've got to go."

She glanced over at his uneaten sandwich, then down at her feet. Outside, a drizzle had begun, and Fletcher was already wrestling with the sleeve of his jacket. She hadn't made many friends in the city since she was usually at work or in her apartment, and it looked like today wasn't going to be the day for breaking that pattern.

She flashed a reluctant smile in his direction and grabbed her coat and scarf. "I understand," she managed.

"The best laid plans…" Fletcher replied, shaking his head.

But, before he could finish the sentence, Gracie was vanishing from sight; out the café door and down the street.

# 4

# Hide And Seek

Wobbling on the cobblestones of Larkspur Close, Gracie approached Tuesday morning with a sense of unflinching determination. It was time to get back to work and, from the jumble of texts that Keira had sent over about the projected orders for the week, it was bound to be a busy day.

She could see the rainwater from the previous evening trapped in the grooves between the stone pavers and watched it glisten as the sun battled the clouds for dominance. Carefully observing each crack and crevice to check for any evidence of life; of a bloom or petal signaling that the street was more spellbinding than just its rugged sandstone façades and slate tile roofs.

Larkspur Close had gotten its name from the stubborn larkspur plants that sprouted in the crannies of the sidewalk and road in late summer. When Gracie had first toured potential storefronts in Edinburgh, none of them had stood out, until she walked up to the one on this particular street. The name itself exuded elegance and status, just like the blooms it was named after. Now number eleven, was all her own—provided she paid the rent on time each month.

As she strode up to the expansive windows she took in the clear, modern sans-serif font spelling out the name she'd chosen, Thistle and Tulip, in wide gold lettering. The trim was painted a deep obsidian green, in stark contrast to the light and color splashed inside of the display window with flowers of every shade and variety. There was no doubt about it, it was the prettiest florist shop in Old Town.

Inside, behind the counter, and engulfed by the overall sage interior, Keira buzzed back and forth muttering to herself about where she could've misplaced the maidenhair fern and biting her lip with worry. Gracie laughed, quietly observing before she stepped into her role as the more organized of the two. The first time they'd met was in a ladies restroom, at a festival in Glasgow, where Keira had lost a contact on the floor and was searching for it on her hands and knees. Despite her chaotic ways, though, Keira had always followed through in her end of things with Thistle and Tulip. From the moment she heard about Gracie's grand plans for it, she had been its number one supporter. Gratitude rose inside of Gracie, and she smiled at the fond memories they made building the place from the ground up.

"Keira, what are ye mumblin' on about? Has the world come to an end again?" she asked affectionately.

"I'm lost, Gracie. We got the order of maidenhair fern for the weddin' bouquets, due Saturday…but I've gone an' left them in a daft spot, nae clue where," Keira replied in distress.

"Oh, Keira. Sixty fern stems just gone into a puff o' smoke, eh? I'll go and see what I can find in the back. You prob'ly just laid them aside."

Keira gave a nod and perched on the stool behind the register, looking defeated. But Gracie wasn't gone a minute before the bell above the door jingled, announcing the arrival of a customer. Quickly, Keira pinched her cheeks and smoothed her hair, hoping to give the impression of a put together florist, and not someone who was just having a nervous breakdown over undergrowth.

Standing in the doorway was a man. He was probably six feet tall or more, from Keira's estimation. As he drew nearer and was no longer backlit from the haze from the street, she saw that his hair was the color of copper with a scruffy beard to match. He wore round, tortoise shell glasses but, beyond those, he had eyes that were like the morning fog.

Keira rose from her seat, suspecting that she should ready herself for him to order something for his wife or girlfriend, since, in her experience, most good-looking men were taken.

"How can I help ye?" she asked, trying to sound chipper.

The man scratched at his beard. "Oh, um, I guess I was hoping to find… I mean, is there a Grace Buchanan in today?"

Keira's eyes widened with curiosity. A smile spread across her face. "Gracie!! Someone's here for ye," she hollered to the back room. Then, turning back to the stranger, she added, "It'll just be a moment."

"Well, I found the maidenhair, but good lord, Keira…," Gracie's voice trailed off as she came into the front room and noticed the man waiting in the entry. "Oh, hello again," she said, cheerfully acknowledging him.

Grabbing Gracie's arm, Keira drew her close and whispered into her ear. "There are *obviously* things we need to talk about." Swiveling around again, she directed herself to the man who had given a polite nod as Gracie laid the fern stems on the countertop.

"So, ye know Gracie, eh?"

"Yeah…well, no. I mean… I'm sorry. I'm Fletcher. Gracie and I met yesterday and didn't quite get to finish our conversation," he replied.

Gracie stood on Keira's left, looking intently at Fletcher as she opened her mouth to speak. "How did ye know where to find me?"

Fletcher's cheeks flushed, and he scratched the back of his neck. "The truth?" he asked with a chuckle. "I Googled you. The top hit online was a Grace Buchanan who owned an enchanting florist shop in Old Town. Who knew it'd only be a block away from mine!"

"Oh, so he's a stalker," Keira murmured under her breath.

Lightly, Gracie elbowed her in the side and stepped around the counter, closer to Fletcher. He towered over her five-foot, three-inch frame, shifting on his feet, nervously awaiting her response.

She eyed him skeptically at first, though she was betrayed by the half-grin on her face. It amazed her that someone would take an interest in a woman they'd met only briefly, over a hungry dog and scattered papers, and seek her out. No one had ever really sought to find Gracie, unless you counted Daniel and their absurdly long games of hide-and-seek as children.

"What was it ye came to say? I hope I didn't accidentally trudge off with one of ye'er important papers," she said finally.

"No, no. Nothing like that," Fletcher said, shaking his head. "I was actually curious if we could talk more about Scotland. I'm doing a research paper on the Highland Clearances and communities. I have plenty of data and statistics, but I'm having a hard time bringing it to life. I was wondering if you'd want to give me some pointers."

"Me? Why me?" she asked. Her eyes search Fletcher's face for any hint of insincerity, but she couldn't detect any.

"The way you talked about Scotland yesterday… you said it was a phenomenon most folks miss. That really stuck with me, and I can tell you have a knack for making things feel fresh and new," he replied.

Gracie looked down at her feet, then at Keira, and back to Fletcher. "Ye've kinda caught me in the middle o' everythin'. I'm not sure if—"

"Go, go, go! I've got ye covered. Have a lovely time and tell me everythin' later," Keira interrupted, grabbing the coat Gracie had discarded on her way in and helping her into it.

"Alright, I s'pose. I'm happy to see if I can help," Gracie surrendered. "But I make no promises."

"Fair enough," Fletcher said. Then, peering sideways at Keira and saluting her, he added, "I'll have her home before midnight."

He swung open the door, holding it for Gracie to exit, and then followed her outside into the brisk air. The two of them stood shivering briefly on the sidewalk and Gracie pulled her gloves out of her coat pocket, busying herself with one finger at a time.

"I was thinking we might go up to Calton Hill," Fletcher suggested. "I know it's a bit cold, but I do have a thermos we can fill with tea, if you want."

Gracie adjusted the last of her fingers and looked at him, her brow lifting slightly. "Up Calton Hill, aye? I hope ye're not planning to make me climb Arthur's Seat next."

A smile tugged at Fletcher's lips. "That depends. Would you?"

Gracie laughed lightly and glanced at him with a sparkle in her eye. "Well, I won't say no to tea. Let's go before I change my mind."

Gracie tucked her hands into her coat pockets, falling into step beside Fletcher as they made their way down the cobbled street. The chill in the air bit at her cheeks, but she found herself smiling all the same. She glanced up at Fletcher, his easy stride matching the rhythm of the city around them. Though she wasn't sure what the day might bring, she felt a quiet curiosity take root. For the first time in a long while, Gracie was content to let things unfold as they would.

# 5

# Walking Backwards

She was shiny. Like a new penny, just minted. Her face beamed like the glint of freshly polished copper. That's all Fletcher could think as he and Gracie navigated the narrow, steep paths leading from Victoria Street to Grassmarket and headed in the direction of Calton Hill.

They'd made a quick stop at The Caledonian Cuppa to fill Fletcher's thermos but he feared, that with the fickle weather, all the efforts might have been for nothing.

*Why on earth did I suggest climbing a windy hill in February?* Fletcher thought. *With a woman who's got a mind to wear a dress in these temperatures!*

As if in disbelief, he shook his head noticeably.

"Regrettin' yer decision already, eh?" Gracie cut in.

Many minutes had passed without either of them uttering anything, and Fletcher realized that he'd been lost in thoughts about shiny faces and pennies and the wind blowing the scent of Gracie's hair into his lungs.

"Oh, I guess I was just lost in thought," he replied vaguely.

"Well, if yer gonna take a strange girl up a mountain, ya might as well give 'er a talkin' to on the way."

"A talking to, huh? That's a tall order for a guy like me," he admitted, though holding back.

"And what kind o' guy is that, Mr. McCullough? 'Cause I'm havin' awful trouble tryin' to pin ya down," Gracie teased, with a twinkle in her eyes.

Fletcher let out a low chuckle. "Maybe I'm just a man of mystery, Gracie. I keep folks guessing."

"Likely story," she laughed. "More like a puzzle who's missin' a few pieces."

"And *you* are far too curious for your own good," he said. Though the wrinkles outlining his eyes betrayed his amusement. "Just let me know when you crack the code, will ya? I've got a few previous therapists who'd probably like to give you a call."

Nervously he adjusted the thermos under his arm and pushed his glasses up on the bridge of his nose.

"I'm gonna bet ye'er not draggin' me out here to tell me 'bout yer life, but we'd better come to some sort o' deal or there's no reason I should tell ye 'bout mine. Research paper or not," Gracie said, trying to sound stern. She furrowed her brows and stomped her foot for emphasis.

"How about we start with the research paper itself. Then you'll have more information and can decide if you really want to keep going down this road," he offered. Glancing around, he added, "Figuratively, I mean. Not this exact street."

Gracie giggled, trying to cover it with a gloved hand.

"That'll have to do I s'pose," she decided in the end.

A few moments passed in stoic silence as the unforgiving breeze swirled around them. Fletcher, content in quiet moments, let his mind drift to the way Gracie bit her lip as she studied the lane ahead.

"So, why *is* there a Danish quote on yer wall?" she inquired, unable to tolerate the stillness any longer.

A gentle smirk appeared, and Fletcher briefly scratched his beard.

"Kierkegaard," he said, his voice thoughtful. "It's a good reminder, don't you think? Easy to get caught up trying to make sense of the past, but it doesn't do much good when you're supposed to be moving forward."

He stole a glance at her out of his periphery. The soft crow's feet around his eyes were carved deeper by a sudden frown.

"It's a principle that rings true and it's stuck with me for a long time. Ever since I was a kid, I've always wanted to know what came before—why it mattered."

"That's poetic of ye," Gracie stated. "Ye have a love o' truth, a craving for findin' things out. That's brilliant."

Fletcher, now fidgeting with the collar of his woolen trench coat, let his mouth go crooked and his brows knit together in consideration.

"I suppose if you find human existence itself to be beautiful. But life… history… it's messy." He paused for a beat, letting questions build between them. But just as Gracie opened her mouth to ask if his own past was something he would describe that way, he cut in.

"But we're not here to talk philosophy—I've got enough of that pinned to my walls. Let me tell you about this paper I'm working on and we can go from there."

Over the next fifteen minutes, and through a breathless, brisk pace, Fletcher described the significance of his project regarding the Highlands in eighteenth and nineteenth century Scotland. Specifically, his research had involved the Highland Clearances. A dark time when many were forcibly evicted from their homes and land. Villages were destroyed, forcing families to migrate to other areas—even as far away as the United States or Australia.

Nevertheless, these strong-willed people managed to preserve their traditions, language, and music. They persevered. They survived.

Gracie nodded as the details Fletcher provided descended on her like light rain. She was familiar with the clearances, however, the tone Fletcher used when he recounted the events made it feel as if he had lived through them himself. His voice hummed with quiet gravity, like distant waves crashing against cliffside stone. Not to speak, but to soak in the sound of his enthusiasm.

Just as they reached a bench facing the Dugald Stewart Monument, with the city of Edinburgh splayed out beneath them, Fletcher was finishing up his dissertation on how Stewart, the Scottish philosopher and mathematician, understood history—not just analytically but morally. His admiration of such an approach was clear to Gracie and Fletcher noticed a look of inquisitiveness on her porcelain face. She looked like a doll in the hazy mid-morning light, and he'd started to expect the endless sense of wonder she seemed to possess.

Fletcher's inherent chivalry took over as he proceeded to wipe off the bench with a handkerchief that magically appeared from his pocket and gestured for Gracie to sit down.

"Sorry if I'm boring you," he apologized. "I can get a little carried away sometimes."

"Not at all!" Gracie exclaimed, truthfully. "I'll tell ya, I'm from Glenrinnes. The clearances hit hard up there. My great-great-great Granny and Granda were driven from their home and t'wasn't til later their kids came back to raise a family. Wi' all the heartache…"

Fletcher observed the way her cinnamon spice hair fell in front of her right eye and her lashes fluttered as her words trailed off. She was beyond pretty. Not the kind of pretty you found in *Hood* magazines at the newsstand. The kind that drew you in, and helped you find out something about yourself you never knew before. The type of beauty that made you feel relaxed and seen straight through. Like when she was looking at him, she could see all the way through his rib cage and to his spine.

Daintily she smoothed her skirt and sat where the bench was now dry, blowing into her gloved hands in a vain attempt at warmth. At this altitude, almost three-hundred-fifty feet above the city streets they'd maneuvered to get here, it felt a few degrees more numbing.

Fletcher took a seat on her left and began pouring the tea from his thermos into the tiny cap that doubled as a cup. Suddenly realizing it was the only cup he had, he silently cursed himself for not being more prepared. He was positively frozen but could only imagine how much more so Gracie was, considering the powerful wind now whipping at her legs, which he could see were bare under her the thin material that veiled them.

"Here," he said softly, offering her the cup.

"Oh, I'm alright. Truly. Ye look like yer beard might grow icicles any minute. Go ahead."

"I'm not the kind of guy who can take the only cup of tea when there is a woman, very obviously stammering from the cold weather I dragged her out into, sitting next to me. Please, take the tea, Gracie."

She blinked once and took the cup without argument. Sipping elegantly, she watched the skyline as he watched her. He didn't do it menacingly, but out of genuine interest. Fletcher didn't consider himself an easy conversationalist or to be all that good of company for anyone other than Tate. But, somehow, Gracie made him want to be personable. To be good-natured. Even if it seemed impossible.

"We could share, ya know?" he heard her say.

She was looking at him now. Her peridot eyes eager as she held out the small, plastic lid, still brimming with steaming liquid.

"That's okay… Honestly, I couldn't," Fletcher replied.

"Couldn't? Ye'er a gentleman, I'll give ya that, Fletcher McCullough. But yer stubborn as a mule, too."

Fletcher sighed heavily and reached for the cup, against his better judgement. His fingertips brushing hers as they made the exchange. Involuntarily, their eyes met, and Gracie gave him a bubbly smile. One he could feel to his toes.

She was sunshine. It was quite clear to him there could be no clouds in her sky. And, in comparison, he was midnight rain. Dark, brooding, mysterious. Everything a girl like Gracie should run from. But here she was. Sitting with him on Calton Hill. Listening to him prattle on about history and philosophy, and the details of a country she already knew everything about. But she was here. And that was something.

Reluctantly, so as not to offend her, he took a sip of the morning brew and savored the flavor. It could've been his imagination, but he swore he tasted the sweetness of her lips along with it.

*Dude, Fletcher. Get it together. You just met this woman and she is definitely not into you. Stop acting like an idiot!* His thoughts berated him.

He cleared his throat and handed the tea back to Gracie.

"We should probably come up with some sort of plan," he suggested. "What I'd really like to do, is get some of your thoughts on the clearances, especially since your family has close ties to it. And then maybe transition to their homecoming and resilience."

"And, obviously the beauty of Scotland can't be overlooked," Gracie replied with another bewitching smile.

*I'm looking at the beauty of Scotland, right now,* flashed through Fletcher's mind.

"Alright," she continued. "We'll start with how they broke the Highland people's homes, but not our spirit, eh? Then how folks made their way back an' managed tae keep their traditions alive. That sound 'bout right?" Gracie finished, tilting her head. Her long locks dancing in a passing gust.

Fletcher couldn't help but let a smile tug his lips upward. His thoughts wandered back to the quote on his cafe wall: *"Life can only be understood backwards; but it must be lived forwards."* It resonated deeply here, atop Calton Hill, where the wind stung his cheeks and a fiery, bright-eyed woman sat beside him.

"Couldn't have recapped it better myself," he said.

# 6

# Archival

Tartan slacks. *Wool* tartan slacks and a cardigan. That's what Gracie was wearing the next time she was to meet Fletcher. He had been unable to keep the concern—or was it disapproval?— in his voice when he'd mumbled something about her bare legs and 'proper attire' the last time they had encountered each other.

To be fair, she hadn't expected to go trapsing up a hill with a stranger, after he had sniffed her out, and had instead started the day out thinking she'd be pulling stems and ruffling petals in the comfort of her carefully curated shop.

*Better safe than sorry,* Gracie grumbled. *But at least I can pull off the smarmy spinster look. It's prob'ly a glimpse at my future,* she mused as she observed herself in the mirror.

In truth, though, Gracie looked every bit the sophisticated historian Fletcher himself did. And she assumed as much when she walked into the National Museum of Scotland and found his mouth slightly gaping. She held a secret smile within, noting his reaction and tucking it away to dissect later. Fletcher had a boorish exterior. But Gracie's hunch was that there was more that made up the indifferent man she saw before her than apathy.

Keira was skeptical and had grilled Gracie after her excursion to Calton Hill. But, from Gracie's perspective, there wasn't a lot to tell. She'd met a man, through the mischievousness of his dog, who wanted to extract information from her, and likely exploit her family. Plus, as far as she knew, she wasn't getting much, besides a partial cup of tea, in return.

After that outing, Fletcher had invited her to the museum to get a grasp on her family history in connection with their eviction from the Highlands and how things had evolved into another generation resettling in the area despite their deep cuts from the past. They had agreed on Thursday afternoon and it was uncharacteristically warm outside, when Gracie whisked into the lobby. Sun beams followed her footsteps inside and she looked as though she was walking on daylight itself.

Fletcher's slate-colored eyes shifted from Gracie to the floor and then to his hands, fingers steepled in his lap. He stood as she approached, looking like a startled Mr. Darcy who'd just discovered Elizabeth Bennet lurking around his home uninvited. Gracie giggled at the thought and considered asking him if he possessed a good fortune and was in want of a wife, but the stern expression he carried and the tension in his stance forced the idea from her mind.

He dug a finger under his collar of his oxford button-up with his left hand, tugging it to the side in an awkward adjustment. His other hand now found the strap of his messenger bag and he drummed a noiseless rhythm on it with his fingertips. Fletcher always looked a little too formal. Overly reserved. Almost as if he was on the verge of saying something and then he overthought it and brushed it into the recesses of his mind instead of bringing clarity into the conversation.

"How'd ye come tae call yer dog Chantilly?" Gracie asked, catching him off guard.

"Pardon me?" Fletcher asked. He blinked, struggling to find the relevance to her question.

"Yer dog, Chantilly. Why is that her name?" she rephrased. "I've been wonderin' aboot it a' week. All I can think o' is Chantilly cream. But she's nae white. Or fluffy," Gracie concluded.

"Uh… good afternoon to you too, Gracie," Fletcher replied, remaining aloof.

"C'mon. Chantilly. Explain, please. And who takes care o' her while yer at work?"

"The name Chantilly means singer," Fletcher sighed, finally relenting. "I named her that because, especially as a puppy, she was always very vocal. Howling and yodeling when she didn't get her way. She's stubborn and always has some opinion or other. Anyway, it often sounded like she was singing in protest to my, no doubt, subpar pet parenting skills. Satisfied?"

Gracie shook her head and laughed.

"No! She's so loveable! How could ye give 'er such a lovely name, then leave her for hours while ye toil away?"

Fletcher's expression flickered—a mix of embarrassment and faint amusement, though he quickly masked it with a shrug.

"I wouldn't say 'loveable.' She has her moments, but she's more trouble than not. And she's not alone all day," he protested.

"She's got good company in *All Creatures Great and Small* reruns. It seemed the least I could do."

Gracie tilted her head, her auburn hair catching the light. "Oh, so ye're a reluctant hero, aye? A knight in shining armor tae a poor, abandoned pup?"

Fletcher scoffed, though the corner of his mouth twitched. "Hardly. More like an unwitting cohabitant."

Gracie laughed again, the sound light and melodic. For a moment, Fletcher simply looked at her, his eyes, now shining charcoal blue, searching hers. Then, noticing the long pause, he turned toward the sweeping staircase in the Grand Gallery.

"We should probably get started. After you," he said, gesturing ahead of him.

His tone had shifted back to business and Gracie dispensed with poking fun at him. There were many reasons she wanted to dig deeper into who Fletcher was but, foremost among them, was to get him to at least look like he enjoyed the life he'd invented for himself.

*No one's mouth should be downturned as often as his,* Gracie considered.

Then she realized she had been paying particular attention to the way the corner of his lips twisted downward, while he was attempting to usher her through the hall. In a few quick steps, she sashayed in front of him and could feel his soulful gaze boring into the back of her neck. The only part of her she'd left exposed and it was now, more than likely, glowing red.

As they wound their way around the various exhibits and concerned themselves with locating key collections of estate papers and newspapers offering significant insight into the times of the Clearances, Gracie's eyes gleamed, nearly pistachio, under the bright fluorescent lighting.

"So, how do you think your family managed it?" Fletcher asked briskly.

"What?" Gracie looked up, concentrating on his wrinkled forehead. She noticed the freckles that dotted his ruddy skin. From his hairline to his chin, there was a smattering of brick hued dots. Not the kind that overpowered his features. Instead, they were the kind that gave him an irresistible desirability.

His red-orange hair, more vivid than hers, flowed fluidly, in a tousled wave, over to one side and his bangs curled back with the help of what she assumed was gel. Fletcher's eyebrows burned with the same flame as his hair, and the coarse, short mustache and beard that cloaked the rest of his face matched them as well.

"Your family," he tried again. "How do you think they felt when all this began? The evictions, the oppression?"

"Ah, me ol' granda worked the land, farming barley an' potatoes. They say he loved the feel o' earth in his hands, under his feet," Gracie said with a wistful expression. "But he was a crofter who couldn't afford his own land. So, when the landlord up an' decided to kick 'em out, there wasn't much he could do."

"Where did they go? You're ancestors," Fletcher asked reflexively.

"Cullen. Not too far, really. Less than an hour from their home. But a totally different life all the same. Granda didn't know much o' fishin' or harvesting kelp so they struggled to find their way."

There was a brief pause, and Gracie twisted a lock of her russet hair around her finger.

"I try tae see it through his eyes sometimes—an' my granny's too," she pressed on. "To go from the soil underfoot to sand. Breathin' briny air, after years o' smellin' Highland mud— squishy, slimy kelp twisting in his fingers instead of the dry heads o' barley. To see nothing but the shore after years o' rollin' hills and the beauty of the glen. I don't know how they did it."

"I'm not sure it's about *how* they did it," Fletcher offered. "Instead, I think it's more about the fact that they managed to instill the past they cherished into their children. Enough for their children to want to go back and try the Highland life again. To honor their parents' legacy."

"Aye. Me Da is still in Glenrinnes, farmin'. Sheep and potatoes. Like he turned out tae be the best o' both worlds. The old Highlands and the new," Gracie mused with a shrug.

Fletcher stopped walking, placed his hand on the top of a glass case, and peered inside. Lying amongst the displayed items were a scythe, a landlord's ledger, and a map of the Highlands that outlined the regions affected by the Clearances. As he traced a finger along the list of names on the page of the ledger, he noticed two names, side-by-side. Malcolm and Edna Buchanan.

"Mhm… Did you say what your great-great-great grandparents' names were?" Fletcher ventured, his eyes still glued to the display.

"Nae. Granda was Mac to ev'ryone who knew 'em. But his birth name was Malcolm. Granny was Edie."

"There's not a chance that your granny's full name was Edna, is there?" Fletcher asked, raising his eyes to Gracie as she stepped closer.

"Yeah, why?"

"Well, because they are listed on this landlord's ledger in the case. Says they were living on the land of a Lord Ewan Fraser," Fletcher stated, pointing to the neat scrolling penmanship.

"Are ye kiddin'?" Gracie's face was now plastered to the glass, searching for the names herself. After a moment, she felt Fletcher's timid hand reach out and grab hers. He unfurled her curled fist until he could guide only her pointer finger over the letters and gently placed it over the line where her grandparents' names could be found.

"I… I can't believe this. How could I not have known this was here?" Gracie whispered loudly. She was trying to conceal her shock and excitement but doing a terrible job at it. She glanced at Fletcher, only to see that his once flush cheeks were now colorless and he had beads of sweat developing on his brow.

"Fletcher? Are you alright?" she asked.

He nodded his head slowly, though his eyes didn't move from the page before them.

"What is it?" she probed again, nudging his elbow.

"Uh… it's nothing. It's just… How many Alasdair and Grizel MacCulloughs do you think there have been on the earth?" he finally responded.

"I don't think I'm qualified to answer that," Gracie managed. "I'm not followin'."

"My great-great grandparents are on this list, Gracie. Four lines down from your family. Do you see it?"

Gracie's breath caught. She leaned in, squinting at the names, then back at Fletcher, whose face had gone pale. His hand, still resting on the glass, trembled slightly.

"You're shakin'," she said softly, her voice stripped of its usual teasing lilt.

Fletcher blinked, as if surfacing from somewhere far away. "I didn't expect to see them here. I didn't expect to feel…"

Gracie stepped closer, brushing his arm. "Ye don't have to explain. But ye don't have to pretend it's not happenin', either."

Fletcher's eyes flicked to hers, searching. "I need air."

Fletcher walked quickly, his messenger bag thumping against his side, and Gracie kept pace without speaking. When they reached the corner, he paused, then turned to her.

"I was headed back to The Caledonian Cuppa," he said, voice low.

He looked at her then—really looked—and something in his expression softened. "You don't have to come."

"I know," she said. "But I want to."

# 7

# Whiskey Neat

An hour later, Fletcher was sitting, yet again, on a barstool in the rear of The Caledonian Cuppa, hunched over a whiskey neat. He had felt flush and sweaty ever since the not-so-subtle discovery of his family's history, side-by-side with a woman who seemed so connected to her own. A pang of jealousy struck him like lightning.

Why had he never known about his own genealogic past? Why had he never delved into it? Was it because he wanted to keep everything about his family as distant as possible, so he didn't have to feel hurt? Or was it because he was so scared he would find something besides pain and accidentally latch onto it?

Gracie appeared beside him, lingering just long enough for Fletcher to notice the hesitation. She didn't seem like the type to hover—he'd seen that in the way she moved, all brisk efficiency and clipped politeness. So, when she didn't walk away, when she lowered herself onto the stool next to his, Fletcher felt something tighten in his chest.

He kept his eyes on the ledger, though the numbers had long since blurred. She'd seen him looking at it earlier—he was sure of that. Pale and unraveling, that's how he must've looked.

The stool creaked beneath her. She didn't speak.

Carefully she placed her tea and scone on the counter and reached for the bottle of whiskey sitting next to Fletcher's glass. He watched as she poured some into her teacup and gracefully spread jam and cream onto her pastry. Her movements, subtle and often unexpected, were mesmerizing. She hadn't spoken yet, but he could feel that she was about to.

Part of him wished she wouldn't have followed him after leaving the museum. He wasn't used to being doted on and the feeling it produced in his gut was something unfamiliar. Foreign emotions were something he attempted to keep at bay. Surprises and unprecedented actions couldn't be contained, and Fletcher liked his world to be contained.

He sipped the strong liquid and let the heat of it blaze down the length of his throat. Blinking into the glass he observed the thickness, the peat, and way it singed his nostrils.

"When I were a wee lass, I used to see Da down a dram or two when I snuck down the stairs at night. I was s'pose tae be in bed, but instead I'd climb down and listen to he and Mam whisper by the fire," she interjected.

Fletcher let a long moment pass before he acknowledged her nostalgia. His heart felt like a stone in his chest and his stare lingered on the twinkling lights of the street outside.

"Yeah? And didn't you land yourself into trouble once they caught you?" he asked, half-heartedly.

"Nah. They might've known I was there, but they never gave me away. I'd sit an' lean my head against the wall. Their voices would float past and I'd stay until I couldn't keep me eyes open."

He scoffed lightly in response. Then, noticing the confusion on her face he opted for vague clarification.

"It must be nice to have such happy childhood memories," he began. "Things to draw on when you feel alone in the city."

"Aye, sometimes. Other times it just ends in loads o' more guilt," she replied.

"What could you possibly have to feel guilty for, Gracie?"

She looked down at her half-eaten scone, took another sip of her spiked tea, and then gathered her hair behind her. The seconds ticked by in agony for Fletcher. He was smoldering, surprised the smoke rising from the embers of his mood wasn't visible.

"Mam passed seven years ago in December," she said, looking at him directly. Fletcher didn't meet her eyes. The tips of his ears grew pink as the regret for asking the question spread.

"Da's been on his own with the farm a while an' I'm forever torn if Edinburgh could ever really be home. The kind of home that doesn't feel like I'm escaping from somethin'. The grief or the memories," she went on.

Fletcher noticed a quiet ache in her voice as she spoke the last sentence. Almost as if she wasn't sure what she was running from. He knew that feeling all too well. Knew what it was like to try and live a life that you squeezed yourself into, instead of one that you embraced with open arms.

He leaned back from the counter and turned to face Gracie, swiveling on the stool. He positioned her knees between each of his and rested his heels on the foot rail. Leaning in ever-so-slightly he could see her khaki green eyes shimmering with the onset of tears. But she blinked them back and her look of bewilderment vanished. She flashed a winning smile as if to say *I'm fine* and patted Fletcher on the shoulder.

"I'm sorry about your mom," he began. "It can't be easy for you to feel so conflicted."

"It's not," she said quietly. "But I'm not sure I have a choice. Mam's inside me. I carry her ev'rywhere I go. And until I can figure out where I belong, I'll always feel like I'm failin' her memory."

"You're not failing anyone. I can promise you that. You've had darkness loom over you and somehow still manage to spread bits of sunshine wherever you go. That's not failure. It's success in its purest form," Fletcher assured her, with a sharp nod.

One of his hands lingered on his glass, still at the bar, while the other rested dangerously close to her knee as he rested it on his thigh.

"You know, I haven't even spoken to my mom, or dad, in probably 15 years," he continued. His eyes were like shiny steel as they bounced from her mouth to her collarbone and then snapped to the front of the shop or back to his lap. He couldn't maintain eye contact. What he was sharing was too intimate, too heavy… something he'd only ever mentioned to Tate.

Fletcher didn't look up when Gracie stood. He heard the scrape of the stool, the soft shift of her weight, and something in him braced. She wasn't one for lingering—he'd seen that. She moved through the world with purpose, not pity.

But now she was beside him, her presence quiet and deliberate. He hadn't meant to let his voice falter, hadn't realized his hand was shaking until the glass clinked against the counter. Maybe she'd noticed.

Gracie's waist was at the level of Fletcher's knees on either side of her. She took a half step forward and her head was tucked under his chin as he stared forward, into the main dining area. Fletcher could feel himself shaking.

"Why not?" she said into the hollow of his throat.

"I...," Fletcher stammers, trying to fight his newfound honesty. But, in the end, he lost the battle. "I was never really close with my parents. I was an only child, on a rural farm, and it was nothing but one hardship after another. My dad, he drank a lot, and his mood swings weren't particularly pleasant..." he said, but his voice trailed off.

Gracie tipped her chin up and examined his features. Bits of blond and strawberry tones in his beard and smell the cedarwood and cardamom on his skin.

Fletched rubbed his palm on the material of his pants while the other hand made rings around the rim of his dram.

*She's so close. Too close. Dear goodness, I can smell the jasmine in her hair.*

"What happened?" she asked in a whisper.

"My dad… He would beat me pretty bad whenever he was in a stupor. My mom never stepped in. Always pretended everything was fine. I used to think that, when I got big enough, I'd fight back. But I never did. He was miserable and frustrated as a young man and nothing changed as the years went by. So, when I got a scholarship to college, it was my golden ticket out," Fletcher finished.

Gracie drew in a sharp breath, and she absentmindedly fidgeted with Fletcher's collar button.

Fletcher could feel the weight of his own words hanging in the air, heavier now that someone else had heard them.

"I'm so sorry. I don't know what to say, 'cept ya deserved better." It wasn't a rush to fill the silence. Just a small truth.

Fletcher didn't know what to do with the gentleness. It terrified him. Because if she saw him this clearly, what else might she see?

"Eh, it was a long time ago now. I just… they aren't a part of my life. It's easier that way," he said, very matter-of-fact.

Fletcher felt Gracie's soft hair against his chin as she moved back to her stool, and he straightened to let her pass. Somehow the space without her in it felt cold and he wished he could retract his last statement.

He missed her presence the moment it was gone. Not because she'd said anything profound, but because she'd stayed. And that, somehow, felt like the kindest thing anyone had done for him in years.

"So, what'd ya know about yer grandparents? The ones in the ledger?" she probed.

"Oh, I've always been a history buff, so I started looking into my family at the urging of a high school teacher I had. But I didn't take it too seriously after the class was over. My sights were set on finding the city of gold and being the next Indiana Jones at the time. I never got back to it."

"But ya knew they were from Scotland?"

"Yeah. I mean, that's kind of where I started. It was a fluke I ended up here though… with you," Fletcher breathed.

"Yeah, kinda strange how that happened," she chuckled, swiveling back towards the counter and knocking knees with him as she swung on the chair. "I'm sure there's lots more tae their story, ya know? Yer family."

"I suspect there is," he said flatly.

"Oh, c'mon! Ye can't tell me ya don't wanna know. It could give ye closure, or hope… maybe both."

"Maybe those things are overrated," he replied.

"Or maybe having a spark of hope is the greatest small act of rebellion amongst this murk we live in," she said with conviction.

"If I didn't know better, Grace Buchanan, I'd think you still read fairy tales."

"And I like them best."

# 8

# Linger

*His eyes are rocky like a riverbed. Deep as a canyon. Grey as the silhouette of peregrine falcon in a cloudy sky.*

Gracie turned these thoughts over in her mind as she walked to work the next morning.

Fletcher's shell was a jagged shield. He was a soldier who had marched into battle too young and was using armor that was unfit to protect him. His mask was slipping, his sword worn. She could see, as they'd been huddled close the night before, that he was still the same young boy waiting for someone to tell him they were proud of him. That he was safe. That he could stop fighting.

Something about his surliness and his overcast attitude fed her
curiosity. Her philanthropic disposition came alive all the more
when he was around. She wanted to know the secrets he held
so close, to solder the broken parts of him together with the
flame of expectations he'd long forgotten.

The discovery of her family's history, so closely intertwined
with his, made the past so much more tangible. Gracie had
always had an appreciation for where she grew up and those
who had come before her. The people that made her who she
was and the quiet life they lived, full of strife and blessings alike,
gave her a sense of determination—to see to it that her own
story reflected some of their aspirations and the advice that had
been passed down through generations.

It wasn't easy, having such a small existence. In talking with
Fletcher, she had realized that there were so many unexpected
challenges that her grandparents had had to overcome. They
had made sacrifices, great and small, to keep themselves moving
forward. Conversing about the things they went through and
the ways they were able to adapt and breathe new life into
changing circumstances that weren't always pleasant, made
them feel larger than life to Gracie. While her own little life was
quiet, repetitive, and mostly solitary.

Fletcher had been kind to say she carried on spreading
positivity despite her own hardships. But, when compared with

the greatness of her ancestors, was that enough? To just be a good person?

Would anyone ever want to peel back the layers of the foreground of her happiness to see what lay beneath? Would they be disappointed if they found a young woman who was just as mystified as the rest of the world?

Gracie listened to her boots scuff the walkway and the birds call to one another from one bare branch above to the other. She observed the way rainwater and debris trickled down the sidewalk in a stream. The uneven roofs and gridded windows stared back at her forebodingly.

As she reached Thistle and Tulip and stretched out her hand to unlock the front door, she noticed a note shoved into the crack above the hinge.

*I don't think I'm even tall enough to reach that,* she considered, standing on her tiptoes. All five feet, three inches of her attempted to swat at the paper and send it free.

Eventually, she managed to wedge the note from its resting place and saw her name scrawled on the front in an erratic print. The handwriting wasn't familiar, and it was closed with a circular wax seal, embossed with a thistle.

Stepping into the dim shop light, she flicked the seal open and glanced at the message with anticipation. Folks rarely handwrote anything in the age of technology and the mystery of who would go about contacting her in such an archaic way kept her in suspense.

Looking down at the uneven letters, a mix of uppercase and lower, she read:

*Gracie,*

*I probably could've called or texted you to say this, but that didn't seem sufficient.*

*Last night, I was far from my usual self, and I fear I laid my burdens on your shoulders without realizing the gravity of the situation. I feel I owe you the deepest of apologies for any information overload.*

*You agreed to assist me with a historical adventure, not to delve into the scars of the Fletcher of my youth. I humbly recant anything I might've overwhelmed you with and understand completely if you would rather sever our agreement.*

*Please, take your time in replying. I know this is rather unconventional.*

*Fletcher*

*P.S. I don't normally do this sort of thing. Is it weird?*

She let out a small cackle after reading the post-script and then re-read the message in its entirety.

When had he left this? It could've been mere minutes before she arrived.

She glanced around outside to see if anyone was watching or if perhaps Fletcher himself was still in view. But the only thing looking back at her was the fluffy alley cat resting on the outdoor plantstand full of cold-hardy pansies. Everything looked as it normally did, but everything felt a little different.

With a blast of cold air, in waltzed Keira, wearing her headphones and singing loudly to The Cranberries' *Linger*. She bopped to the music and dropped her purse in the usual heap on the counter next to the register. Giving Gracie a quick once-over and then a bemused look, her eyes fell to the letter in Gracie's hand.

"Oh me gah, did we get an invitation to make flower arrangements for the palace? Wait, the King didn't die, did he?" Keira asked, rapid fire.

Gracie rolled her eyes playfully. "No, Keira, he didn't die. And the only funeral arrangements we've gotta make this week are for Mr. Barclay, poor man."

"Then, what's with the fancy paper? A love note from a secret admirer?"

"I wouldn't say that," Gracie began. "Ye know that man who came in to see me? Needin' help with his Scottish history paper?"

"How could I forget? The redheaded stalker with the Irish dog?"

"He's not a stalker, Keira! Anyway, the note's from him. An apology."

"What's he apologizin' fer?" Keira asked genuinely.

"Um, things kinda took a turn when I met 'em at the museum yesterday. Turns out we've got more in common than we'd have thought. And it led to a lot of drinkin' and talkin'… ye know how that goes, eh?" Gracie replied.

"Ha! Do I! But I never pictured ye havin' a dram with a history nerd from America," Keira admitted.

Gracie gave an exasperated sigh. "Here. Have a look at the letter."

There was a long moment of silence while Keira read and reflected on the contents. Then, she let out a long, swooping whistle.

"Well, he's got it bad for ye. That's what that is," she appraised.

"Oh, please. He does not," Gracie protested, though she felt her face grow warm.

"No man takes the time to write a letter to a lass unless he's a feardie or he's got a crush. I'd say maybe both in this case," Keira said with a nod. "Either way, something's gotta hold of 'em."

Gracie rolled her eyes again, more exaggerated this time.

"I'm not getting' into that, right now. But I *am* goin' to pick us up a couple o' coffees."

And with that she rushed back out the door, leaving it to Keira to open the shop, and her full thermos on edge of the counter.

# 9

# Planting the Seed

Just as Fletcher was engrossing himself in a parish register of Alasdair and Grizel MacCullough's marriage, alongside a giant cappuccino, Gracie yanked open the door to The Caledonion Cuppa and stormed in. Her hair in the wind, lips parted, pearly skin—luminous.

*Is she mad at me? What if writing that note was idiotic?* Fletcher wondered. *I hope she didn't take it the wrong way.*

"I was hopin' I'd find ya here. I didn't know if ye'd be at yer office," she said as she strode over to the table.

"I probably should be," Fletcher said, and his lips quirked up tentatively. "But lately that office seems more like a coffin than a sanctuary."

Gracie nodded, acknowledging his conflict.

"I got yer letter. It was…"

"Stupid?" Fletcher offered.

"No!" she exclaimed and raked a hand through the ends of her hair. "I was gonna say, it was… sweet. Not that ye felt bad, just that ye… were concerned." She stumbled through the words, struggling to find the right justification for his actions.

"Well, self-preservation in the presence of a lady, such as yourself, is always a concern. I've got a reputation to maintain," he replied teasingly.

"Naturally," she said. "But if I were a lass who required an apology after ye sharin' yer past, would ya expect me to share mine with ye?"

This was an angle Fletcher hadn't considered. Slowly, he stood from his seat and pushed back his laptop. It wasn't something he did often—pause in the middle of work to address something personal. But things were feeling quite personal with Gracie.

"Gracie, I think I've been going about this all wrong. I'm just not the kind of person who enjoys confrontation or awkward silences. It seems I've encountered both, more than once, in the last couple of days. It's not easy for me to be… caught off guard," he explained.

"I'm just someone who wants tae help," she answered, looking up into his face.

A blast of crisp air circled them as the door to the café swung open once again, and in rushed Tate. His strides were quick and he crossed the entry halfway through a sentence already.

"…never guess who I just saw, mate. Sophia! And she said she's been missing you and hoping you'd call," he said, stepping past Gracie and pointing playfully at Fletcher's chest.

Fletcher's eyes cut to Gracie at the mention of his ex-girlfriend, and he saw something unreadable there. Jealousy? Annoyance? Not that it mattered much, considering Sophia was the furthest thing from his mind and he had no intention of getting back together with her. Still, the expression Gracie wore, however brief, troubled him.

"Tate, this is Grace Buchanan. She owns the florist shop up the street and I've recruited her to help with my research project.

Which, so far, has proved to be pretty enlightening for both of us, I think," Fletcher said, nodding in Gracie's direction.

*Or maybe I should just come out and say it,* Fletcher thought. *This is Grace Buchanan, and I can't stop thinking about her no matter how hard I try to stop.*

But he swallowed the notion and listened to Tate and Gracie politely exchange introductions.

It was true, Gracie, her proximity, her gentleness, and need to mend had all be on a steady film roll in his head. Nothing seemed to erase it. Not the rest of the bottle of whiskey he finished after she'd left the previous night, not trying to stuff away his problems and dismiss it all with a letter of cowardice, and definitely not standing here watching her giggle at one of Tate's idiotic anecdotes.

Fletcher cleared his throat and interrupted just as Tate was about to launch into another flirtatious line, catching him by the elbow.

"So, what was it you were coming in to talk about, Tate? Because I'm sure Gracie needs to get back to work. In fact, isn't that were *you* should be?"

"As a matter of fact, I should. But it just so happens, I quit," Tate rebutted.

"Quit? What for? That was the best job you've had… ever!" Fletcher exclaimed, clearly unhappy.

"Eh, they were holding my creative spirit back. I'll get 'em on the next one," Tate said with a wink and pounded his palm against Fletchers bicep.

"I do need to get back to the shop in a few, but I came to propose somethin' a little unconventional," Gracie spoke up.

Both Tate and Fletcher raised their brows with interest.

"A woman proposing to man. I've never seen it, but they say it's done more often nowadays," Tate laughed.

Fletcher let his eyes roll back and feigned amusement but quickly regained composure and urged Gracie to continue despite his friend's ignorance.

"I know this isn't somethin' we've discussed, but what if we took the research yer doin' on the road?" she asked.

"On the road?" Flecther repeated. "How so?"

"I mean, since we found out about my ancestors, and yers, livin' near the same place an' such, durin' the Clearances, I thought maybe takin' a little road trip to that area might give some more… what's the word ye like tae use? Perspective?"

"I don't know… It seems like a lot of investment into something I could probably just piece together with our notes, conversations, and online research," Fletcher began.

"In the coffin office?" she replied.

"Fair point," he said, his smile broader than he'd allowed with her before. She was smart and quick-witted. Gracie kept him on his toes, and he liked that. The idea of being on the road with her on a research trip, though, was a bit overwhelming.

"Me Da has room for us to stay. Tate can come, too, if he's got free time. I could invite Keira, too. I keep promisin' her a holiday," Gracie continued.

"So, it's a research trip or a holiday? Because I'm not coming if I'm going to be on a wild goose chase," Tate stated.

Gracie laughed again at his openness and Fletcher felt a twinge in his stomach. Something urging him to reach beyond the obscurity he lived in and search for something greater, more fulfilling. Maybe even something that could make him feel whole again.

"Why not a bit o' both?" Gracie suggested.

"And how long would this hybrid trip be?" he asked skeptically.

"I've got orders to fufill this weekend already, but next week looks light. I could work around those and leave on Tuesday morn if that is good fer ev'ryone. Including Chantilly, because she is invited, of course," Gracie said with a grin.

"I'm starting to think you like her more than you like me," Fletcher joked.

"She lights up a room, what can I say?" Gracie teased.

*So do you. You're a candle in the window on a dark night, and I'm finally seeing it through the driven rain,* was Fletcher's silent response.

Tate shifted on his feet and threw up his hands in enthusiasm. "Well, count me in! I say, what is there to lose?"

He and Gracie both looked expectantly at Fletcher who was scratching the cowlick at the back of his head and staring intently at the floor. It almost seemed as if he was trying to bore a hole right through it.

Realizing he was now the center of attention, let his shoulders slump and let out a resigned sigh.

"It's been awhile since I've lived outside of a dimly lit library-like rooms, I suppose," Fletcher admitted.

"Where's your ol' Indiana Jones spirit?" Gracie nudged.

"Fletcher? Indiana Jones? Ebenezer Scrooge is more like it! Haven't you heard him muttering 'Bah! Humbug!' when he's particularly enthusiastic?" Tate chimed in.

Gracie let out a high-pitched squeal of laughter and Fletcher felt his lungs collapse. Watching her radiate happiness wherever she went quite simply took his breath away. Her smile warmed him in a way the sun never could.

He let out a long, slow exhale, counted to five, and then punched Tate in the arm.

"That's for the Scrooge reference," he explained and then turned to Gracie. "And as for this trip… It's not something that's typical for me. But maybe something unexpected is warranted right now. Especially considering something I dug up after I went home last night."

He grabbed his laptop off the nearby table and turned the screen toward Gracie. Pointing to each name on the document, he explained that it was the marriage registration of his great-great-grandparents, Alasdair and Grizel.

"But there's something unique about it, that I didn't realize could be significant until this morning," he continued. "There's the name of a witness listed here. See?"

"Edna Murray," Gracie read aloud. "I'm not sure I understand."

"I didn't either, until I remembered that your granny's name was Edna, too. So, I did some digging, and it turns out that Edna Murray and Edna Buchanan are one in the same! Your granny was at my grandparent's wedding, Gracie," Fletcher announced.

He watched as Gracie's mouth formed a small o-shape, and her brows knit together. She was so cute when she was thinking. And when she did everything else he'd witnessed, too.

"But, how? I mean… she couldn't have been more than—"

"Eighteen," Fletcher finished her sentence. "My grandparents were 29 and 30 years old at the time, so she must've grown up around them or become friends with them at some point."

"Fletcher! This is amazing! We *have* tae find out more," Gracie insisted, tugging on his sleeve.

Tate silently took in the scene and peered at Fletcher knowingly, with his hands behind his back. He looked like it was taking every ounce of strength he had to behave himself.

"Alright," Fletcher conceded, holding his hands up in surrender. "It would seem I have no other choice."

"Bless," Gracie breathed. "I've got tae get back, but I'll text ye later with details. After I convince Keira to come along," she added, and headed out the door with a wave.

Tate circled around Fletcher and watched until Gracie was out of sight. Then, faced Fletcher with a smirk on full display.

"What did I just agree to?" Fletcher asked, running a hand through his hair.

"To go on a road trip with a girl you're mad about, mate. And I get to sit back and watch the whole thing unfold," Tate replied. He took a seat and put his hands behind his head, as if he was settling in for a good show.

"What are you talking about?"

"Ah, ah, don't try to throw me off the scent. I know a lovesick puppy when I see one," Tate poked.

"Don't you have anything better to do than psychoanalyze me?" Fletcher said, sitting opposite and taking a sip of his now lukewarm coffee.

"Not really. Besides I don't know that I've ever seen you this invested in a girl. I've only seen you look at ancient tombstones the way you look at her."

"Oh, that is *not* true," Fletcher denied.

Tate quirked an eyebrow. "In any case, she's not getting the Sophia treatment from you. You like her. And now you are going to ride off into the sunset together."

"More like into the foggy moors."

"Whatever," Tate rolled his eyes. "Mark my words, McCullough. She's the one."

# 10

# Fire and Ice

Wandering back up the street and into Thistle and Tulip, Gracie couldn't help but wonder who this infamous Sophia was that Tate had mentioned upon his arrival to The Caledonian Cuppa. Fletcher had bristled at the mention of her name and seemed to want to avoid the subject, at least while Gracie was there.

On the other hand, her cup was overflowing with excitement about the trip to the Highlands and finding out more about her granny Edna; how things had transpired between her and the MacCulloughs. Gracie hadn't been particularly drawn to history in school, but finding out more about her own clan and the way the story of her life had been written until now felt like the slow unwrapping of a gift. And Fletcher had been the one to give it to her.

She'd never met anyone like him. He was handwritten notes instead of phone calls, stacks of books instead of hands covered in dirt. There was a quiet strength about him, in contrast to the brute force of other men. And the warmth inside of her when he was around was the same warmth she felt after drinking mulled wine—tingly and relaxing.

"Where are the coffees?" Keira asked, bursting into Gracie's thoughts.

Gracie looked down at her hands and then blinked at Keira. She'd left the shop and said she was getting coffee, but now realized, in the emptiness of her arms, that she'd truly gone in search of Fletcher. In search of making sure things were alright between them. To reassure him he was still worthy of her time.

"Ya ran into 'em, didn't ye?" Keira asked. "Fletcher."

"I guess I didn't happen upon him as much as I went lookin' for 'em. Just couldn't leave the note alone, I s'pose."

"I figured when I saw ye'd already brought yer thermos," Keira chuckled. "Not like you to be the scatterbrain. That's my job."

Gracie laughed lightly. "I'll admit it, he's got me in a twist. I can't put me finger on it, but—"

"But ye like him," Keira interrupted.

"It's a weird connection. And now with this shared history… I can't help but wonder if we were supposed to find each other. If for no other reason than tae make sure that history isn't forgotten."

"Whoa… that's deep."

"Is it?" Gracie asked, busying herself with a bucket of black parrot tulips. Then, suddenly, she turned back to Keira. "By the way, I volunteered ye for a sort of… field trip."

"Sorry, a field trip?" Keira asked warily.

"A holiday really. I might've asked Fletcher to come back to Da's so we can do more research in the Highlands. His friend, Tate, is comin', too. It'll be…fun," Gracie spat out.

"Gracie, you just invited a man you've known for nae two weeks to go home wi' ya and meet yer Da?"

"It's for research," Gracie said firmly, tying on her apron.

"Mhm. This chaperone thinks otherwise," Keira replied, pointing towards herself.

Gracie flew over to her and hugged her tightly, overcome with relief. "So, you'll come with us?!"

"I don't think there was ever a question in the invitation, was there? Besides, someone has tae play wing woman," Keira winked.

With another squeeze, Gracie conceded to her friend's intuition. There was no way around it; Fletcher was different than other men she'd met. They all seemed like silly schoolboys. But Fletcher was mature and mysterious, if not a bit troubled and sensitive under his no-nonsense attitude. She considered this as she dove into the work week.

By the time the following Monday evening arrived, Gracie and Keira had fulfilled two hundred sixteen orders for floral arrangements and shuffled their remaining orders for the week to other possible dates or other florists. Their bags were packed, and Keira's daily inquiries about whether Fletcher had checked in were at an all-time high.

The truth was, Gracie hadn't really gotten more than a few disgruntled correspondences from him since they had initially discussed the trip to Glenrinnes. She filled him in on some travel details and asked a couple of questions about the itinerary, regarding some of the historical sites they might visit. But even that hadn't gotten much of a response. He hadn't asked to meet her to go over any more findings or get any further insight into her family tree, what she knew about the Clearances, or even just to say hello.

She'd managed to refrain from going to The Caledonian Cuppa for nearly a week just so she wouldn't seem too eager if she bumped into him there. Even if she *was* craving their specialty Hebridean tea with a freshly baked fruit scone on the side. Somehow, she'd gotten by with plain black tea and milk, but with every sip she saw visions of a cold day on Calton Hill.

*Maybe I've gone daft,* Gracie considered, as she closed the shop. *Not even a note in the hinge has gotta mean somethin'.*

She shook her head and turned the key until she heard the lock click into place. Then, fumbled to put her keys in her purse as she stepped out into the sidewalk, suddenly colliding with another body. Gracie, wobbled and nearly landed in a pot of winter cyclamen.

"I'm so sorry! Let me help," said a familiar voice.

Gracie stared at the outstretched hand waiting to help her up. Following the extension up the arm, across the shoulder, and to the face that went with the voice she'd heard. Blinking, she recognized Tate, who looked mortified.

Before she could speak, she began to laugh. Heartily and uncontrollably. Tate's expression shifted from embarrassment and worry to confusion and soon, his shoulders were shaking with laughter of his own.

"I'm sorry again, Grace," as she took his hand and was helped to her feet. "I promise, I really am much more astute than that."

"Nae bother. T'was 'bout time I sat down anyway. Been on my feet all week," she said with another giggle.

"In that case, I'm happy to have been of service," he said, tipping his imaginary hat.

"Why thank you, kind sir," she replied, curtseying deeply.

"How chivalrous," came Keira's voice from behind Gracie.

Whirling around to face her, Gracie immediately saw the amusement in her eyes. From Keira's angle it probably looked like a flirtatious exchange between the two of them. And Gracie didn't want it to be misconstrued before they embarked on their journey together.

"I got halfway home and realized I forgot me keys," Keira explained, after a long pause.

"I'll let ye in. Tate was just apologizin' for mowing me down," Gracie stalled. "In fact, you two haven't met yet. Keira, this is Fletcher's friend, I was tellin' ye about. He's comin' to Glenrinnes wi' us."

A spark of recognition flashed across Keira's face, and then a wide smile. "Ah, I'd thought a knight in shinin' armor had come to sweep this lass off 'er feet."

Tate chuckled. "I think I could carry off the armor, but sweeping ladies off their feet isn't my forte, I'm afraid."

Keira smirked, crossing her arms. "A shame, really. Could've made a great spectacle, you twirling Gracie through the air like some grand ballroom affair."

Gracie rolled her eyes but let out a soft laugh. "I prefer keepin' my feet on the ground, thank you."

Tate grinned. "Well, then, it's settled—I'll stick to my strengths and leave the sweeping to someone else." His gaze flickered toward the shop door. "Speaking of, I assume you two are finishing up before heading north?"

"Aye. We've got so many orders out the door… I'll probably sleep the entire time we're there," Keira yawned.

"Well, I know you're exhausted, but I'm just out to meet Fletcher for a dram before we leave tomorrow. You both should come," Tate encouraged.

"I don't know… we've got an early start and I wouldn't want tae wreck yer plans," Gracie replied.

"Ignore her," Keira spoke up. "We'd love tae come an' take a load off. Especially if this holiday really does turn into a history lesson."

She immediately looped arms with Tate and off they marched in the direction of Fletcher and his awaiting spirits, leaving Gracie to ponder if they would even notice if she snuck off and went home. But it would only make things worse in the morning, if she didn't face the inevitable tonight.

Trudging into the bar area, at least five minutes behind Keira and Tate, Gracie felt windswept and anxious. Why hadn't Fletcher been in touch? Maybe he didn't want her help anymore. Maybe he was going in a new direction or wanted privacy to go through his family's records. But wouldn't someone who was invested enough to give her a handwritten letter give her more than just radio silence if he didn't want to see her anymore?

Scanning the area, she spotted Keira and Tate snickering in a corner as if they were grade school friends, passing secret notes and playing pranks on the teacher. Their friendly chemistry was palpable and brought a smile to Gracie's face.

As her eyes traveled over the room, she noticed Fletcher, standing at the bar, glass in hand, looking intently in her direction. She felt as if the room was suddenly in flames, but she was unable to move away from the danger. His cool gaze did nothing to ward off the heat.

He nodded in her direction and raised his glass a bit in recognition. Her fingers tightened around her purse strap.

*Oh great. He knows I'm here. Now what?*

# 11

# Halfway to Nowhere

Looking up and seeing her across the room was like seeing a mirage, after days in the desert with no water. Fletcher wasn't sure she was real. It had been several days since he had seen her and now that she was just a few steps away, it felt like they were meeting again for the first time. He wasn't sure what to do or say. Then again, was he ever really clear on those things?

She'd caught him staring and all he'd done was raise his glass and nod. He tightened his grip on the dram; his second of the evening. Fletcher was quite sure he was seeing Gracie clearly, but inside things felt uncertain. She was always fluid and free, but tonight, she seemed far off. A dreamy haze encircling her as she stood at the threshold.

He didn't want to just leave her there. She needed to be closer. Almost unknowingly he was clinging to her bold capacity for joy. Loud, audacious joy. Gracie looked for light in everything and when she found it, it lit her up from head to toe. Beams of it shot out of her fingertips and the ends of her hair. She became a beacon. A beautiful representation of all things good.

Fletcher dared to steal another look at her, and she tilted her head as if sensing his hesitation.

*Agh. She hasn't looked away.* He gritted his teeth.

Five seconds later she was standing in front of him while he stared into the glass he had bottoms up, draining every last drop of whiskey from it. Noticing her nearness, he wheezed, and the drink ignited his lungs. He pounded his chest with his fist and cleared his throat, hoping for a smooth recovery.

"I was just about to come say hi. Didn't think you were going to show," he blurted.

"Didn't know if there was a reason I should," she countered.

"Listen, I know I've been really quiet this week. I've been slammed at work and I'm not great at checking my phone but, that's no excuse—"

"Maybe a carrier pigeon wi' a handwritten note of some sort then?" she quipped.

Fletcher let out a short laugh, shaking his head. "You'd have better luck training the pigeon than getting me to send a timely message."

Her deadpan expression shattered with his response and Fletcher felt the sweet relief of her smile rest on him.

"Can I tell you something?" he asked, but didn't wait for a response. "I have spent my entire life trying to put things into words. Trying to make everything neat and orderly. Trying to get it to fit into some sort of mold that would make it make sense."

Gracie listened patiently, waiting for him to continue. Fletcher breathed deeply and scratched his temple in thought.

"I'm not sure if words ever help me gain clarity though. I've read so many books, attended lectures, and written countless papers about people and places the world over. Some of which don't even exist anymore. And nothing seems any clearer than it ever was," he concluded.

Gracie reached out and let her hand rest on Fletcher's shoulder.

"Mony a mickle maks a muckle," she said. It sounded like pure gibberish to Fletcher.

"What does that mean?" he asked, perplexed.

"Means that small things, a lot of them, over time, lead to big things. Surprised a professor like yerself didn't know that," she teased. "Anyways, if ye think of ev'rythin' you've accomplished—all yer hard work—it's led ya right here. Maybe right now, it doesn't seem big. But look. You're on track to find family ya knew nothin' about. It's a new adventure."

"I might not be as brave as I once was," Fletcher admitted.

"There's still time for ye tae be who ya want to be."

Fletcher let these words settle over him like a blanket of clouds on a mountaintop. Could he really trust that there was more to come? More happiness? More peace? Or, was it all too good to be true?

"How do you stay so confidently optimistic?" he asked finally.

"Joy is recyclable. You can be happy about the same things over and over again and never get tired of them because you love 'em. Findin' the little things ya love even in the bigger things ye don't, that's the key."

"What if the things you love stop feeling good? What then?"

"Love is like history. It never really disappears—it's just waiting for someone to rediscover it."

Her words resonated deep within him, causing ripples of emotion that grew into waves. He felt like a small child again, lost in a corn field in Pennsylvania. The hot summer sun beating down on him and squinting up into the bright sky for any sign of home. The revelation of his grandparents' life in Scotland and the undoubted parallel to Gracie's family had caused questions that he'd never considered.

"What is it?" Gracie asked, bringing him back to reality.

"I… My dad, sober or not—but especially when he wasn't— always made sure to tell me how lonely I'd end up. How this world would take everything from me no matter how hard I tried to make something of myself. So, I ran somewhere far away and tried to prove to myself that it wasn't true. But up until now, it hasn't worked," Fletcher confided.

"Until now?"

"Spending a couple weeks with a walking, talking ray of sunshine will make you question your own callousness."

"Wow, I never knew I had this effect on folks," Gracie said, obviously pleased.

"Oh, you have quite the effect, Gracie."

"So, does this mean you'll still come on the trip?" she probed.

"If I say yes, does that mean I'll have to drive?"

If Fletcher was being honest, he was hoping the answer was yes. Being confined to the front seat, squished next to Gracie for nearly four hours was likely to be the best kind of torture. If anything, a good distraction. One that might make his arrhythmia act up.

He wasn't a masochist, but even knowing he was no good for a girl like Gracie, keeping her close—letting her rub off on him—felt like enough. At least that's what he told himself.

"I can drive. I know those roads like the back of me hand. Ye can be copilot in case we need to make an important historical stop," Gracie replied.

Fletcher huffed a quiet laugh, shaking his head. "Copilot, huh? That means I get to control the playlist, right?"

Gracie shot him a knowing look, already anticipating a battle over music choices. "Aye, if ye want us tae lurch o'er a cliff to Nirvana."

"Oh, c'mon. It would probably be Audioslave, but who's making the rules?"

"My car, my rules," Gracie said, tossing her hair over her shoulder.

"I thought rules were made to be broken."

"And is that who ye are, McCullough? A rule breaker?"

He could feel her searching his face for the answer.

*A rule breaker. I could be that. For her, I could try to be anything.*

Instead of leading with this, though, he looked away, ordered another whiskey, and steeled himself against falling into the trap of honesty. Deceiving Gracie wasn't easy, but lying to himself had become easier over the years. If he told himself not to care, willed away the stirring he felt inside, then he could stay in control.

After a long silence between them, Gracie let out a sigh. "Yeah, I'm not much of one either," she said to no one in particular. Pausing to order a pastry and a kettle, she brushed a hand over her forehead, collecting herself. Then, added, "I was an only child so, I always felt pressure to show up exactly how me mam an' da expected. They were kind parents, but I became a perfectionist tryin' tae make 'em proud. I think that's why I'm torn between the shop and bein' wi' me da. Me mam would've loved the shop but me da… I don't know."

Fletcher bit his lower lip in hesitation, afraid to say something prying. But saying nothing wasn't really an option. A few seconds passed, and finally he opened his mouth to speak; right or wrong.

"I know what you mean, about the only child thing. Brothers and sisters were something I dreamed of as a kid, but, at the same time, I wouldn't have wanted them to experience the childhood I did. Trying my best in school and keeping my head down when I was at home, getting my chores done… I got it all down to a perfect science so that I could stay relatively invisible to my dad," he told her.

"Did it work?"

"Sometimes. Most of the time. When it didn't, I just told myself that I hadn't tried hard enough. Hadn't been good enough at blending into the surroundings."

Gracie placed her petite hand over his, the contrast almost laughable. Fletcher flinched slightly at her touch. Physicality wasn't something he was overly fond of. Most of his memories of physical contact weren't pleasant. Even his mother had only hugged him a handful of times that he could remember. The last time was when he'd left for college. Probably because she knew he would never come back.

Despite himself, he let Gracie linger there. In the quiet understanding of his pain and the sweet, unfamiliar pleasure of comfort.

The bartender came by and placed a small plate with a lemon tart next to the kettle he'd brought for her, breaking the protective barrier of their mutual compassion.

"Me mam used to make these ev'ry spring. The whole house smelled of lemon, lavender drying in the eaves, an' she'd put forget-me-nots on top. She always said that if I ate them, they'd grow memories o' her in my heart so that no matter how far apart we were from each other, I couldn't forget her," Gracie sniffled.

Fletcher fidgeted with his vest chain and checked the time on his watch. He took a swig of his fresh drink—liquid courage.

"Seems like she was a special woman. I'm sorry I won't get to meet her," he said softly.

Gracie gave him a wistful smile, tracing the rim of her teacup with a fingertip. "She would've liked ye, I think."

"Eh, nothing much worth liking, really," he said shaking his head. "But I'm flattered you think so."

A beat passed, warm but tinged with something unspoken. It wasn't just about her mother anymore—it was about the memories people left behind, the spaces they carved into others, whether they realized it or not.

"Are you two done circling each other?" Tate asked from over Fletcher shoulder.

Fletcher fist clenched at his side, almost as tight as his jaw. Tate was his best friend, but he certainly knew how to ruin a moment.

"Perfect timing, Tate. As always," Fletcher muttered.

"Well, you'd think you two are the only ones in the room," Tate whispered to him.

"I think I'll go see Keira, if ye'll excuse me," Gracie nodded.

"We are going to be in the car with these two women for several hours tomorrow. Could you just not be so Tate-ish when that happens?" Fletcher remarked.

"Sorry, mate. But it's exactly for that reason you'd got to get your head out of your hind end. Gracie seems like a great girl. She puts up with you and your moods, if that says anything. Maybe try to crack a smile once in a while."

"I'm sure that'll make all the difference."

"Don't know until you try, my friend," Tate replied, clapping Fletcher on the shoulder.

*The step I'm hesitating to take might be the one that changes everything. But, what if it all changes for the worse instead of better?*

Fletcher exhaled, checked his watch again—as if time could give him an answer. He drained his drink, then strode toward the table. To new friends, old memories, and a future that still felt uncertain.

# 12

# Glenrinnes

Playful banter with Fletcher was becoming addictive. It was like a high—one that kept her climbing, reaching, because once she earned even the flicker of a smile from him, it was as refreshing as the smell after a heavy rain.

Sitting in the car with him, one hand on the gear shift, and one on the steering wheel, she could feel his presence more permanently. The dim daylight, trademark of their early start, filtered through the trees and the space was filled with Keira's chatter and the scent of fresh morning brews. Gracie took a long inhale, savoring the cinematic mood and sound of Chantilly's snoring in the backseat.

They were approaching Queensferry and passing by the Forth Bridge before Fletcher shifted from his stillness of observing all the things out the passenger window to gazing forward through the windshield. He hadn't said much on the ride so far, but Gracie was getting used to the way things were when he was around. More relaxed, reserved. Nothing rushed. No drama. In a way, it was nice to know what to expect.

"Hard to believe I've lived here this long and have never really left the city," he mused.

"Never?" Keira asked.

"There was one sporadic hiking trip to Skye with a coworker. But it was badly planned, and I think I ended up with nothing more than a handful of photos of Tilly in the Fairy Pools."

"And ye never tried again?" Gracie chimed in.

"In case you hadn't already noticed, dear Gracie, Fletcher here is a creature of habit. Those habits don't involve a lot of sunlight or human interaction," Tate replied.

Gracie huffed a quiet laugh, shaking her head. "So, what I'm hearin' is that ye barely breathe but claim to be livin'?"

"Tate tends to exaggerate," Fletcher said.

Keira snorted from the backseat, stirring her coffee. "If ye don't do sunlight and socializin', how did Tate manage to befriend ye in the first place?"

"He weaseled his way into my affections somewhere between the last glazed donut at a university mixer and the maniacal poem he wrote about the first girl who ever broke his heart."

"Correction. The *only* girl to break my heart. I've been much more skilled at playing the field since then, thank you," Tate teased.

"The details might be fuzzy, but I recall you calling her a two-faced murderous witch who deserved nothing more than to be fed to the dogs like *Jezebel*," Fletcher replied.

Tate placed a hand over his heart in mock offense. "I was a poet, Fletcher. A tortured soul. You wouldn't understand."

Keira hummed, taking a sip of her coffee. "And what happened to *Jezebel*, exactly?"

"I certainly wouldn't know," Tate said, sticking his nose in the air. "I was in artistic anguish. Couldn't be bothered to care if she fell off the face of the earth."

Finally, Tate gave in and gave a more elaborate answer on how the two men had met than Fletcher had cared to offer. Once Keira stopped peppering him with questions about Cambridge and how exciting campus life must've been for someone of his popularity, the conversation lulled. Tate quickly fell into a slumber that was only comparable to that of a toddler; fitful one moment and deathlike stillness the next. Meanwhile, Keira donned her earphones and began sketching Thistle and Tulip's stall design for the Scottish Garden Festival.

Fletcher, the only one besides Gracie, fully immersed in the quiet shifted uncomfortably in his seat and adjusted his glasses. He seemed suddenly unsettled.

"Ev'rything okay?" Gracie asked.

"Mhm," Fletcher murmured.

"Ye sure? 'Cause it doesn't look it," she pressed.

"I'm just too much of a giant for European cars, ya know? Leg cramps and back aches. It all comes with the territory," he replied, giving a crooked smile.

"Ah, yes. I believe I've heard o' those over thirty complainin' of aches," she teased. "If I'm guessin' yer age right."

"Not all of us have drank from the fountain of youth."

"And here I was thinkin' ye were a regular *Tuck Everlasting*."

Fletcher let out a sound somewhere between a laugh and a stifled snort. Then, realizing he'd nearly let good nature show, he carefully buttoned up his expression and cleared his throat.

Gracie couldn't deny he was good at deflecting. But the way he argued with her in a mix of history quips and pop culture references was overwhelmingly charming. She was beginning to crave the way he challenged her energy and quickened her cleverness.

Keira had implied that Gracie had a crush, a growing attraction to Fletcher. But it was something more than that. It was the finite details of the way he glanced at her out of the corner of his eye when he thought she wasn't looking. The way he bit his lip out of insecurity when he was about to share something vulnerable. Gracie liked to think those moments belonged to her alone.

*I'm being silly*, she thought. *I'm just a means to an end. A source. A glorified fact checker.*

She reached to turn on the radio. Certainly, some musical relief from thought was welcome. But, as her hand reached the knob, so did Fletcher's and they clumsily fumbled over one another. Their hands brushed and each of them stilled, as if lightning had passed between them.

Fletcher's gaze flicked to her, and she could feel them rove over her face, down her arm, and to their hands—almost joined. His eyes were the color of worn denim, and his hair was still mussed a bit from sleepiness. He was wearing a baggy hoodie instead of his usual button-up and vest.

*This is it. The almost unguarded version of Fletcher McCullough.*

"Are we going to start a thumb war over the radio?" he said, breaking into her thoughts.

"I wouldn't start anythin' yer not prepared to lose," she suggested, placing her hand back on the steering wheel.

"Bold of you to assume I wouldn't win. I might not talk much, but I have other ways of getting what I want," Fletcher assured her.

He casually turned the knob until a melody overcame the static on the radio station. James Blunt was singing about an angel who planned for him to be with the girl of his dreams and then all his hopes were dashed.

Gracie silently wondered why James eventually concluded that he and the beautiful girl he'd met on the subway could never be together. It seemed bittersweet, the idea of meeting someone, however brief, and knowing you belong together, only for it to fall apart in the end.

"This guy sounds like a chump," Fletcher stated.

"Why d'you say that?"

"He sees some girl and he thinks they are fated by an angel to be together and then he just doesn't do anything about it? I mean, c'mon. Then he just decides, 'oh we'll never be together'?

He literally stood by and did nothing. No wonder they wouldn't work out," he said, sounding frustrated.

Gracie glanced at him, half amused, half intrigued. "So, if it were you, what would ye have done?"

"I'd like to think I'd have at least made an effort. Talked to her, given her flowers…something before I found myself the punchline of an angel's joke," he shrugged. "At the very least, Chantilly could've been the segue into something."

Subtle tension lingered between them as the radio DJ switched the song to Paolo Nutini's *Last Request* and, when Fletcher didn't bother to change the station, Gracie contemplated whether he had a gooey warm center after all. Like a freshly baked chocolate chip cookie. Or was he more like a shortbread biscuit? Crisp and crumbly.

As Paolo continued to croon about his doomed relationship and traveling down a one-way road from which he couldn't return, Gracie wondered if maybe she was on a similar path. Was the journey she started on with Fletcher bound to end in heartache?

The open road stretched out before the four of them and they sped along peacefully until Ben Rinnes was in view. On a clear day you could hike to the top of that hill and see all eight of the surrounding counties. Gracie had done it once with her Da. Her favorite view was looking north, past Aberlour, to Elgin and beyond, to the North Sea.

"If ye ever try hiking again, ye shouldn't miss the view from up there," she said to Fletcher as she pointed out the landmark to the group. "Me Da took me when I was little. That's where I learned a lot about my grandparents an' their parents an' such. Those long walks were my history lessons."

"I'd try it again… with you. For historical reference, of course," Fletcher blubbered.

Gracie didn't reply. Something about letting him sit in this awkward admission amused her. The way his complexion colored when he said it, or the curious look he gave her—as if asking, *Do you feel it, too?*

It wasn't long before they were passing the Glenrinnes Distillery and Keira was making remarks about how they should go for a tasting while they were in town.

Turning onto a narrow side road, they made their way closer to the croft house. With it drawing ever nearer, Gracie's stomach flip flopped with anxiety. She wasn't just bringing a friend home, but strangers too. Outsiders to the community. How would they be received? If the neighbors found out it was for a position, they likely wouldn't be the first to open

The Highlands was full of close-knit communities and folks who valued their personal space. Newcomers had to earn trust and Gracie worried that, if favors needed to be asked of the locals to advance Fletcher's research, they might not be met with benevolence. No matter how well meaning their intentions.

Convincing her Da has been easy enough. He'd do anything for her. But keeping the likes of Mrs. Grant out of their business was another thing entirely. Plus, this was yet another trip home where she didn't tell Daniel she'd be visiting. Heaven forbid he come knocking on the door again!

Gracie blinked out at the sprawling pastures and fields. There was one thing that inevitably came with homecomings. The experiences that changed you while you were away.

Maybe there was something to the perspective Fletcher was always talking about. Ultimately, the distance from Glenrinnes didn't change her values or beliefs, but her world view had been broadened. He was partially responsible for that.

She would've never thought that her opinions, past, or perceptions would carry weight with someone the way they seemed to with Fletcher. He might've been a bit scratchy at first, but she'd worn down the grain. At least enough to see that what lay underneath was a great deal smoother.

# 13

# Blurred Edges

As the car pulled down the drive, filled with potholes and puddles, the stone house came into view and the breathtaking scenery surrounding it made Fletcher, Tate, and Keira gasp collectively. Chantilly, now bright eyed and tongue flapping, sat erect in the middle of the backseat, as if she too was taking in the view.

All the signs that winter was melting into spring dotted the landscape. Small patches of colorful buds could be seen from the road and the deep greens of the terrain were returning with the season. Overtaking the umber and olive of wintertime.

Fletcher could sense Gracie's appreciation of their impression. Her home was deeply personal, and she was sharing her farm, her family, and her history with them. Inviting them into her place of shelter, somewhere that held so much happiness and, simultaneously, so much pain was not only kind. It was brave. An act of courage rather than simple hospitality.

Reflecting on this, Fletcher realized that he wouldn't have had the same transparency with others. Not even Tate had heard the entire story about his childhood. It was something he kept close, locked away and only took it out occasionally to look at. Then, he'd tuck it back into its hiding place and ignore it for another few years.

Suddenly, the car jerked to a stop, and he broke free from his rumination, only to find they hadn't stalled in front of the house, but in front of a large wooly sheep.

"Clover! Ye are a bad lass, ye are!" Gracie exclaimed as she hopped out of the driver's seat and started toward the imposing animal.

"Should we help her?" Tate asked, leaning forward to take in the scene. But his inquiry was a few seconds too late, as Fletcher was already unfastening his seatbelt and climbing out of the car after her. The sound of Tilly's yipping echoed after him. Her paws scrambled against the seat.

"A friend of yours, I assume," he states, coming up behind Gracie.

"Ye use the term friend loosely. This one's always been a stubborn escapee," she replied.

Fletcher had to admit that Clover did look rather indifferent to the fact that she was out of the pen and away from the flock.

"Is there something I can do to help?"

Gracie's gaze went from Clover to him and back to Clover. It seemed as if any moment the sheep might decide she was altogether against returning to the ninety-nine others, turn-tail, and run.

"Go open the hatch an' look for a rope," Gracie directed.

Fletcher obeyed wordlessly and found the rope, neatly wound in the trunk, with no trouble. Handing it to her he retreated to the other side of the sheep in case he needed to run interference. Not that he really knew how to do that with a sheep, but he assumed it would be like when he was a child, and the cows got out. Only on a smaller scale.

He watched as Gracie gracefully intertwined the rope with itself to form a noose-like hoop. Gathering her intentions were to slip it over Clover's neck, he moved ever-so-slightly forward. Gauging his proximity, the sheep moved a couple of inches closer to Gracie. Apparently, she didn't like strangers, and that was fine by Fletcher.

"Great," Gracie whispered. "Now, close the gap so she doesn't retreat, and I'll go 'round the front."

Fletcher took a few steps to the left and Gracie stepped to the right. Crouching until she was almost face to face with Clover.

*About six more inches and she'll be ours,* Fletcher thought, moving at a sloth's pace to hopefully coax Clover forward.

Carefully avoiding a large water-filled rut in the driveaway, he skirted around towards Clover's rear. But, with eyes fixed ahead, he didn't see that a brittle twig was in the way of his next step. With a loud crack, the stick snapped under his weight. The sound startled Clover and she bolted to the left while Gracie lurched to the right, landing face first in the massive muddy puddle.

Fletcher raced to cut Clover off but slipped and ended up on his backside in the culvert.

For a moment, he and Gracie laid in their own embarrassment and defeat. Then, looked at each other in disbelief. Clover trotted towards the house as if their downfall was her goal all along.

Gracie heaved herself up from the ground with audible groaning and Fletcher dusted himself off, though, ultimately, only ended up spreading the mud around. He steadied his gaze on Gracie as she surveyed her ruined dress. A winter white, long sleeve, linen ensemble covered in a wildflower pattern and ruffles along the hem, now covered from the collar down in thick dark sludge.

*Even knee deep in a pool of muddy rainwater, she's a goddess.*

Somewhere in the hazy background, Keira was honking the car horn and hollering out the window, asking if they were okay. Chantilly anxiously barked something in morse code. But all he could focus on was the cherubic woman, glowing in the lane before him.

Looking from her dress to her gritty hands, with a bit of earth smudged across her cheek, and then to Fletcher, she offered a wobbly smile. He was surprised how strong the urge was to walk over and smooth away the stripe with his thumb. Instead, he put his palms up and shrugged.

"Wanna walk?" he suggested.

"Are you guys coming?" Tate called, joining Keira with his head out the window.

"We'll meet ye at the house," Gracie said, shaking her head.

*She chose the pause. The walk…with me.*

Fletcher's panic started to surface as the realization of the quarter mile walk in front of him with the girl he was slowly unraveling over settled on him. This wasn't a library or a museum. It wasn't going to be easy to hide behind a conversation based on work or study. This was different, casual, and decidedly more intimate. Walking a woman to meet her father, in the most deplorable condition with inescapable desire.

Between here and the front door, he wasn't Fletcher the historian. He was just Fletcher, the man bringing Gracie home in soaked clothes with raw feelings.

As he joined Gracie in the middle of the driveway, he held out his hand to help her out of the cloudy pool she was still standing in. And, like a lady would, took it, while holding her frock up with the other, regardless of the fact it was far from being salvaged.

"Sorry about your dress," Fletcher said. Though he wasn't sorry at all. In his opinion, he'd never seen her look better than she did right now. This, right here, was honest and unfiltered.

"S'alright," she replied cheerily. "*I'm* sorry *you* got into this mess."

"Yeah, this *was* my favorite sweatshirt," he poked.

"Maybe Clover will pay ye back one day wi' a new sweater."

"Not sure I'd trust anything Clover calls a gift."

"She gave us this walk," Gracie observed quietly.

Fletcher stopped walking and let Gracie get a few steps ahead. He was truly taken aback by the rose-colored world she saw, when he only saw grey. She was *Pollyanna* on steroids, and he was hooked.

The scary thing about starting to fall for someone is, you never know just how far in you are until the water is so deep, you're drowning. As far as Fletcher was concerned, his heart was in the middle of the North Sea, floundering, and surrounded by killer whales.

He was treading dangerous, uncharted waters with no hope in sight.

"You didn't ask from my opinion," he huffed, catching up to Gracie. "But I'll tell you what I think."

"Ha! That's a first. Fletcher volunteering information," she laughed, elbowing him.

He gently reach out and grabbed her by the elbow, turning her to face him. A fine mist began to fall and collected on her lashes and the strands of her hair. She looked like a mermaid, stuck on land with a grumpy sailor. She was shivering and Fletcher realized she'd forgotten her coat in the car.

Whipping off his soiled hoodie, he swiftly slipped it over her head and tucked her into it. Gracie's gratitude was more than just a murmured thanks. It was evident in the way she snuggled into the fabric and her lips stopped quivering.

"I think you're rare, Gracie. Not just people like you, but you specifically. You've got a whole world living inside of you that you carry around wherever you go."

The rain began to fall harder. Fletcher's hair fell into his eyes, which were growing in earnestness.

"The freshness of your flowers, the intensity of your happiness… They color that world and you splash that color around this grey planet with the grace of a skilled artist," he panted.

Gracie's dress clung to her legs and the sweatshirt hung on her small frame, even heavier now soaked with rain. She'd been staring straight at Fletcher's chest throughout his speech, her head barely reaching his collarbone. Now, she looked at him in the face.

*Finally.*

Reaching up, Gracie carefully removed Fletcher's fogged glasses. The blurred world around them stained greener than before. The trees, the grass, the bushes. As if they were held in the palm of the earth.

"Seeing more clearly now?" she asked.

"I think I'm beginning to."

Just then they heard a loud whistle coming from the direction of the house and, taking it as a signal, took off in a jog towards it.

Arriving at the door out of breath and laughing, Gracie leaned against the wall and gasped, followed closely by Fletcher who sat on the step wheezing. Each of them unaware of the audience at the window.

"Not much to entertain around here, huh?" Fletcher asked, his pulse slowing. He pointed to the noses he'd suddenly noticed, pressed to the glass.

Keira, not ashamed of her curiosity, banged on the window. "What took ye so long? Can't walk and talk at the same time?" she yelled, as she motioned for them to come inside.

"Ye know, she seems set on causin' a scene. About as much as Tate. Maybe we should play matchmaker," Gracie suggested, wiggling her eyebrows suspiciously.

"Two drama queens like them in a relationship? I don't think the world is ready," Fletcher replied.

"Yer prob'ly right," she sighed. "We'd better get in there before they get a wee bit too crazy."

She yanked the door open, and Tilly came running out to greet them. Nosily, she nudged Fletcher's knees and sniffed his ankles. Fletcher watched as Gracie gathered her long, wet tresses and began to ring them out before stepping inside. It wasn't going to be much use, trying to look presentable, until they could get out of the mucky clothes they were in. A shower was definitely in order.

Nevertheless, he liked watching her preen.

There was no debate, Gracie was a simple girl. She'd grown up on a farm. She'd just tried to lasso a sheep. She wore little to no makeup, as far as he could tell, and was never overdressed. Gracie was understated, unassuming. And it suited her all too well.

"You two look positively dreadful," Tate announced, as made way for them to come into the small entry. "And I won't pretend you smell better than you look."

"How sweet of ye, Tate," Gracie said sweetly, while violently swatting at him like an annoying housefly. "If ye like this, ye'll love where yer sleepin'."

Fletcher squinted his eyes at Tate, giving him a wary *I'm warning you* look and Tate put his hands up in surrender.

"Is me Da in?" Gracie asked.

"Nah, he's out in the barn. Housekeeper said so," Keira replied. "I put some tea on for ye two. Figured ye'd be freezin' after gettin' caught out there."

Fletcher looked around, noticing a bright copper kettle on the stove, a fire roaring in the hearth, and the overall coziness of the space. He imagined what it must've been like for Gracie to grow up around such warmth and love. What would it have been like for him to grow up in a home like this? With parents that adored him? So much that he never wanted to let them down. Never wanting them to hurt or suffer at his expense.

He felt Gracie's eyes on him and let the thoughts go as quickly as they'd come. Who was he to be envious of something she didn't have any control over? Gracie deserved this life. She deserved everything.

"Ye alright?"

"Yeah, all good," he said. "Just wondering where the nearest shower is."

"Right. Come wi' me upstairs an' I'll get ye straighten out," she said, and motioned for him to follow.

As he went with Gracie up the stairwell and down the hall, he could see some of the rooms had doors that were cracked open, others were locked. But towards the end of the passage there was a room whose door stood completely open, as if inviting him inside. He paused at the threshold.

The space was neat and orderly, but not in an obsessive way. There were floral accents, woven baskets that housed plants, and small canvas paintings on the wall. A large window let in whatever sunlight Scotland was generous enough to provide. The bed was made up with a bright yellow quilt and dainty doily coverlet hanging off the edge. The whole room oozed yellow radiance.

This was Gracie's room. He felt it. Her presence was there even though she had disappeared into a closet to find bath towels.

*Yellow is my new favorite color. Yellow is the loveliest color of all.*

"Ye get lost?" came her voice from behind him.

His cheeks turned rosy as he turned and took the towel she was offering. "No, I… I was just admiring what I assume is your room."

"Aw, yeah. Da insists on keepin' it like this even though I've gone off on me own. I think seein' it stay the same makes him think I always will, too."

But, before Fletcher could answer, she ushered him back down the hall to the bathroom and shut the door behind her, leaving him alone with his thoughts.

So much had happened in the course of the morning and sorting through it would have to wait. The priority was getting to the root of this newfound family history and figuring out what, if any of it, he could apply to his research paper.

While he hung onto the shower curtain rail, waiting for the water to get hot, he closed his eyes and exhaled, the steam curling upward as warmth settled over his skin. The world outside was still gray, still drenched, still blurred—but behind those dusty blues, all he could see was yellow.

# 14

# Fragments & Foundations

Gracie reentered the room in a faded pair of cargo khakis and a blue knit sweater, featuring a swan on the front. She looked relaxed and refreshed compared to the chaotic, mud-covered version of herself that walked into the house an hour ago. Glad that Da hadn't been there to see Fletcher on her heels, she felt she could take a deep breath and sip her tea in peace before his arrival from the barn.

After Gracie had called things off with Daniel, Da had become a bit more protective of Gracie. As a father, she assumed he felt it his responsibility and right to make sure her heart was cared for. But it was always a bit awkward to talk about her love life, or lack thereof, with him. Those were times she really ached for Mam.

As she sat back on the sofa, listening to the sound of the rain and scratching softly behind Chantilly's ears, she thought back to what Fletcher had said when they were alone on the path. That she colored the grey world with a rainbow of color. A shiver went up her spine. Were his experiences in life so grim that he viewed someone like Gracie as a lighthouse in the storm?

Fletcher wasn't exactly someone who threw compliments around like confetti. This one felt personal. Like she had unknowingly begun to peel back the disguise he lived in and was starting to see who he was under the surface. Who she hoped he was, if only for her.

*Oh Mam… What do you think?*

Gracie's silent question filled the air. The emptiness of the room, of the house without her mother in it, and the gnawing feeling that something was shifting consumed her. And as the drops of rain slowed, she could hear the cackles of Keira who'd gone out to the chicken coop to take selfies with the hens.

"Where is everyone?" Fletcher asked as he walked through the doorway. The floorboards creaked under his weight and Gracie noticed how he filled the space, much like her Da. A solemn, strong man holding his heartbreak together with a string.

"Keira is documenting her city girl meets country life series. Not sure 'bout Tate," she answered.

Tilly looked up from where her head rested in Gracie's lap. Big brown eyes pleading for Fletcher to join them.

"I think Tilly likes you better than me," he observed.

"Nah. It's just that us women have tae stick together," she said with the last swig of her tea.

Her mind quickly went to Sophia, whom Tate had mentioned previously, and she wondered if this was the kind of relationship they'd had. Something unspoken but powerful. Did she and Chantilly cuddle on couches and share wordless secrets?

Fletcher had never mentioned her. Was that because she wasn't important to him? Or was it because he had his walls so fortified that Gracie could never really penetrate them? Perhaps getting through the first line of defense was all the farther he would allow her to go. Enough to be the recipient of his crooked smile and honest admiration, but nothing more.

"What are you thinking about? You've been quiet for a long time." Fletcher was now seated opposite her in an armchair, staring at her intently.

"Sorry. I was just lost in dreamland."

"Was it at least a good dream?"

"Who is Sophia?" she asked bluntly.

"A dream with her in it would decidedly *not* be good," Fletcher responded.

"Who is she?" Gracie insisted softly. "Is she—"

"My ex," rushed out of him. "She's my ex-girlfriend. Emphasis on the ex."

Gracie giggled. "I don't mean tae pry. It's just… Tate had said somethin' about her the other day and… I thought maybe she was why you hesitated 'bout comin' up here."

"Do you think I'm the kind of guy who would come here and take advantage of you and your family if I had a steady girlfriend?"

"I think I'm still figuring out what kind of guy you are," Gracie replied. "But, no, I don't think ye'd do that."

Fletcher's shoulders visibly relaxed. "Gracie, you should know by now that I don't spend my time with anyone who I feel would waste it. Just know that *you* are the exact opposite of a waste of anything."

Gracie wasn't sure what to say. There was so much she wanted to detangle in those sentences. But forming a coherent thought in reply seemed impossible.

He let out a deep sigh. "I was thinking, now that the rain has stopped, we might go to Cullen and do a little bit of sleuthing."

"Not tired of bein' in the car?"

"I've got a contact up there who might be able to shed some light on where to track down more information on your grandparent's life in that area."

A loud bang and heavy footsteps interrupted as Gracie's Da entered the house. Gracie got up and floated over, arms outstretched and embraced him lovingly. He looked like an ogre in comparison to her. Rough beard and hands, dominating stature. But oddly, she seemed to belong in this ogre's arms.

Fletcher stood out of respect and needlessly adjusted the cuff of his shirt, as he waited to be acknowledged and introduced. Gracie could see the discomfort in his demeanor and the way he shifted from one foot to the other.

Finally, Da stepped forward, taking in Fletcher. His height and broad shoulders were comparable enough to Da's, though his countenance was decidedly different.

Gracie watched as Da extended his hand and Fletcher took it with his own. Something unsaid passed between them, though she couldn't pinpoint what it was. She only hoped Da wouldn't scare Fletcher off. She had tried to convey how important his research was and how it tied to their family, but now she wondered if she'd done a good enough job.

"Ye must be Fletcher. Welcome," Da said confidently.

"Thank you for having me, Sir," Fletcher replied.

"Call me, Lach, please. Sir makes me feel old," Da chuckled. "Gracie tells me ye're uncoverin' some Scottish roots."

"It would seem that way. I'm hoping to follow the trail as far as I can."

"I hope ye find what yer looking for," Da stated, eyes shining.

Gracie stepped up beside Da. "We were actually 'bout to head to Cullen for the afternoon."

"Back in the car, again?" Keira whined from somewhere in the kitchen. Gracie hadn't noticed her come in, but now there was unmistakable sounds of her rummaging through the refrigerator. And after a moment she appeared with a freshly made sandwich.

"Who's goin' tae wake Tate from his third nap to tell 'em?" she added.

"Eh, let 'em sleep. Ye two get goin' so's ye don't get back too late. Does yer dog know how tae herd sheep?" Da said.

Fletcher chuckled nervously. "I don't *think* so. It's not exactly a skill I felt qualified to teach."

He looked at Chantilly, abandoned on the couch. Her head was resting in the empty space left by Gracie, and she dozed peacefully.

"If yer sure, Da. Be back 'fore long, promise," Gracie said, pecking his cheek.

"Keira, you sure you don't want to tag along?" Fletcher offered, though Gracie knew the answer.

When Keira shook her head and chewed on a mouthful of bread and meat, her assumption was confirmed. Even if Keira hadn't been completely engrossed in her sandwich, she wouldn't have wanted to go down the rabbit hole of history. Plus, Gracie knew her well enough to know that this was a setup. Keira was dying to see Gracie and Fletcher confirm her suspicion of unrequited love.

"Suit yourself," he said, as he followed Gracie towards the door.

Armed with umbrellas and the thrill of discovery, meandering the curvy roads of the Highlands for the next hour didn't seem so bad. Maybe the air would clear—of both the clouds and the wordless notions that hung between them.

Gracie's stomach growled as she climbed into the passenger seat, letting Fletcher take the lead. She wasn't sure where exactly they were going and he wasn't familiar with the area, on top of it all, she was hungry. But she tried to push her appetite aside.

"I didn't realize that we'd missed lunch until now," Fletcher mentioned casually. Gracie knew it was because he'd heard her belly scold her. But she pretended not to notice the connection and waved off the thought of food.

"We'd be better off gettin' tae Cullen and stopping for food later," she suggested.

"Ya know, if you wanted to pretend you weren't starving, you should've picked a quieter stomach."

"And if ye want tae finish yer paper we'd better get a move on," she retorted. "We can throw back a pint and yap after. Unless there's some reason tae put it off?"

"No reason at all," Fletcher replied. He slammed the car into gear a little harder than someone who had nothing on their mind.

Gracie let the response settle without answering. Though it was hard to suppress the desire to explore the reason behind his dismissive tone.

So far that day the energy between them had been piping hot. Nearly boiling over. But now, Fletcher seemed to have cooled off. He was distracted and distant. It had to have been for more than just her insistence on skipping a meal. However, Gracie was sure that if she continued to press the subject, she'd be met with dogged determination to evade an explanation.

Instead, she bounced her knee against the door handle and looked out the window. She looked out at the rolling landscapes of Moray—the lush farmland and the rugged hills that define Speyside. All while tepid stillness occupied the driver's seat.

The only noise that occasionally colored the bleakness of the drive was the robotic voice of the GPS telling Fletcher to *turn right in three hundred feet* or *continue straight for two miles.*

*Apparently living in Scotland hasn't made computing kilometers any easier,* Gracie observed.

By the time the quaint, seaside cottages and wet, sandy beaches of Cullen came into view, Gracie was chewing the inside of her cheek raw from her resolve to not be the first to speak. It should've been a site she felt was welcoming her, like she had during her summer trips there with Mam. But right now, the dark pounding waves and circling seagulls felt oppressive.

"Looks like another storm might be rolling in," Fletcher offered, as if they hadn't just spent the last fifty-six minutes in silence.

Gracie didn't let herself look at him. She could already tell there would be a quiet pleading in his eyes—for her to open up, connect. Perhaps he didn't even know that his eyes had that effect on her. He could've made her spill her deepest desires with only a bat of his lashes or a longing stare.

"Where are we going?" she replied to the bleary window.

"I thought you'd never ask," Fletcher chuckled. "We're headed to Fordyce Parish Church. So not exactly in Cullen. But I found some leads that suggested your family might've attended there while they lived in the area and thought maybe you'd like to check it out." He nudged her with his elbow. "They have records that date back to 1665."

"What d'ya expect tae find?"

"Not exactly sure, but I've got a hunch this a good starting point. I've been in touch with a local archivist who pulled some of the most relevant material for us to sift through."

It was then that she turned to him. Two hands on the steering wheel as if he was trying to keep himself in control. Of the car, or his own emotions, she wasn't sure. His profile was prominent—sloping forehead to a distinguished nose and full lips partially hidden beneath his scruff. He was handsome, she couldn't deny that. And she wondered what had made him turn out gentler than his father.

"Are ye sure that delvin' into me family isn't takin' away from yer research? If anythin' shouldn't ye be focused on yer own discoveries?" she asked innocently.

"I don't know why we can't do both," he reasoned. "I could be wrong, but for the first time in a long time, history is more to me than just facts. It's familial truth. And I give you all the credit for that."

"Aren't ye scared of what ye might find?"

"Honestly," he sighed, "I'm more scared of what will happen if I don't even bother looking."

"Ah, is that hope I'm sensing from the grumpy professor?" she laughed.

"Well… right now, I figure if I wear it like a parachute, maybe it'll come in handy during the freefall."

Gracie pressed her lips together and cocked her head to the side. She couldn't figure out if she was witnessing Fletcher's metamorphosis or mental breakdown. Either way, she was cautiously excited to find out what was next.

As they passed through the small village of Fordyce, drifting by Fordyce Castle and continuing a short way east, Fletcher recounted several details about the town and how one of the ladies-in-waiting to Mary Queen of Scots was laid to rest not far away, near Findlater Castle. It was entertaining for Gracie to see the past of her people through the eyes of someone who grew up so far removed from this life of clans and claims to the throne.

She was so consumed by these thoughts of tradition and monarchy verses the freedom of what should've been Fletcher's childhood—the childhood he was robbed of—that she didn't realize the car had come to a stop in front of a weathered stone building. The pitched roof, stained glass windows, and peaceful kirkyard all stood as hallmarks of its era.

Its quiet dignity and untold stories clearly beckoned Fletcher, since he had already rounded the front of the car and was attempting to open her door. His earnest face peered in at her as he mouthed for her to unlock it and gestured toward the handle, waiting for his actions to register.

Once she grasped his request, she collected her Harris tweed backpack and slipped her cell phone inside. Stepping outside she noticed a chill in the air and thought back to the soft fabric of Fletcher's hoodie wrapped around her. It had smelled of aged paper and patchouli and, even though it was four sizes too big, felt just as comfortable as her favorite sweater.

Fletcher led her to the entry of the parish and the two of them went inside, wide eyed with a sense of wonder. Together they wandered through the main sanctuary and were met near the pulpit by an older gentleman with ink-stained fingers and sagging shoulders. He wore a black gown, white clerical collar, a Geneva band and introduced himself as Reverend MacKenzie.

His already welcoming presence seemed to relax even more as Fletcher explained the reason for their visit and the documents that he understood were set aside for their review. The reverend nodded and led them down a narrow hall to a small, dim vestry. It was a quiet, functional space full of shelves lined with ancient books and records. A wooden table, worn smooth by years of use, sat at the center surrounded by sturdy handmade chairs.

"Please, take as much time as ye need. I'll be just up the hall if ye need anythin'," Reverend MacKenzie assured them before excusing himself to attend to his duties.

Graced glanced around, in awe of the amount of information contained in such a tight space. The generational insight held within the walls of the archive room was weighty and impressive.

"Yer move, McCullough. Where do we start?" she asked. Flecks of dust floated in the air, and she felt Fletcher nearby, taking in the wealth of knowledge he was about to hold in his two hands.

"Gracie, have you ever felt like everything was crumbling and you couldn't fix it?"

The question caught her off guard. She wasn't sure how to answer or where the response might lead once she found it. Fortunately, Fletcher wasn't watching her. He was moving toward the table in the middle of the room and scanning the contents splayed out on it. He looked like Nicholas Cage about to find the *National Treasure*. All grit and courage.

"I've felt like that almost my entire life. But places like this," he went on. "They make me feel like if I could soak up the wisdom of the past—the mistakes, the lessons, the successes… that maybe I could fix it after all. Maybe I'd find the piece that's been missing and rebuild that crumbling world."

"I'm not sure what ye're looking for exists in a book," Gracie stated. "Ye're not the one responsible for fixing what happened to ye."

"Maybe. Maybe not."

"Fletcher." He looked up at the sound of his name. "Ye're not less of a man 'cause somebody didn't know how to love you. The piece ye're missin' is loving yerself."

She watched as his adam's apple bobbed and he swallowed, not just his pride but tears he refused to shed. Gracie took a step closer and tilted her chin up to look him in the eyes. They glistened with recognition loaded down with years of unworthiness.

He tried for a shaky smile, but it melted into more of a grimace. She linked her elbow through his and steered him toward the forms and certificates on display.

"Alright. Now, let's get tae work."

# 15

# Holy Ground

The small clock that hung on the wall provided a satisfying ticking sound that seemed to match the rhythm of Fletcher's heartbeat as he and Gracie inspected every scrap of paper before them. He traced the edge of each parish register with the pad of his thumb, the documents soft and worn beneath his touch. He scanned the words carefully, afraid to miss a crucial detail.

Across the table, Grace slouched over her own stack of files. Her nose was scrunched and freckles on it seemed to dance with each other as her facial expressions went from frustration to enlightenment and back again. Every now and then, he'd catch himself staring for a moment too long, watching the way her lashes touched the top of her cheeks and the crease in her forehead deepened as she read.

Never would Fletcher have thought he'd be up to his eyeballs in a project that started out as a simple retelling of history, but that turned out to be intimately connected to him as an individual. He was a man who had spent his adult life running from his past and disguising it as a career choice. Now, he was getting up close and personal with the side of his family he had always wished away.

But his curiosity outweighed his avoidance. The closer he got to finding more information about his lineage, the weight of it started to feel less like a burden and more like something that was worth understanding. He had been invested in work before. This was different. It wasn't just a job, it was the key to accepting who he was. Where it could all be going.

The light coming through the diamond-paned windows had changed from stark and white to a golden glow. The clouds were finally giving way and early evening was setting up to be beautiful. Fletcher rubbed his beard and hummed lightly, running his finger down the page in his hand.

At the bottom of the page, he noticed a faded, but visible, coat of arms symbol embossed in the corner. Looking closer, he could see it featured a shield with a lattice pattern and above that a knight's helmet with visor. Atop the helmet were feathers and around the coat of arms was mantling, scrolling and elaborate.

He sucked in a sharp breath. This wasn't just any symbol. It was the MacCullough family crest. The one his father had worn on a signet ring on his pinky finger when Fletcher was a child. He'd recognize it anywhere.

Scanning the page again, he realized that it wasn't just a haphazard record of any community member. It was the loose leaf of a contract with the church regarding bookbinding. The document stated that the MacCullough family had opened a bindery in Fordyce following their displacement during the Clearances and that, as an act of charity from the church, were gifted a small cottage and parcel of land.

It appeared to Fletcher that the church's recognition of the MacCullough's transition from displaced farmers to skilled tradespeople was an acknowledgement of their legitimacy in the community. Perhaps this led to their creating ties with influential families, expanding beyond ecclesiastical works and into the preservation of other important books. Anything was possible.

"D'ya find something?" Gracie asked. Her expression was hopeful and open. "Anything about me granny?"

"I… I can't believe what I found, actually," Fletcher stammered. "Proof that my family relocated to Fordyce during the clearances. They learned a new skill, opened a book bindery, and rose in status thanks to the recognition they got from it. This paper is part of the contract they had with this very church."

"Really? That exciting!"


"The MacCullough crest is stamped down here in the corner. I remember my dad having it on this ring he wore. I'll never forget that ring…" Fletcher's voice broke. "The ring that contributed to more than a few of my busted lips and bruised cheekbones," he said through gritted teeth.

"Why did your family drop the 'A' from their name?" Gracie asked, steering the conversation away from Fletcher's dark memories.

Fletcher's eyes flickered to the wall ahead of him, and then back to Gracie. He tried to focus, but his mind was abuzz with the influx of information. "It could've been any reason, really. Simpler spelling, an error at the port where their immigration to the US was recorded… Don't think I'll ever know for sure."


Gracie rounded the table to look over Fletcher's shoulder at the new evidence. She hovered above him and he could feel the

hitching of her breath, the increase of her pulse. He could sense
how invested she was in this search; in the testimony he was
unearthing. Gracie was cheering him on, even in his solemnity.
Even when the memories that surfaced were ugly.

"Well, what are we waiting for?" she finally asked.

"Waiting for?"

"The location o' the cottage is on here. Let's go check it out!
It'll be dark soon."

Without hesitation, Fletcher took a photo of the document with
his cell phone and collected the rest of the papers into the
center of the table; the way they'd been when he and Gracie
had arrived. They quickly thanked the reverend for access and
apologized for rushing off in such a hurry, explaining that
they'd made an exciting discovery that couldn't wait.

According to the mechanical voice of the GPS, they were going
to arrive at their destination within five minutes. Fletcher's
hands trembled as he tapped his fingers on the steering wheel.
He was certain the cottage wouldn't be inhabited, which meant
that little would be left standing. Maybe there was nothing to
walk around and admire at all. But even stepping on the ground
it once stood upon would be a sacred moment. The thought of
being so close to tangible evidence of his family's resilience

crumbled his defenses. He couldn't hold back the excitement he felt.

Only a couple of miles down a one lane road, Gracie spotted a structure on the left. The unmistakable ruins of a home. Moss and lichen clung to the stone walls and ivy twisted through the cracks. As they approached, the land around the house looked windswept and wild. Frost lingered at the edges of the thistle leaves and the smell of damp earth permeated the air.

With no clear distinction between the driveway and the yard, Fletcher pulled over to the shoulder of the road and put his hazard lights on. His breathing was heavy, and he clutched the seatbelt where it crossed his chest.

*It's only a house. They aren't here.*

Still, repeating this to himself didn't get rid of the ghostly presence he felt getting out of the car.

Gracie followed close behind, stepping over vines and twigs; careful not to encroach on Fletcher. He wanted to reach out and hold her hand. To grip onto something he knew was real. Because, right now, everything else felt like a fever dream. Vivid, pearlescent, and distorted. It was magical and mystical and terrifying.

Moving through what used to be the doorway and going up the disintegrating stairs into the living space, he could see the remnants of a bed built into the wall and a collapsing stone hearth. The floorboards were rotting and splintering; warped and swollen. He imagined what it would've looked like in its prime, when it was a residence instead of a ruin.

Besides the common areas, there looked to have at one time been a small stable built onto the side of the house. However, the roof had long since collapsed and the walls caved in.

Standing amidst the emptiness, Fletcher somehow felt full. This lack of anything was simultaneously everything he had ever needed. It was proof that he was more than the estranged son of an abusive alcoholic. More than the two generations of Pennsylvania farmers that came before him.

Gracie's voice invaded his thoughts then. "I'll bet this place used tae be beautiful."

He nodded in agreement. "It still is, in its own way. There's something aesthetic about everything it's not. Everything it used to be," he replied softly.

Suddenly his eyes fell on the corner of an obscured chest under the space where a window had once been. He moved toward it, taking note of the weeds growing around it, through the floor, and the debris from years of storms. The kist was carved with intricate floral details, namely thistles, and the rusty hinges barely held the lid in place. Some might've seen it as future kindling for a fire, but Fletcher saw a potential treasure trove.

Lifting the lid enough to peer inside, he could see weather-stained papers, small keepsakes, and a scrap of mildewed fabric. After pushing the top off completely, he noticed something else tucked into the corner. A thick leather pouch and, under it, a few worn leaves of Fordyce's Sermons.

Gracie crept closer and crouched next to Fletcher. "Are ye goin' tae open it?"

Fletcher didn't respond. Instead, he unraveled the strap that was wound around the outside of the pouch and hung it over his knee. He turned the leather, smooth and well preserved, over in his hands. Then, briefly, he closed his eyes, as if saying a silent prayer that the contents would be of value.

Carefully unwrapping the bundle, he revealed a stack of envelopes, fragile with age. The ink on the outside was faded, but legible. And, in addition to the address, a name was written. Finlay MacCullough.

"D'ya know who that is?" Gracie probed. She now had one hand on Fletcher's shoulder, steadying herself as she huddled next to him.

"My great-grandfather," Fletcher said. "That's my great-grandfather's name. The first of our family to come to America or so I read on Ancestry.com."

He turned one of the envelopes around. On the back flap was written:

*P.S. I wish you were here.*

Fletcher's eyebrows shot up and he hurriedly opened the envelope, which was no longer sealed. Inside, there was a letter. Small, neatly folded, and covered front and back in scribbled cursive handwriting.

Very slowly, Fletcher unfolded the paper and smoothed it against his thigh. He skimmed it quietly and then began to read aloud, from the beginning.

*My Dearest Finlay,*

*The days are dim and lonely now that you've gone away and it feels as though I may never see the light of day again. I spend my time preoccupied with thoughts of us meeting under our favorite hawthorn in the spring, wishing for those days to return to me. For you, my love, to return to me on the western wind…*

After reading the first paragraph, he paused and ran his fingers along each line, finally reaching the signature.

*Forever Yours,*

Fletcher sat frozen, his hand floating at the edge of the letter, his lips pressed into a hard line. Gracie felt the weight of his silence and knew that, in that moment, something had shifted.

# 16

# Tangled Threads

Thirty minutes later, Gracie sat next to Fletcher, pressed into a booth at a local pub in Fordyce. The Wandering Stag was atmospheric, warm and storied. The perfect place to hole up with Fletcher's laptop and investigate his great-grandfather, Finlay, and his beloved, Aisla.

From what Fletcher could recall from his limited ancestry research before leaving Edinburgh, Finlay would've been about forty-three years old when he immigrated to the United States. However, the details on whether he went alone or he was accompanied by someone, particularly a wife, were fuzzy. Gracie peppered him with questions to which he had inadequate answers. Plus, they still hadn't found the information regarding her family that he had held out hope for.

She sat with her chin in hand, elbow propped on the table, awaiting her cottage pie and ale. Perhaps some food would help the gears turn a bit faster and she could be of more help to Fletcher. Hunger was clouding her ability to do anything other than create more uncertainty.

Fletcher adjusted his glasses, typed a few words into the empty search field on the website homepage that filled his screen, and then adjusted his glasses again. Gracie couldn't help but notice how adorably focused he was. How nuanced his movements were and the redness of his bottom lip from chewing it as he read various forums and online records.

He looked away from the monitor in time to catch her staring and her cheeks grew pink. Goosebumps prickled her arms. Fletcher offered a relaxed smile and went back to typing and clicking various boxes on the form in front of him. Gracie had never seen him so intent, and in his element. It was fascinating to her that he never seemed to tire of searching.

As their meals arrived, and Gracie took a swig of her Belhaven brew, Fletcher's arms shot up in triumph.

"I've got it!" he exclaimed.

"Got what?" Gracie asked, barely swallowing the rich, malty beverage.

"Aisla. Have you really never heard that name before?"

Gracie shook her head. "Not that I remember. Should it mean somethin' tae me?"

"Aisla *Buchanan* was your great-great-great aunt, Gracie. Malcolm's much younger sister."

Hysterically, Gracie began to laugh. The sheer improbability that Aisla Buchanan was the lost love of Finlay McCullough seemed incredulous. But Fletcher's face remained elated, frozen in the thrill of the moment.

"You don't believe me?" he finally asked, doubling down.

His challenge struck a nerve. Slowly she regained her composure, but there were lightning strikes in her eyes. Computing this was impossible. Her stomach twisted with doubt, but her heart lurched with possibility.

"Here, look for yourself," Fletcher said, shifting to put his right hand on her lower back and he moved the computer closer. Gracie felt a shudder down her spine at his touch and instinctively leaned in. His left hand lowered to her thigh and his eyes met hers.

"What if…" Gracie began, her breathing shallow.

"They weren't married, Gracie. Please, look."

Bracing herself, she turned to see what he had uncovered. He slowly removed his hand from her thigh and pointed at a

chronological timeline on the screen. His hand shook, and he
cleared his throat, as was his habit.

"If you see here," he began. "Aisla's timeline doesn't start til
seventeen years after Malcom. By the time Mac was married to
Edna, Aisla was a preteen. And here, when their family tree
expands? That's about when Aisla would've been writing to
Finlay. She was probably no more than sixteen."

*Was Aisla too young to make decisions for herself? Did Finlay leave
believing they had time, only for history to interfere?*, Gracie wondered.

"But if you look down the line farther," he pointed to a date,
typed neatly under Aisla's name. "She passed away at eighteen.
Dysentery."

Gracie instinctively pulled back and stared at her cottage pie,
now getting cold. The yellow light hanging above the booth
suddenly seemed too bright. The warmth of the pub, too warm.
She felt light-headed and dizzy. So much lost potential. A love
cut short before it had the chance to be something lasting. An
aunt she never knew existed. Why had no one ever told her?

The hum of the tables surrounding them dulled in her ears, her
pulse roaring louder than all else. Grief for a life that never fully
unfolded filled her as she felt Fletcher move and then both of
his hands were on her shoulders. Begging her to focus on him.

His lips parted, preparing to speak. Then, he clamped them shut. Only to open them again and ask the question she hoped wouldn't come.

"What are you most upset about right now?" he whispered.

He waited patiently, uncertain of how she would respond. Watching her look away, grip the handle of her glass. He heard her let out a shaky breath.

"I'm not upset. I'm confused. Sad. I wish I had known she was a part of my story. Our story now, I guess," she said quietly to the table.

"Edna and Mac must've moved to Cullen before she died. I'm guessing she stayed in the highlands with her parents and was heartbroken when Finlay had to leave, during the Clearances, with his."

"I'm sorry," Gracie replied. "I'm sorry that this is the start of yer time up North, that yer not finding better information for yer paper." She sniffled lightly and brushed her sleeve under her nose.

"Gracie, this isn't about a paper anymore. Don't you see? This is a legitimate connection I've craved for my entire life. And I never would have started down the path of finding it if it weren't for you," he admitted. "And getting to know more about your family, about you, it's the feather in the cap. The extra objective I didn't realize I was looking for. Except now that I've seen it, I can't look away."

Gracie paused, absorbing his words. There was a shift. The warmth of the pub softened. Fletcher reached for his own beer, gulped a couple of times, and set it back on the table.

"I'm not sure what to say. I always thought I knew who I was, what I was meant for. Then I lost me Mam and I've been torn since. Thought about closing up shop and coming back home. This adventure has made me question what home really is."

"I've never really felt at home anywhere," Fletcher shared.

"Maybe it's closer than you think," she said, with a half-smile.

Fletcher's fingers gripped the table as he leaned back, needing space to process her words.

"We should get back," he announced. "You gonna eat?"

"I'll admit, I'm not all that hungry anymore. I'll take it tae go. Da will be wonderin' where we got off to anyway."

Gracie seemed drained. She rubbed her arms feeling a sudden chill and the mood sat heavy between her and Fletcher. Watching him carefully, she wondered what he was thinking as he stood from the booth and rolled his shoulders. Suddenly there was darkness under his eyes and a weariness in his stance.

"C'mon, sunshine," he sighed. "Let's get you home."

# 17

# A Frenzied Flame

The next morning Fletcher awoke in the sparsely furnished loft above the sheep pen. Converting it had obviously been an afterthought, due to the lack of insulation and privacy. But he'd slept well enough. The emotional journey he'd taken yesterday, and the discovery of the Aisla Buchanan's letters had worn him out. Outside a rooster crowed.

He looked over at Tate, splayed out on a camping cot, on the far side of the room. His mouth hung open and he snored softly. He looked like a cat stretched out in the sunlight and Fletcher shook his head in disbelief that someone who napped so often could ever sleep soundly at night.

Fletcher turned onto his back and stared up at the ceiling. His mind wandered to Gracie. Was she awake? Was she thinking about him too? Something had been changing in their dynamic lately. He'd felt pure electricity when he was tangled up with her in the booth at The Wandering Stag. Letting his guard down when it came to research and family was one thing, but the fondness he felt for Gracie was something else. It was borderline infatuation; with the way she moved, the way she spoke, the cadence of her laughter. All the intimate details of how she existed in the world—in his world—were committed to memory.

Suddenly the loft felt confining, and Fletcher shifted restlessly. He could hear the ruffling of feathers from the chicken coop and the soft bleating of a lamb. There was no way he would be able to go back to sleep now. He ran a hand over his face and decided to sneak outside into the milky sunrise.

Chantilly lay under the small window, content to continue lounging, as usual.

Letting a cardigan hang open over his plain white undershirt, and shoving on his boots, he crept down the stairs and into the open air. It was a crisp morning, and the scent of fresh hay clung to the breeze. The farm sounds and the slow awakening before the day was fully alive reminded him of his childhood. When he was ten or eleven years old and was up before dawn, scrambling to do his chores before the school bus arrived. Knowing his dad's belt awaited if things weren't done just right. Fletcher's stomach tightened, but he shook his head and let the thought vanish.

Gracie's farm was different than the one he'd grown up on. It was homey and quaint; quiet when it should be, loud when there was joy or humor. The Highlands, he decided, were unexpectedly grounding and peaceful.

Just then, he noticed movement at the far end of the barn. Then, the crash of a bucket and harsh words being hurled at someone, or something. He moved closer to the commotion with steady strides. His boots crunched on the gravel and crushed stray bits of hay.

"*Tha mi a' priodadh*," he heard a voice say. "I'm losing my patience with ye, Aleine."

It was Gracie's voice.

Fletcher held back a bit and peered around the corner of the stall where the noise had come from. He could see Gracie with her arm around the shoulders of a large Holstein cow, whispering into its ear, and a spilled bucket of milk at her feet.

After a beat, he straightened and rounded the corner. "Exchanging early morning secrets, are we?" he teased.

Gracie whirled around, eyes zeroing in on the intruder. Realizing it was Fletcher, she softened and continued petting Aleine. The naughty cow flicked her tail in defiance and attempted to shift away. Allowing distance, Gracie knelt to collect the pail and kicked a mound of hay over the pooling milk.

"Eh, she's a headstrong one," she said. "Been kickin' the bucket since she were old enough to be milked."

At that, Aleine stomped her hoof and Gracie shook her head, smirking. "See what I mean? Quite the personality."

"Oh, I'd say you've got enough tenacity to match it," he chuckled.

Gracie giggled in reply and shrugged, neither confirming or denying whether his statement was true. Fletcher noticed her hair was pulled halfway back, not tendrils framing her face as usual. She had it tied loosely with a ribbon and the length of it tumbled down her back. Her legs were bare and he observed that their paleness was being overtaken by a red cast due to the cold.

She wore only a pair of cotton boxer shorts, an oversized sweater, and wellies, but she was the most glorious thing he'd ever seen.

"Are ye cold? We can go in and I'll put a kettle on," she suggested, oblivious to his stare. "I know the loft isn't the coziest. But there's plenty more blankets in the house, and ye can warm up by the fire."

Fletcher swallowed and looked away briefly. Suddenly he was overly aware of everything. Of the way her hands deftly untied the rope Aleine was attached to, her constant concern for his well-being, and her dusty rose lips as she spoke.

They were about two-hundred feet from the house, but Fletcher wasn't ready to go in yet, wasn't ready to relinquish this quiet moment between the two of them. They were the only ones occupying this instant in infinity and he wanted to hold onto it.

Gracie paused mid-step, on her way past him, glancing inquisitively at his thoughtful posture.

"Ready to go home?" she asked.

Fletcher couldn't hold it in anymore. He felt like a rocket ready to shoot into the atmosphere. The word home was like a trigger that Gracie was pulling back on and had finally released.

He reached out and put a hand on her upper arm, gently pulling her back a step. Now, she was directly in front of him, looking up at him with confusion, but something else too. Was it anticipation? Desire?

"Ready to go home…" he repeated, more as a statement than a question. "Don't you get it, Gracie? You *are* home to me. Warm and safe. With you, I'm wrapped in a blanket in front of a fire, always."

Her eyes, olive in the muted morning light, shined with the sparkle of a million diamonds.

"I'm…I'm nobody really. Just a girl," she replied.

"You're so much more than that. You're dessert before dinner, the sun that peeks through the clouds, the gentle reminder that there is good in this world. And, for better or worse, I'm falling for you," Fletcher confessed. "Maybe I'm grumpy and scarred, but I'm yours, if you'll have me."

She reached out and brushed her fingers against the inside of his wrist, down his palm, and finally, intertwined them with his. Taking one step closer, then two, she was toe-to-toe with his boots. Then, she stood on her tiptoes and kissed him gently on the cheek.

Fletcher was undone. The need to reach her had replaced every trace of restraint. He didn't speak—he simply stepped closer, touching her like memory, like hope. Her fingers clung to his sleeve, grounding herself in the stillness between them.

He dipped his forehead to hers, their breath mingling. She gave a soft nod, but he'd already begun to lean. The moment had always been coming.

He drew her close.

Time stilled.

And there in the quiet, wrapped in unspoken truths, they held on—not just to each other, but to everything they'd been afraid to want. She melted into him, and he let himself feel the weight of finally belonging. It wasn't passion that gripped him, but the ache of having found something he hadn't dared to dream of.

Together, they shivered. Not from cold, but from the overwhelming hush of hearts aligning.

In the distance, Fletcher heard a high-pitched bark, the honking of disturbed geese, and Tate's voice calling for Chantilly. Breathless, he and Gracie broke apart, though his eyes didn't leave her lips.

She took a step backward, catching sight of Tate at the other side of the yard. Bedhead and pajama pants, running after Tilly and clapping his hands. But Fletcher reached out and tipped her chin until she was looking at him again. Until she gave him a smile that put the sun and stars to shame.

He exhaled and let out a quiet laugh, as if acknowledging the depth of what just happened and the reality they were about to get dragged into. Everything had changed, but the world outside was oblivious. Fletcher wondered if they should keep this development to themselves, as if it was too holy to be touched by outsiders. And what would Gracie's Da, Lach, think?

"We'll figure this out together, yeah?" Gracie says, as if sensing the sudden weight of his thoughts.

He nodded, elbowed her gently, and rounded the corner in search of Tate.

# 18

# No More Secrets

*It's almost too good to be true.*

That's what was on repeat in Gracie's mind as she washed up from milking Aleine and stoked the fire.

*The cynical introvert falling for me? And me for him?*

She was bursting with the leftover sensations of the kiss. The way Fletcher's arms felt like a tether attached to the warmth she'd been missing since Mam passed. How nothing else seemed to exist when it was just the two of them locked together, suspended in the what ifs and maybes. Choosing a future instead of sitting solely in the past.

Her thoughts drift to Mam and her kind, friendly face. She would've liked Fletcher, despite his flaws and pessimism, would've laughed at Chantilly's antics and smiled at Gracie's fondness for the pair of them. Mam wouldn't have questioned if the timing was right or if Gracie was sure. She would've been able to sense the certainty of it, the way Gracie could now.

She sat and folded her hands on the table, the way Mam used to, imagining that this is what it feels like when your life starts to come together. How quiet, subtle moments begin to be your favorite because suddenly you're not alone. Gracie wished she could ask her Mam if this is how she felt when she met Gracie's Da. If that's when living really began.

Her mind flicked to whether Mam knew about Aisla. If she was just a passing thought or a pressing family secret. Gracie knew she'd need to ask Da to explain before she could move on. If she and Fletcher were ever to grasp what came before them.

She felt her thighs press into the chair underneath her and shifted from one side to the other, back and forth, rocking to the rhythm of her thoughts; realizing that the idea of knowing the truth about Aisla and Finlay filled her with anticipation but not dread. Finding out the details of their parting and of Aisla's death would bring a sense of closure. Right now, the lack of knowledge felt like a gaping wound.

"Mornin', lass. Thought I heard ye up before the break o' dawn. D'ya go to the barn?" Da asked, as he entered the room noiselessly.

Gracie nodded but her gaze was steady on her hands.

"Who was Aisla Buchanan?" she said. Her voice came out a little too bold, but the effect was what she desired. Da stopped halfway to the kettle on the stove but looked straight ahead.

"I haven't heard that name in thirty years," he replied gently.

"Why haven't I ever heard it from ye? Or Mam?" she urges.

Just then, sounds of Fletcher, followed by Chantilly, enlivened the space. Though when he felt the uneasiness of the room, Gracie was sure he would regret coming in at all.

"Should I come back later?" he asked, on cue.

"No," Gracie assured him. "I was just asking Da about Aisla."

Fletcher's eyes widened, and he gripped the chair in front of him with both hands.

"Da, we already know Aisla was Finlay MacCullough's sweetheart and that they were separated, that she died before she was even grown up… But there's something missin'," she continued.

Da let out a heavy sigh. "Aye," he managed. "Lots were lost where Aisla was concerned."

Gracie glanced at Fletcher, silently asking if he was ready to hear what was about to be revealed. The room felt charged and the only sounds were Chantilly whining at Fletcher's ankles and the crackling of the fire.

"But, love, it's nothin' for ye tae concern yerself wi'," Da insisted.

"With all due respect, sir, it's a story that affects my family, as well as yours," Fletcher cut in.

"This isn't somethin' we can just walk away from now," Gracie said.

Da finally turned and took in the two of them, child-like impatience on their faces. Gracie could see his resolve weakening from the way he dragged his hand along his chin and slumped his shoulders. Fletcher pulled out the chair next to her and sat, waiting—interest piqued.

"Aisla was somethin' of a wild thing," Da began. "From the whispers I've heard, no one had a hope of controlin' that girl since she was a babe. They used to say that getting her to do anything was like tying down the wind. Had a mind of her own, that one."

There was a hint of nostalgia in his voice, though Gracie wasn't sure if it was because of his affinity for these family skeletons, or something else entirely.

"During the famine years of the Clearances, Mac and Edna left the homestead. Survival was nearly impossible, and they wanted to start a family. Cullen was overcrowded already, but they had better odds there."

Fletcher clutched the edge of the table and Gracie ran her smooth palms over the familiar feel of the dark wood. She wondered if willpower and hope had been enough for Edna and Mac back then; whether they had really lived or just existed. Then again, here was her father, living proof that they'd successfully made their way.

"Too many people were sleepin' in the same room back then, food was scarce… ye couldn't even call it gettin' by. But Mac's Mam an' Da were stubborn. Insisted they'd survive if they didn't give up. Felt like everyone who left was selling out," he went on.


"But, even their own son was leavin'!" Gracie exclaimed.

Da flinched at her interjection. Gently he pressed his finger to his lips and then pointed upstairs. Keira was still asleep and, unless they wanted an audience, it was best they kept their voices hushed.

"Sometimes survival overrules duty at times like that," Fletcher offered. "Tough choices. I've seen that pattern over and over again in my career."

Da gave a solemn nod. Gracie, though, couldn't help but wonder what the choice her great-great-great grandfather made had meant for Aisla. Could she have escaped death if she'd have gone to Cullen with Mac and Edna?

"Anyways, Mac was old enough tae make the decision. For him, his wife, and their future children. But Aisla was no more than a child herself. There was no option for her once her Da said they were stayin'. The only thing that kept her sane was takin' tae young Finlay."

The memory, although it wasn't her own, felt unfair to Gracie. To lack agency over how your life might turn out. To carry all the questions of what might have been to your grave. Tears sprung to her eyes and she looked at her lap, allowing them to silently trail down her cheeks.

"Ye're sure ya want tae hear this now?" Da asked. But it was more so directed to Fletcher.

Out of her periphery, she could see Fletcher shake his head yes. It was the answer she would've given, too.

"Alright...," Da exhaled, as he took a seat opposite. "Finlay, the nice lad who lived a few farms over, was the son of Edna's friends. Ye prob'ly already know that bit. Well, Finlay an' Aisla couldn't stay away from each other. He was like forbidden fruit an' she had tae have a bite."

Gracie wiped her cheek absentmindedly and raised her head. Da's voice was rougher now, tighter. She'd never heard her father tell her a love story, but she imagined it would be like this. Discomfort. Things not meant to be said out loud. She wondered if Fletcher was three steps ahead, tying up the loose threads of the story, the way he pictured they would end. If he could sense the echoes of his own pull towards her.

"Finlay couldn't have been more than seventeen when his own parents decided to leave the Highlands a year later. I was always told that Mac could hear his sister wailing all the way at the seaside when she found out Finlay was goin' away. It broke her heart. And what she'd not told him was that she was pregnant, at sixteen, only not with his child."

Gracie's hand immediately flew to cover her mouth, and she let out a small, mournful cry. Fletcher's arm wrapped around her shoulders and he drew her closer, steeling them both for the next bit of information. Da's gaze flickered between them and Gracie pondered whether he saw the same inevitability in them that was once seen in Aisla and Finlay.

"He suppos'dly promised he'd write to her every day. That he'd come back for her and they'd get married when he had some money," Da added. "Only Aisla was already promised to someone else. An older man who was cold, an' saw her more as property than a partner. But the man… he took liberties no decent soul should."

"We've got evidence that Aisla wrote to Finaly, but whether those letters were answered is a mystery," Fletcher said.

"To me, too," Da answered. "Either way, Aisla had the babe. Alone and under the weight of an unwanted engagement. Her parents called it a future. It was a trap. But there was nothing to be done. She was forced into a loveless marriage and kept the boy til he was a year old or so, but that's when she came down wi' sickness. No proper doctor nearby, no food tae speak of… she was gone in days." Da's voice faltered with emotion then. "The man she married, went off to protest against landowners a week later. Things got violent and he was shot. Died on the spot."

Fletcher lowered his head and sucked in a breath while Gracie clutched his arm. The fingers of the other hand curled into her palm, making small halfmoon shapes with her fingernails. She could feel another lump forming in her throat. The hopelessness of the situation settled deep within her.

"What happened tae the son?" she asked.

"Aisla's parents didn't feel they could take him on and, ultimately, they were ashamed o' their way of life. They put the child up for adoption at an orphanage."

Gracie could tell that this snippet of family history sat heavier with her father than he expected. He stared blankly at the tabletop and gripped his knee, though it still shook. Fletcher's brows were furrowed and his hold on Gracie tensed.

"Why not send him off to Mac and Edna? Why an orphanage?" Fletcher inquired.

Gracie could feel Fletcher's frustration, his own unresolved feelings about heritage and family. Da shifted uncomfortably, hesitating to answer. Gracie reached across the table for his hand, and he took it. She felt the callouses and rough skin that told of the hard worker he'd been over the years and she ran her thumb over his knuckles, sending him a sign of support.

Da cleared his throat and blinked back emotion. "Mac and Edna never knew o' the boy. Aisla's parents made sure the truth about his conception was buried deep enough it couldn't be found without the proper resources. An' no one would ever go lookin' for someone they didn't know existed."

Da's voice dripped with an agony Gracie could feel to her core. Her stomach twisted with the pain Fletcher must've been tortured by. The depth of the secrecy, how Aisla's son felt to grow up never knowing his family, and what it meant for the Buchanan's family line. Only one question remained in Gracie's mind.

"Why all the secrets, Da?"

"I've only tried tae tell ya the good things 'bout our family, lass."

"I know, Da. But it's not just Fletcher anymore—this is about me now." Grace looked at Fletcher. He tried to give her a grin, but it was like he'd forgotten how to arrange his face into anything resembling happiness.

"The boy, Aisla's son, eventually traced his roots. He'd been adopted by an affluent family in England, and they spared no expense to help him find his birth family. By then, Mac and Edna had a stable life, a respectable name… the truth was too painful to face. They didn't want the scandal." He shook his head, as if he was trying to rid his brain of the information. Trying to forget the Buchanan's had cast aside Aisla's son, not once but twice.

Gracie couldn't disguise her shock, audibly gasping. Fletcher set his jaw and refused to make eye contact. Each of them grappling with the injustice of it all. The fragility of the truth.

Finally, Fletcher's voice cut through the thick silence. "That's not just history, that's erasure. The complete dismissal of another human being's existence and actively making sure other people keep the secret for you, for generations… It's barbaric." He rose from his place at the table and paced behind Gracie's chair.

"I know, lad. But what's tae be done?"

"What's tae be done?! Da! We've gotta find this man's family! To make things right," Gracie screeched.

Da rubbed at his temples, carrying the weight of both past choices and present possibilities.

"Maybe your dad's right," Fletcher said. "I mean, what are you going to do? Show up on their doorstep and beg for forgiveness for something that happened almost two-hundred years ago?"

"They deserve that an' spades more!" She was yelling now, but she didn't care. "If that man was resilient enough to move on and have children and live a beautiful life in spite of my family, then an apology is the least they are owed."

Fletcher stopped pacing and put his head in his hands. Gracie sensed his exasperation, but she was ready to go another round. She was running on adrenaline and disappointment. With or without Fletcher's help, she was determined to make amends for the sins of her ancestors.

Da was watching them with a face full of despair. But something else was there too. Pride? Worry? Gracie couldn't tell.

"D'ya know his name? Aisla's son?" she pressed. But when Da said he didn't, she believed him. She let out a long sigh. "Well, I don't know where to start, but there's got tae be somethin' that can point me in the right direction."

"Woah there, *Lone Ranger*. Don't go thinking I'm letting you do this on your own," Fletcher replied.

She studied his face, realizing that, despite his frustration, he's committed to seeing this through. The fire crackled louder, her breath came quicker, and Chantilly sat erect next to her chair—excited from the shouting.

Suddenly, there were footsteps on the stairs and then Keira's face, still locked in a sleepy expression, peered around the corner. She rubbed her eyes with the sleeve of her pajama shirt and yawned.

"What's all the ruckus about?"

# 19

# Soft Edges, Sharp Shadows

Hours later, Fletcher was still draped over his cot in the loft, restlessly combing through each letter from Aisla to Finlay. Aisla, the daughter of parents likely in their mid-forties when she was born, pined for her lost love in each line. Some even looked to be tear-stained, although Fletcher chalked that up to his vivid imagination.

He wondered what Finlay's thoughts must've been as he read the letters. Did his heart ache for what he'd left behind? Or did the distance between them cause his feelings for Aisla to eventually dwindle? Did he answer any of the letters, or slowly let her slip away in silence?

With the papers spread out on the floor in front of him, Fletcher could see the subtle differences between the handwriting in each. Some looked rushed, as if she was finishing just in time to slip it into the post. Others were long and deliberate. But, regardless of length or composition, none of them mentioned her pregnancy or the birth of her son.

A pang of sadness went through him as he considered the silence that must've been forced on her by her parents. Frustration, too, at the fact the boy was deliberately left out. His fingers twitched over the pages.

Finlay's parents would've been around the same age as Aisla's. Did they have strict rules about his relationship with her? Did they forbid him to stay in contact after they moved to Fordyce?

There was also the possibility that, if each of the families had known about the children's affection for each other, they had conspired to keep them apart. Perhaps it was an active separation that paved the way to Aisla's engagement to another man. Maybe Finlay let himself be controlled by expectations, instead of sticking up for their love and the life they wanted together. There were endless possibilities.

All he and Gracie had now was speculation. No certainty. Just gaps in time where love might have survived if circumstances had been different.

Fletcher picked up an envelope. And, though it was empty, it seemed to have weight. He examined the front. The scrolling letters of Finlay's name and small flowers drawn in upper lefthand corner. His fingers tightened around the edge as he wished for just one iota of proof that would confirm all that had happened. For Gracie's peace of mind, if nothing else.

He traced his fingers over the flowers, imagining Aisla sketching them as a farewell whisper. This envelope had held the last letter in the bundle, and from what Fletcher could piece together chronologically, it was the final letter Aisla ever wrote to Finlay. The contents of the note inside hadn't been overly drawn-out, but it was full of sorrow and yearning just like the others.

Skimming the words for the millionth time, Fletcher's eyes fell on a few lines he'd not fully grasped before.

*And for all the memories we made, there is but one that remains my favorite. I send a remnant of it back to you, my sweetheart. That you should never forget me, so long as we both are living.*

Fletcher's pulse quickened. A remnant. Something sacred she sent to him. Not just a gift—a message, a vow, a plea not to let time erase what mattered. But what was it? *Where* was it?

He shook the leather pouch which had housed the letters but found nothing. He shifted the papers around but only heard the rustling of one against the other. His eyes flicked back to the envelope.

*All these others are light as a feather, but that one is heavier. Why?*

Picking it up again, feeling its weight, he turned it upside down and shook it. Nothing came out, but he heard something rattle lightly. Reaching inside, he felt something long was coiled into the corner. It was smooth and cool against his fingertips. Lifting it out, he let it unravel, daylight exposing its delicacy.

Fletcher still wasn't sure what the memory Aisla had referred to was, but surely it was the moment this string of pearls passed between them. Likely a gift from Finlay she thought she'd see again one day, only to have those days severed.

Being part of a poor family, Finlay couldn't possibly have been able to afford to buy the necklace outright. And the lack of an expensive chain solidified the idea. Instead of gold or silver, thin frayed string was intricately wound around each small pearl and connected to the one beside it. Fletcher ran his fingers over the string, smoothing the tattered bits.

Now kneeling beside the cot, with the necklace resting in his palm, he imagined Aisla's reaction to the humble gift. It had obviously been priceless to her, regardless of its handmade nature. He thought of Finlay tying it around her neck, hands shaking; of Aisla clutching it in times of despair and loneliness. It was likely her most prized possession.

How many nights had she held this, praying for a letter, hoping the wind might carry him back to her? How long had Finlay kept it, tucked away with the letters he couldn't bear to read again—each one a page from a life unlived?

Perhaps Finlay had been out fishing for mussels in the River Spey, hoping to find his next meal, and happened upon the pearls inside. Had he used horsehair fishing line to string the pearls together? Was this necklace part of a larger promise to Aisla? That they would be together regardless of what came their way?

Fletcher lifted the necklace again, letting the pearls sway like a pendulum between his fingers. Questions weighed on his heart. This keepsake wasn't just a simple pact between friends. It was a covenant between lovers.

Fletcher swallowed hard. The loft was quiet, save for the soft creak of the timbers above him and the faint rustle of paper as he shifted the letters back into their pouch. His hand hovered over the necklace for a moment longer before he tucked it gently inside, resting it on top like a final punctuation mark to a sentence left unfinished.

He drew in a breath and stood, knees stiff from kneeling too long on the wooden floorboards. The low ceiling pressed close around him now, the air dense with dust and memory. He tucked the pouch into the pocket of his coat that rested on the makeshift bed and wondered when the right time would be to tell Gracie about the necklace.

Fletcher longed to see the light in her eyes as she read the letter that accompanied it, now safely inside the compartment he would zip close to his chest. He wanted its reveal to be as special as the first time it was presented to Aisla. For it to represent, not only the past but, every feeling about Gracie that was swirling around inside of him. From the moment he met her at The Caledonian Cuppa to kissing her downstairs that morning and everything in between.

He slipped on the coat, and zipped it shut. His fingers lingered on the fabric, as if sealing a secret. The next step had to be intentional. Fletcher was determined to let the words land first, before he placed the string of pearls in Gracie's hand.

Just then, he felt a presence behind him. Not oppressive or lurking, but gentle and observant. He turned and noticed Gracie in the doorway. Casually, she leaned against the door frame. It was the first time he'd ever seen her in jeans and everything about the way she looked in them made it hard for him not to cross the room in two long strides and take her in his arms.

She wore a sweater, cropped at the waist and a quilted chore jacket over it. Fletcher envied the way the corduroy collar rubbed her cheek, and pink rose all the way to the tips of his ears as he thought about how much he wanted her to be his. Only his. There hadn't been any time to discuss what the morning meant and where to go from there. He suddenly felt like a floundering fish.

"Don't look so happy to see me," Gracie teased. But his face was still twisted in confusion at his own feelings. She stepped closer and looked up at him for a long moment. "Why, Fletcher McCullough, ye aren't goin' soft on me are ye?"

He shook his head slowly and put his hands on her waist. So soft that it was almost as if he wasn't touching her at all. He bent his head to look her in the eyes. They were dark like a lush forest, and he was just a boy, lost in the woods.

Gracie didn't speak, but her breath caught—just faintly—as though she felt the weight of the moment curl itself around them. Her hands slid up his arms, slow and sure, anchoring him in the here and now.

"Only you could have that affect on me, sunshine," he replied. He let out a low laugh, shaky at the edges. His forehead rested against hers, and for a breathless second, the world shrank to two heartbeats and the space between them.

"Good to know," she said with a wink. "I came tae see if ye wanted dinner at the pub wi' the lot o' us."

Fletcher lingered in that pause, forehead still grazing hers, as if leaving that small space might break whatever quiet spell had settled around them.

"I do," he said at last, voice low.

Gracie searched his face, something shifting behind her eyes—tenderness, curiosity, maybe a flicker of the same ache he was learning to name. She stepped back with a small breath. "And don't disappear up here for hours again. Chantilly might be good company, but she falls asleep far too easily."

He chuckled, tension easing. "Deal."

She smiled at that—one of those small, off kilter ones that tugged at the edge of her lips and at something deeper in Fletcher's chest. Turning to go, she reached for his hand; fingers trailing across his knuckles. His fingers threaded through hers and they headed down the stairs. But at the sound of laughter in the driveway and the sight of Tate and Keira waiting by the car, Gracie released him and stepped into the fading daylight.

Fletcher paused on the last stair, watching as Gracie stepped outside, her silhouette momentarily golden in the light as the sun dipped low behind the hills. He heard her voice folding into the warmth of the friendly conversation. It was almost like he'd been hearing it his whole life. Maybe he had. Maybe his world had been waiting all along for someone like her to slip into its quiet places and stir everything up.

Fletcher lingered a second longer, hand resting on the stair rail, heart still a little off rhythm. He could still feel the trace of her fingers along his own. Still see her smile like a half-spoken thought. And just inches away the necklace waited—not just Aisla's story, but a bridge to whatever island he and Gracie inhabited when they were together.

He stepped outside. The cool air greeted him with the scent of heather and cypress, the sky veined in pink and blue as twilight settled upon them.

"There he is," Tate called out, lifting a mock toast with his water bottle. "We were starting to think you'd vanished into the archives."

"Not quite," Fletcher replied with a half-smile, walking toward the car. His eyes found Gracie's again, and the unspoken moment passed like a tide between them—full of things no one else needed to know.

Keira popped the passenger door open with a grin. "Hurry up, lads! I want chips before I waste away entirely."

The pub wasn't exactly what Fletcher expected. Its façade was dark and menacing. It looked like it belonged to a work of fiction. And, as they approached, he noticed the warped wooden sign with a coiled serpent wrapped around a Highland dirk. The snake and the dagger were sitting atop the words *The Adder Arms*, the name of the restaurant.

A place with a name like that didn't exactly scream *cozy evening out*, but Fletcher didn't dare judge based on it's signage—or its serpentine décor. Still, the snake's unblinking eyes followed him as they ducked through the door, and he couldn't help the shiver that ran down his spine.

Inside, however, was an entirely different story. The air was thick with the scent of butter, bourbon, and something sharp and herbaceous from the kitchen. A fire crackled in a deep hearth, and the low murmur of conversation curled around exposed beams and tartan-covered benches. Flickering sconces cast gold light on the dark stone walls, softening the menace into something oddly familiar.

Tate was already waving him over to the booth he and Gracie had claimed, and Keira was flipping through the menu like she was reviewing battle strategy.

Fletcher crossed the room slowly, eyes adjusting to the flicker of firelight and dimly lit lamps. The walls, though rough-hewn, seemed to hold stories of their own—battles and ballads, whispered confessions over ale. He slid into the bench opposite Gracie, who glanced up from her napkin with the smile that always managed to undo him.

"You survived the serpent's lair," she said, voice low enough to belong to the shadows.

"Only barely," he replied, shrugging out of his coat.

A server arrived with a tray of tankards and a grin. Keira ordered without looking up, rattling off something involving salt, vinegar, and reckless amounts of cheese. Tate added his with the theatrical flourish of a man certain he was composing a narrative, not just a meal.

Fletcher caught Gracie's eye again. For a second, the din of voices dulled. They were back on that invisible island, just the two of them, lost in something neither had named yet.

When the server turned to him, Fletcher blinked.

"Oh—uh, the haggis and mash. And a dram of the house whisky, if it won't kill me."

The server winked. "Only on Mondays."

As she walked away, Fletcher leaned in a little closer across the table, preparing to reveal that he had a surprise for Gracie. However, just as he opened his mouth to speak, a man's slurring speech came from behind him. He didn't recognize the voice but, from the tense look on Gracie's face, she did. Soon the massive hand that accompanied the disturbance came down on Fletcher's shoulder.

"Imagine findin' *you* here," the voice drawled behind him, breath soaked in whisky. "And ye didn't think to tell a guy, Gracie-girl. I'd have done somethin' special for ye."

Fletcher turned to find the face of a man, likely close to his age, towering over their table. His eyes were sleepy, and his face was flush from his overindulgence. He hiccupped and it was like a drunk annotation in the margins of his inebriation. Despite it all, he was grimacing in an attempt to smile seductively at Gracie.

"Do you know this guy?" Fletcher asked loudly.

"*Know* me?!" the man sounded offended by the insinuation that Gracie wouldn't know someone of his caliber. "I'm Gracie's soulmate. We've been it for each other since we were just kids. Isn't that right, Grace Mairi?"

Another hiccup.

Gracie cupped her hands around her eyes, trying to make a tunnel of vision that only allowed Fletcher to remain in view.

"Danny, please, don't do this. Go home," she commanded, more than asked.

But Danny's frightening grin only grew wider and more wicked. "C'mon now, love. Don't be shy in front o' your new fella. Tell him the truth. You an' me—we've got history. The kind folk around here don't forget." Then, he reached out and took hold of Gracie's wrist and began to pull her from the chair and into a snug embrace. She wriggled her arm and tried to get free, but Danny's long fingers were locked tight around her.

Fletcher stood, slowly, his chair scraping gently against the floor. He didn't puff out his chest or raise his voice, but the shift in his posture was enough—measured, deliberate, unafraid.

"She said go home," he repeated, voice even.

Danny's smile faltered. He looked Fletcher up and down, swaying slightly where he stood.

"And who are you supposed tae be? Her knight in a secondhand coat?" he slurred.

Fletcher didn't flinch, but the air between them was thick with an unspoken dare. He took a step closer, calm as a summit in fog, and looked Danny in the eyes, losing patience. Tate was now standing too.

"I know she said no. That's all that matters," Fletcher remarked. His jaw clenched and his hand flexed at his side.

Danny's fingers twitched but didn't let go. Gracie winced, her free hand pressing against his in protest.

"You might want to rethink that grip, before someone does it for you," Fletcher added.

"Oh yeah?" Danny laughed. "An' who's gonna do that? You?"

"You keep a finger on her, and I promise you'll regret remembering how."

The bartender was already rounding the bar, sleeves rolled, her boots heavy on the wooden floor. Behind her, the room had turned—a few patrons standing, others watching with the slow stillness that comes when a scene teeters on the edge.

Danny's whiskey fog thinned just enough to realize he wasn't the biggest man in the room anymore. The shame and disapproval of the patrons of the pub was obvious. His hand loosened. Gracie jerked her arm free and stepped back quickly, shoulders squared despite the tremble in her breath. She grabbed Keira's arm for support.

Fletcher moved between Gracie and Daniel and spoke with finality. "Come near her again, and it won't just be words that fly between us."

Danny scoffed, but there was an understanding in his eyes. He glared at Fletcher, but the fight was leaving him—his resolve no longer loud enough to shield him. He muttered under his breath and staggered backwards, pointing at Gracie. "It's always gonna be you and me, G. Ye'll see."

Then he turned and shoved the door open, disappearing through the serpent guarded threshold.

The silence he left behind held its breath for a moment, then slowly unraveled. Conversations resumed, low and tentative. The fire crackled again.

Fletcher took one look at the tears welling up in Gracie's eyes and wasted no time. He grabbed her hand and led her through the maze of seated couples and friends to a dim hallway just outside the kitchen. Ducking into it, he pressed her against the wall, smoothing his hands over her shoulders and down her arms.

"Just breath for a sec, yeah?"

Gracie lolled her head back and let the tears fall. They leaked out and down her cheeks and temples. "I'm so sorry," she whispered.

"Sorry? For what? That guy was a jerk. He is the one who should apologize. Not that I'd let him near you again."

Gracie shook her head, eyes squeezed shut. "I didn't expect my past to stroll in an' try to lay claim to me tonight. You didn't need that."

Fletcher cupped her face gently, thumbs brushing the tears at her temples. "Gracie, you aren't responsible for how that guy chose to treat you. I don't know who he is, but he definitely doesn't deserve a say in your life."

She opened her eyes then, lashes wet, and looked at him—really looked. As if trying to see if his steadiness was real or just another mask waiting to slip. Her breath hitched. Then she leaned forward and rested her forehead against his chest, like she needed shelter and knew exactly where to find it.

"Danny… we were together for a long time. I think it was always more about owning me, for him. About having me to himself. Us having grown up so close… But when he asked me to marry him…"

"You almost married that guy?" Fletcher asked, quietly.

"I thought about it. He wasn't the guy ye saw tonight back then. Still, I knew I wouldn't be happy."

"Well, I can't blame him for wanting to gatekeep you," Fletcher replied, with a shy, half-hearted smile.

"Thank you, for defending me. I mean, I don't know how that would've gone otherwise. I've never really seen Danny like that."

"My dad…" Fletcher paused and shook his head with memories. "My dad would get that way with my mom when he drank. Always handsy, always aggressive. Seeing the way Danny's hands were on you tonight… it brought a lot back. And I hated it."

"Hated what it brought up?" Gracie asked gently.

"Yeah… but I guess I also just hated seeing him act like you were his," he admitted.

Fletcher felt his stomach turn at the thought of Gracie encircled in Danny's embrace. He pictured Danny down on one knee with a ring in a small velvet box, proposing to her. It was enough to make him feel nauseous. His protective side had shown itself tonight and he wasn't ready to put it away.

Gracie didn't move from his chest. "I'm not his, ya know. I've never belonged anywhere the way I do with you."

He closed his eyes at that. Relief bloomed within him. All at once, a cloudy hallway that smelled of grease and stale beer was the most romantic place he'd ever been.

"Me either, sunshine." Then, he planted a kiss on top of her head. "I found something this afternoon," he said gently. "Something Aisla left for him. Something I think you should see."

Gracie lifted her head just enough to look at him. "Do you think it'll lead to anything?" she asked.

Fletcher met her gaze and shrugged. "Even if it doesn't, it deserves to be seen. *You* deserve to see it."

She nodded, not ready to let go just yet. So, he held her—between the ghosts of what was and the quiet promise of what might be—and decided he could wait just a little longer.

# 20

## Full Tilt

When they returned to the table, it took everything Gracie had not to beam—not to spill over with the weight and wonder of everything that had passed between her and Fletcher in a single day. That morning's kiss felt impossibly distant and impossibly close, like something dreamt and remembered at the same time. Fletcher, ever the gentleman, hadn't pressed her in the aftermath of Danny's outburst. Instead, he'd kissed her cheek—soft and sure—and nodded with a quiet kind of pride when the tears had stopped. He'd placed his hand at the base of her spine and ushered her into the dining area without saying another word. And somehow, that silence had said the most.

Keira, noting Gracie's puffy eyes and tear-stained cheeks, patted the bench next to her and reached out to put her arm around her friend. "What was *that* about?" she asked, adding a mouthed *Wow* and raising her eyebrows.

"Gracie's a heartbreaker, didn't you know?" Fletcher cut in, with a wink in Gracie's direction. She gave him a grateful smile for the attempt at redirection.

"*Of course,* I knew," Keira said as her eyes darted between the two of them. "She's beautiful, smart, funny, and kind. I'm surprised it took you this long to figure it out."

Fletcher turned to Keira and took a long look at her. Gracie wondered if he was contemplating her sarcasm, deciding how to respond. It was obvious what she'd said struck a chord, because he was rubbing his hand along his jaw; something he seemed to do a lot when he was deep in thought.

"Ya know, Keira, I'm surprised, too," was what he settled on.

Tate clapped Fletcher on the back in approval. Keira smirked, clearly pleased with herself, and took a theatrical sip of her drink like she'd orchestrated the whole exchange for maximum entertainment. Gracie stifled a laugh, cheeks warming.

The server returned with their food then, providing a momentary shift in attention. Fletcher's haggis and mash were set down with practiced precision and Gracie's stew arrived still steaming, aromatic with thyme and roasted root vegetables. Gracie looked around the booth as everyone tucked in. The tension of earlier had ebbed, replaced by something quieter— more grounded. She caught Fletcher looking at her and his lips quirked into a soft smile. One that said *I see you.* And, for once, she didn't mind feeling so vulnerable.

Keira nudged her under the table with her knee. "So… you gonna tell me what happened, or do I have to drag it out of you after dessert?"

Gracie shot her a look, then reached for her spoon, trying to hide the grin tugging at her lips.

They ate to the sound of Tate telling a tale about an English butcher who trained his pigs to respond to opera. Apparently, they preferred *Carmen* to *La Bohème.* They loudly protested if he played anything too modern. Then, he announced to the group that his goal over the coming summer was to see as many classic operas as possible, although his opinion on Tchaikovsky wasn't fully formed yet, and to start writing again.

Gracie let the rhythm of the chatter wash over her. Her spoon stirred the stew absently, but her attention drifted to the man sitting across from her—the one who had faced so many different versions of her past already and hadn't looked away.

Keira admitted that she found the opera boring and poetry an overrated, overdramatic declaration of love. "If someone wants to get their point across, they should just come right out an' say it," she stated. This sparked a heated debate between her and Tate about Lord Byron, and Gracie giggled watching the unlikely friends.

Then, she felt Fletcher squeeze her knee under the table and electricity shot up her thigh. Once he'd gotten her attention, he noiselessly passed her the letter, folded in his other hand. But it hadn't gone unnoticed, and Keira snatched the paper from Gracie's hands with wide eyes.

"Ooh! What's this? Passin' love notes now, are we?" she clucked in mock disapproval. She was teasing, and Fletcher played into the opportunity.

"Actually, that's exactly what we're doing," he said innocently.

Tate looked shocked at Fletcher's honesty and Keira seemed baffled by the admission. She obviously hadn't been expecting the truth and sat frozen with the letter in her hand. Keira speechless was its own kind of irony.

Fletcher's mouth curved into a smile, and suddenly he was laughing. Heartily. Fearlessly. It was a deep rumble that started far beneath the surface, and when it escaped, it sounded free and booming; like rolling thunder on a stormy night. Gracie basked in the way it vibrated through her. She hadn't heard him like that before, and she wanted to bottle the sound. It was the kind of laugh that filled all of her cracks and echoed in her ribcage.

Soon they were all cackling and doubled over, nearly in tears, together. It burned Gracie's lungs and squeezed her heart. She had never felt so unburdened. Even in all the light she'd given to others, she had secretly always felt as if she were standing in the shade. In the shadow of something bigger than herself that she couldn't see clearly. But, at *The Adder Arms*, on a deliciously dark night in February, with her pulse fluttering on the wings of hope, the sun shone on her brighter than ever.

Once they'd all caught their breath and were heaving collective sighs of happiness, Fletcher reached over, plucked the letter from Keira, and laid it next to Gracie's place setting. His eyes seemed to radiate the message *It's time* and Gracie nodded almost imperceptibly.

"Guys, I think it's time we let you in on what we've found up here. If Gracie's comfortable, maybe you two can help," he said.

"Fletcher McCullough asking for help? I never thought I'd see the day," Tate replied with a look that said *Have you been body snatched?* But Fletcher looked to Gracie to take the lead.

She exhaled deeply and then began to speak. "It's all very unexpected," she started. "Fletcher started out just wanting to talk about my family's history in the Highlands. But everything we've discovered so far… is less about me and more about *us*. Our lives, entwined in ways we never could've imagined." Gracie swallowed and glanced at Fletcher.

The next several minutes involved a complete run-down of their findings, from the beginning to that afternoon. Gracie watched as Tate shifted in his seat and took in every word, poised and calculating. Keira nodded along and interrupted for the occasional question or clarification. Gracie was aware it felt like something out of a Kate Morton novel—sweeping, unlikely, and more tangled than fiction had any right to be. But the truth of it was etched into her soul.

"Whoa," Keira exhaled when they had finished. "I always thought Taylor Swift was full of it when she sang about invisible strings. But this is amazing!" She took Gracie by the shoulders and shook her gently, emphasizing her enthusiasm.

"So, then, what's in the letter Gracie's got over there? Is it a tell-all exposé that's going to give us the key to everything?" Tate leaned in and rubbed his hands together, as if conjuring magical powers.

"I wish," Fletcher replied. "It's something special. Just not quite everything we need. Go ahead and open it, Gracie. I think this one was meant especially for you."

The paper seemed to groan as she unfolded the creases. How many times had this letter been read and reread? How many eyes had seen the words on this page? Something told Gracie it was likely that only Aisla and Finlay had been privy to the contents before now. A part of her wanted to put it back where they'd found it. Another told her to press on; that this was only the next clue.

She took in the handwriting first. It was deliberate and drawn out. Almost calligraphic. The ink had faded in some spots, but it was still legible. The tone of the first few lines was beautifully aching, and it took a moment for Gracie to realize that the group was staring at her in expectation. She looked at each face, to their shining eyes, and then back to the letter itself. Gracie cleared her throat softly and, carefully, she began to read aloud the words written so long ago, letting them reverberate in the present.

When she finished, she traced her fingers over each letter of Aisla's signature. The last goodbye. But before she could ask about the keepsake Aisla hinted at in the letter, Fletcher pressed something into her palm. He cupped her hand in his and slowly revealed what he'd placed there. A long string of freshwater pearls, held together with frayed fishing line.

"This was coiled into the corner of the envelope. I think it must've been a gift from Finlay. One that she just couldn't hold onto without it breaking her heart," he finally said.

Gracie shook her head. "I think her heart was already broken when she sent it. I think that's *why* she sent it," she said in a low voice.

"I agree," Keira commented. "It's like when women get broken up with and they get a new hairstyle. This was Aisla's way of letting go."

Tate hummed in concurrence. "I think what you focus on next is the son," he states. "You said he tried to reach out once he was old enough. So what if they turned him away? He deserves to know someone's out there looking for him. Caring about him."

Fletcher rested his thumb on his bottom lip and his brows knit together. "What do you want to do, Gracie? Should we keep going on this quest or leave the past in the past?"

"You already know the answer to that," she replied. "But ye should be the one to decide. It's yer project." She slipped her hand into his. "Do ye want keep chasing? Things might change."

His gaze drifted from her hair, over her face, down her arm, and rested on their joined hands. "I think it's too late for that," he said as he gave her the most devastating smile she'd ever seen. "Why not go full tilt?"

# 21

# Something Like Love

The following day, gathered in the den, Keira was mid-monologue about the absurdity of royal titles and the possibility that Aisla's son had been adopted by a wealthy English family.

"His family could be the Dukes or Earls of something or other by now," she insisted.

Gracies's face was pinched in concentration, as she listened, and she traced a finger along the creased edge of the old map splayed across the coffee table. They'd begun compiling a list of the most plausible orphanages where the boy could've been taken as an infant. Trying to trace his whereabouts with a series of guesses wasn't looking as promising as she'd hoped.

Nevertheless, the group's curiosity was stitched together with hope. The dream that, one day, they would be face-to-face with a descendant of Aisla that everyone had tried to deny existed.

Fletcher stood resolutely from beside her and made his way to the kitchen, Keira still prattling on about the privilege she was sure had made up for the lack of family connection in the boy's life. Dishes rattled and pans clanged, but she barely noticed the racket Fletcher was making. It wasn't until he returned with a stack of plates in one hand and, piled high on a serving platter, a three-tiered strawberry shortcake with cloud-like chantilly cream filling that she was audibly stunned.

"Okay," he said, clearing a space beside the map. "I figured we deserved something a little sweet before diving into lost sons and family secrets today."

Taking out a large knife, he cut generous slices of the thick golden shortcake. Macerated strawberries glistened on top. It was exactly as it should've been—too lovely to rush, too sweet to resist.

"You *made* this?" Gracie asked, eyes wide with astonishment.

"Sure did," Fletcher replied. "I couldn't sleep last night and just needed to keep my hands busy."

Keira blinked. "Wait—so he cooks, he broods, and he tracks down nineteenth century bloodlines?"

Gracie just laughed and picked up her fork. But, before she took a bite, she looked over at Chantilly, staring out the window from her perch on the armchair. She looked regal and distinguished with a bit of soft charm, just like the dessert on the platter. Staring at the dog now and remembering how she and her namesake had brought Fletcher into her life, Gracie felt her heart go gooey.

*It's official*, she thought. *I'm ruined for normal men.*

"You could cook like this when we were in university and yet we survived on microwavable fish pie?" Tate cut in. "You're a cruel, cruel man, Ther."

Fletcher smirked as he handed Tate a plate. "Consider this my official apology for the trauma to your gut," he said.

"Who taught you to cook?" Keira pried.

Fletcher looked taken aback by the question. He opened his mouth to speak and then shut it, rubbing the back of his neck absentmindedly. "I was kind of a latch-key kid. My parents were usually working—either their nine-to-fives or on the farm so, if I got hungry, I usually had to fend for myself. One day, in the cupboard, I found a vintage *Better Homes and Gardens* cookbook.

It started as curiosity and necessity. But I actually ended up really liking to cook," he finally said.

"It's a skill I'm sure me mam wishes I was keener on," Kiera laughed. "She always tells me that my porridge would run off any marriage proposal. But what she doesn't know is, I don't care!" She cackled again and Gracie couldn't help but giggle too. Not just because Kiera was always so straightforward and unapologetically herself, but before February had begun, Gracie hadn't seen herself getting into a serious relationship with anyone. Let alone someone like Fletcher. Now, she saw the possibility clearly.

Sitting cross-legged on the floor and surrounded by the ambience of the afternoon rainstorm raging outside, Gracie wondered if, deep down, she'd always known a future like this might find its way to her. It was a risk to believe that there was a place for you to belong, a place where you fit and maybe fill a gap in someone else's life. Having feelings for another person was a precarious position, too. Love didn't always hold two people together just because they wished it would. Aisla and Finlay were proof of that. Maybe she and Fletcher could be different.

From across the room, Fletcher caught her eye and gave a goofy grin, mid-sentence in conversation with Tate about whether the weather would improve in time for Saturday's rugby match. His eyes, the color of the bluest flame, burned bright in the pale afternoon light.

As Tate's voice rose and he got more animated, gesturing, and ranting about how superior the Wales Rugby Union was to Scotland's, Fletcher nodded along, but Gracie could tell that his mind was working on a thousand different ways to get back to the work at hand. He scratched at his beard, scrunched his eyebrows, then raked a hand through his hair. She'd never seen him so fidgety before, but it seemed like the closer they got to opening the door to Aisla and Finlay's past, her son, the more agitated he became.

Gracie cleared her throat softly and tapped her teacup with a spoon to get everyone's attention.

"I just want to take a moment to thank each of ye for making this a true adventure. It might not have been the holiday Keira or Tate expected, and it certainly wasn't the kind of sleuthing I had in mind, but I'm glad we're doin' this. We're doin' something brave and, even if we don't find him—whoever he is—I'm glad we found each other."

"I'm totally not crying *at all*," Keira sobbed while wiping at her eyes. Tate gave her a platonic pat on the shoulder and Fletcher chuckled as Keira threw a pillow at him, a clear declaration that she was just fine without his comfort. Gracie let out a contented sigh. This was the rhythm she'd come to know and adore since they left Edinburgh.

Without anyone noticing, Da had slipped into the room. One moment, Gracie was watching Chantilly eye the shortcake with determination, and the next, there he was—standing just inside the doorway, hands tucked behind his back, gaze unreadable.

The set of chairs and the small table in the middle, under the window, had belonged to Mam. It was where she always sat to do needlework, read her favorite florist journals, and have an afternoon cuppa. Da looked oversized and out of place in the dainty furniture. He moved uncomfortably until he finally perched on the edge, appearing like he might get up and walk out again.

Everyone had fallen silent and was now waiting for whatever was about to tumble from his mouth. Four sets of expectant eyes rested on his tired face and the twitching of the fingers that rested on his knee. The warm found-family dynamic that had filled the room just moments before was replaced with a chill.

"I've done some diggin'," he began. His chapped lips quivered as he struggled to find the words he wanted to say. He gave a tight smile and his windburned cheeks turned plump. "I ask me Mam tae give me as much information as she could about the orphaned boy. Gracie, ya know how Nan can't remember much. But what she could recall might help ye."

Gracie leaned forward, her hands clasped tight in her lap. A flicker of hope sparked in her eyes. "What did she say, then?"

"Her mind is so far gone now, ya know. But she kept repeating something about an Edinburgh hospital." Fletcher began furiously typing something into his phone. Da wiped the back of his hand across his forehead.

"The Edinburgh Orphan Hospital!" Fletcher exclaimed a moment later. "I don't know how I didn't think of that before!"

"Probably because it's not within the radius we made," Keira pointed out dryly.

"But Aisla's family wouldn't have traveled all the way to Edinburgh with no money an' starving as they were, would they? It would've been awfully hard, especially wi' a baby in tow," Gracie considered.

Da shook his head. "Aye... it's possible," Da said quietly, eyes distant. "They might've sent the boy with a traveler—someone who could deliver him to Edinburgh. Instructed them to leave him at the orphanage, maybe?"

Gracie's eyes narrowed as she unclasped her hands and began twirling a piece of her long hair around her slender finger again and again. "What if they didn't go there for help? What if they went because someone *told* them to?"

Keira's brow arched. "Told them?"

"A benefactor," Fletcher said slowly, catching on. "Someone who arranged for the baby to be left there."

"Mhm, I think they might've arranged for the boy to be adopted from afar. For him to meet his new family in Edinburgh," Da said, choking on the words. Gracie could tell it was emotional for him to discuss this, and she was a little surprised he had done so much thinking about it. There was no doubt it had caused him pain. Nevertheless, she was proud because she knew he had done it all for her.

"That's genius, sir," Fletcher grinned. "I'm going to have my colleagues in Edinburgh go through the records from the hospital at that time. There might at least be record of someone bringing in an unnamed infant from the Highlands."

Gracie stood and went to her father, took his hand in hers, and gently kissed his knuckles. "Thank ye, Da," she said with tears in her eyes.

"I just want ye tae be happy, Gracie girl," he replied, stroking her cheek. "And if he'll give it to ye then who am I tae stand in the way?"

"Finding out what happened to Aisla's son will be a breakthrough, *if* it happens."

"I don't mean that, love. I'm talkin' about Mr. McCullough over there," Da said, nodding his head in Fletcher's direction. "I've not seen ye smile so much since yer Mam…" his words faded.

"Da…" she gave him a squeeze around the neck. "Ye know that my heart is wi' you, and in this house, and all around the glen… I'll never ever leave you, not really. Not so long as ye can stand me," she whispered.

Gently, Da patted her arm and ruffled her hair a bit. He stood but, before leaving, he turned back and said, "I'm glad yer lettin' people see you again, lass. You need them, Grace, but they need you, too." And, with that, he left.

Kiera and Tate chatted in the background about all the possible results that would be emailed over from the other professors in Edinburgh and what it might mean for the discovery of the descendants of a forbidden love, as Fletcher stepped into the next room to make the phone call. But Gracie kept her eyes fixed on the window and watched her father through it, blurred by the rain. His back was turned but it looked like he was wiping tears from his face before heading in the direction of the barn.

She didn't move, didn't call after him. There were some moments you honored best by letting them be.

## 22

# What's In The Dark

Friday arrived as slow as treacle being folded into scone batter. Everything was hazy around the edges with the murkiness of morning. Crisp frost covered the ground and would've glistened if there was any sunshine, but none was in sight. It was shaping up to be another dreary day by the time Fletcher dragged himself from the thick blankets of the cot in the loft, driven by a need for coffee and to see Gracie's smile.

Tilly, stretched out in the corner, had her eyes closed and the pattern of her breathing told him she was taking the morning to sleep in. Clearly in no rush to go for a walk or stir up the chickens around the barnyard today, she let out a sigh and flicked her tail. *Do not disturb.*

Notifications slid onto the glowing screen as Fletcher unlocked his cellphone. None of them looked particularly interesting, except… Was that an email with the documents from Edinburgh Orphan Hospital he'd asked for yesterday? His colleagues hadn't been sure they could get him the records before the weekend, and that uncertainty had dampened the group's spirits, including Gracie's father, Lach. After he'd been able to provide such a valuable lead so they could continue their search, Fletcher had hoped he would be able to give something back to him. Some kind of thanks for the insight and the hospitality.

*Oh, and I'm in love with your daughter.*

It was too risky to say out loud to someone like Gracie's father. But the thought brewed in his mind and swelled in his chest until he could hardly breathe. There wasn't a moment now he could imagine without Gracie by his side. And no memory he wanted to revisit without her in it.

With a long exhale he pressed the pad of his finger to the screen and opened the email. In it was the usual two sentence explanation for why it was being sent, along with a nondescript signature, and several file attachments. Fletcher looked through the file names, one-by-one, until his eyes landed on the final document. *Register of Admitted Children.*

As the file loaded, Fletcher could feel his pulse quicken. Was the child they hoped to find listed among the hospital's admitted after all? When the page was fully downloaded, he could see that Professor Morven Baird, his associate in the city, had taken the time to make digital mark-ups on the page—specifically circling a section of interest in red. But Fletcher couldn't make out the tiny words on his phone, no matter how much he squinted through his lenses or tried to zoom in. The font, worn with time and distorted from scanning, would need to be read after being printed.

In the house, he hadn't seen a computer or any evidence of wireless printing. Or even the internet, for that matter. He'd been using cellular data and hotspots wherever they'd gone since leaving Edinburgh. Maybe the local library was an option? Still, he needed to read those documents—soon. Time in the Highlands was running out.

He checked his watch. *8:07 AM.* There was no way he could delay until later in the day. By then, a crucial opportunity could be missed. They'd been supposed to head back to Edinburgh on Sunday, to prepare for the week ahead. But now, it seemed the hands on the clock only moved in a pattern that matched up with the past. It was as if, ever since they'd arrived, they'd stepped into an alternate timeline. One parallel to Aisla and Finlay's. To the Clearances. To confessions of love made under hawthorn trees.

It was the stuff historians dreamed about.

With no time to linger in his thoughts on romanticism and the possibility that he and Gracie might renew the sentiments that had been expressed by their ancestors so long ago, he headed toward the house. His gait was determined and steady. There was no way he could walk away from unearthing what had been buried with the ages.

The house groaned with the swaying of the trees outside as it settled on its ancient foundation. As Fletcher stepped into the dim entryway, a sudden gasp cut through the dark. He stumbled backward at the sound and nearly tripped over a footstool. The clatter of something hitting the floor sounded through the space.

"Goodness, Gracie! What are you trying to do? Give me a heart attack?" he sputtered.

Gracie's shadowy figure rose slowly from the armchair where her father had sat the day before, deep in thought.

"What are *you* doing sneakin' into the house like that?" she retorted.

"I'm *not* sneaking," he insisted. "I was coming to find you. Who sits around with no lights on anyway?"

"Aw, McCullough. Not afraid of the dark are ya?" she teased.

"Not the dark," he said, taking a step closer to her. He ran a hand over her shoulder and down her arm, letting his fingers linger on the delicate skin inside her wrist. "Only what's in it."

"Don't you mean *who*?" she baited and closed the gap between them. Standing chest to chest, Fletcher paused. Then, slowly, he let his gaze trace her. He started at her hairline, where burnt pumpkin strands hung down onto her forehead. Her fringe was mussed with sleep and was adorably seductive.

His eyes then flickered to hers. They were inky, like a spruce just before daybreak, shimmering with dew.

Next, her lips. The color of pure desire, like the terracotta roofs he'd once seen in Tuscany. Not too red, or brown, or pink. Fletcher's own lips quirked up with the thoughts flooding his mind.

Slowly, he looked down at her neck. Her skin was the shade of white water lilies dancing in moonlight on the lake. Pale freckles dotted her skin like stars in the night sky. And lying between her collarbones was a string of pearls. The ones Finaly had given to Aisla.

Instinctively, her hand shot to her neck when she saw his eyes linger on the necklace and her cheeks flushed.

"I… I was just trying them on. It makes me feel closer to her, I guess," she stammered and reached around her neck for the makeshift clasp. But Fletcher caught her hands in his and brought them back down to her sides.

"Don't hide from me." His voice was low and gravelly. "I've been wondering how those would look on you since I first found them. And now I know, they were always meant to be yours."

Gracie blinked, lips parted as if to speak—but nothing came. The necklace sat cool against her skin. His words, bloomed with heat.

Footsteps on the stairs were echoing as dawn transitioned into daylight. Without much thought, Fletcher pulled Gracie to the corner of the room, away from whoever's prying eyes would interrupt their private moment. He pressed her to him, and they listened together to slippers shuffling across the floor, the kettle being heated, a yawn. The moment stretched forever, but with Gracie clinging to him, arms now around his waist, Fletcher didn't regret his decision to dash out of sight.

Gracie's breath warmed the fabric of his shirt, her fingers curling slightly at his back. After a few moments though, they heard the stove shut off and someone quietly walked back upstairs. Reluctantly, he loosened his arms around Gracie and leaned his head back to see her sheepishly smiling up at him.

"What was that, *James Bond?*" she laughed.

But Fletcher's expression turned serious, and he trailed his fingertips down to the small of her back, gripping her T-shirt in his fist. "Sometimes I'm just selfish," he said with a shrug. "Sometimes I'm not ready to share you with other people. I just wanted to pretend it was just me and you for another minute. Like there was no one else here."

"It *is* me and you, Fletcher. I think it has been all along."

He smiled at that and placed a tender kiss on her lips. It wasn't grandiose or especially sultry. Instead, it was a reminder that they had found each other and that he was determined not to let their time expire. If only Aisla and Finlay had had that chance.

The message seemed to translate because, once he pulled away, Gracie gave him a small reassuring pat on the bicep. It was as if she was saying *I believe in us.* His pulse picked up, but he cleared his throat and adjusted his glasses, attempting to stay calm. He was all too afraid that the next thing to fall from his lips would be three little words that he wasn't sure she wanted him to say. Sometimes the way she looked at him coaxed the sentence to the tip of his tongue. But he always swallowed it down—like he did his anxiety, one breath at a time.

"Uh… do you have any printers around here? The records I requested from Edinburgh came through, but I can't seem to decipher them on my phone," he exhaled.

"We do, out in the manager's office. It might take a minute to boot up, but it should work," she replied. She touched his elbow lightly, as if anchoring them both back in the moment before nudging him toward what came next.

Fortunately, it didn't take long for the files to fill the tray of the printer. All of them had some sort of annotation from Professor Baird. Arrows marked dates or names here and there, a few locations circled in red. Each of them leaned in and blinked a few times to make out the pixelated words on the pages. A magnifying glass would've been helpful, but there wasn't one in sight.

"It says something about a male infant being taken in on this date here," Fletcher said, pointing to an arrow on the far right of the page. "And down here," he moved his hand to the bottom right edge, "there is mention of the health condition of the child."

Gracie slipped a sheet from his hands and held it to the colorless light trickling in through the small windows of the office. "This page says the date of his official adoption and," her finger traced down the page, "that he was left with a note, found pinned to his shirt. It's listed among the belongings. Here." She pointed to a small box of brief text.

"It doesn't say the contents of the note anywhere," Fletcher frowned.

"No, but it does say the name of the person who picked him up from the orphan hospital. An Arthur Windsor signed the form."

Fletcher repeated the name under his breath. It sounded ordinary enough. But in a record like this, even ordinary could echo. He didn't recognize the name, but why would he? By now, one thing felt relatively certain. They would have to check into the records in England to follow the thread Arthur began sewing in Edinburgh. Thankfully, there was an address, albeit an old one. Still, it was the strongest lead they had.

*15 Langford Terrace*

*Mayfair, London*

"What's wrong?" Gracie asked, interrupting his thoughts.

"I'm just wondering how much time all this searching is going to take. Trying to decide how we can do this quickly, in case something else needs to be explored in the Highlands before we head back."

"Hmm…" Gracie rested her chin between her thumb and forefinger in thought. "What if we start with the address? We can see if the Windsor family still owns the residence?" she suggested.

"Brilliant!" Fletcher beamed. It wasn't that he hadn't thought of that possibility already. But watching Gracie's mind reach the same conclusion made him float in quiet euphoria. Researching side-by-side with her had become more than a project. Now, it was a passion, and he hadn't felt that way in years.

Outside, the wind swept through the glen, just as it had been doing for centuries. Whatever waited in Mayfair, it had already begun to whisper through the Highlands.

# 23

# Barrel-Aged Absence

By late that afternoon, Gracie was fast asleep with her head rested against the passenger window of her car while Fletcher drove West, toward Inverness. The sunlight danced on her freckles and the warmth of it created a cocoon of golden slumber.

He glanced at her only once or twice, distracted by the weight of the research and the ache in his shoulder. She looked peaceful, but even that couldn't pull him out of the spiral of thoughts tightening around him.

At one point, Gracie murmured something half-asleep—maybe a question, maybe just a dream—but Fletcher didn't respond. He was too deep in the logistics, the archives, the fear of what they might find. She shifted, then settled again, and he told himself she hadn't noticed.

Tate hadn't taken much convincing to tag along, and Keira, of course, leaped at the chance for adventure. At this point, they all felt invested, for one reason or another, in the story between the Buchanans and McCulloughs. Whether in the love story written generations ago, or the one unfolding right before their eyes.

Fletcher's shoulder and outstretched arm ached from the tense hold he had on the steering wheel. He had reached out to a connection in London, someone with whom he'd graduated university, to see if they could possibly check The National Archives for the historical ownership records of the address they found belonging to Arthur Windsor. It would be helpful to know if the property had stayed in the family throughout the years.

The group had also gathered around the laptop at Gracie's and connected to the only thing available—dial-up internet. Not surprisingly, Lach hadn't been the type of man eager to upgrade to a more modern alternative. Nevertheless, they were able to check the HM Land Registry's online database to see the property summary and current ownership information. However, the only name listed on the website was a Mrs. Audrey Browning. While Audrey *could* be a descendant of Arthur, they'd have to wait for the official records from London to know for certain.

Honestly, the trip to Inverness fed more into a spur of the moment need to get away and breathe than furthering their research. Even Fletcher had to admit—a step back to see the bigger picture might be exactly what they needed. He felt they were getting close to a breakthrough, but each barrier they had to break down brought back a little bit of the fear he had about finding this long lost man's relatives. Each roadblock or new detail stirred something quiet—familiar echoes Fletcher couldn't quite place, but he knew where they came from.

Every now and then, he would get a call from an unknown American number and wonder if it was his mom. Maybe she was calling to apologize for the way things were all those years ago. Perhaps she was looking for forgiveness. But he would never know because he never had the courage to answer the phone. It had always seemed best to let that part of his life slip away into the unknown.

Only on days when he was deep in the recesses of his own dark thoughts would he pull out his computer and look up obituaries from his hometown and death records, to see if his parents were still living. He'd check the deed to their property next—to see if they still owned the farm. Of course, they did. His dad, as hard as he had to work to keep it up, would've never left that land. Those Pennsylvania fields lined with haybales and the pale blue skies watching from above.

Sometimes he wondered if his parents were still married, but he couldn't find a record of their divorce anywhere, so he figured that his mom had stuck it out. Though he couldn't help but wonder why. As a boy he'd resented her for not being brave. Now, when he pictured her—those hollow eyes, those weathered hands—he felt only emptiness.

*Toiling for absolutely nothing.*

"What's got your smile turned upside down?" Gracie's voice sliced through his brooding. She was stretching and yawning. Rubbing her sleepy eyes.

"I was just thinking about how these are the kind of research projects I'd hoped to do when I was a kid. Meaningful and mysterious," he lied.

"Thinkin' about yer parents then?"

*Gosh, she can read me better than anyone.*

"Yeah. I haven't thought about them this much in a long time. I know it sounds silly. But part of me still hopes my mom would be proud. Even if she didn't do what she should've when I was younger. In a weird way, I think we all want our parents' approval, despite what kind of human beings they are."

"I'm sure that yer parents would be amazed at the man you've become. Especially doin' it all on your own," she replied confidently.

"Hey!" Tate exclaimed from the back seat. "He wasn't *all* on his own. What about his most loyal friend?"

"Oh, right! You forgot to mention Chantilly," Keira laughed. Tate's smug smirk was replaced with a look of hurt and shock, which only made Keira crack up all over again.

Fletcher chuckled, shaking his head as warmth bloomed in his chest. Maybe he hadn't done it all on his own after all. He glanced at Tate in the mirror. Loyal, ridiculous, irreplaceable. Everything you could want from a best friend.

"If Tate can stop acting betrayed for a minute, maybe he'll let me buy him a dram and all will be forgiven. Because we're here," Fletcher announced.

"Where is *here* exactly?" Keira asked, peering out the window.

Between them and what appeared to be dunnage warehouse building stood only a broad stretch of concrete. It was, in fact, the parking lot, but Fletcher had to agree that it looked a little rough around the edges. Okay, it looked abandoned. And the lack of other cars made it seem even less impressive.

Gracie glanced from the warehouse to Fletcher and back, a silent question in her eyes. *Are we really going in there?* The sparkle in them, though, told him she'd likely follow him anywhere. And the trust she had in him nearly made him melt.

"This is *GlenTrèigte*," he said, gesturing ahead to the oversized gray, stone building in front of them. It didn't look like much more than a cellar, at best. "It's a distillery that flies under the radar. They don't have a ton of awards or anything, but they make a mighty fine whiskey."

"How did you find out about this place?" Gracie asked.

"They were one of the first distilleries that took a chance on working with me when I was opening the back-room bar at The Caledonian Cuppa. They don't distribute widely, so having a few bottles set aside for us made it feel special," Fletcher explained. "I've never visited them in person, but the website says they have a tasting room and pretty great food."

The building gave nothing away from the outside—but then again, neither did most hidden gems. When none of them objected or prodded further, he gave the smallest nod, then stepped out of the car, the gravel crunching beneath his boots like the opening chord of a song long forgotten.

As they got closer to the still house door, Fletcher could see that the long building sat at the crossroads of a narrow road, named Thistlehame Lane, and under the steel-framed industrial windows, was a simple sign: Distillery Road. The windows were tall and arched with a sooty patina from decades of use, and on the other side he could make out the gleaming copper of the stills themselves.

Though the day was now bathed in rare Scottish sunlight, the lights on the inside of the building shone brightly and splashed through the window panes, onto the walkway outside. *GlenTrèigte Distillery*—the name was etched proudly across the weathered stone. A few feet down, there were black paned French doors labeled: Tasting Room.

Nearly as soon as they entered, Fletcher could see Gracie's imagination churning. He knew she was probably thinking that the peculiar air of the place could be lightened with some bunches of flowers on the tables or some landscaping outside. She was always searching for ways to incorporate blossoms and stems into her surroundings. And, of course, from what he'd seen from the inside of her shop, they obeyed her command to grow wildly with glee.

The scent of malt and woodsmoke drifted out as he pulled open the door. It was a smell he'd grown to love. If he had more time, he would've loved to delve into the making of whiskey itself. How to instill just the right flavors and balance. But working in an office five days a week and The Caledonian Cuppa being his second home, he just couldn't squeeze anymore in. Not even if he thought it might bring him a rare kind of satisfaction. History, especially now, ran through him like the blood in his veins. But whisky was a passion he felt in his bones.

Gracie's fondness for plants had been blooming inside of her since she was a little girl. She'd told Fletcher about how her mother would take her walking in their small wood and teach her to identify different varieties of flowers. It was something she'd been born knowing. She had learned it practically still in the womb.

He felt that his love of history and dead things was coming to a head at this point in his life, and it was starting to cloud everything else. Even the people he cared about. He'd barely spoken to Gracie on the drive, too wrapped up in the ghosts of the past to notice the warmth beside him.

How long could you spend chasing after what was fading from existence without completely fading from it yourself? Life had to be lived forward. Just as the wall at his café said. Then, why was he always looking for a way to go back?

Fletcher had spent the majority of his life ducking his head and hiding. Working toward something, but what? Not really building anything for himself. What did he have to show for all his efforts? A few plaques on a drab beige wall in an office he often dreaded going to. He let out a breath he didn't even realize he had been holding.

From beside him, he heard a gasp and turned to see Gracie's mouth agape. She was staring up at a large flag-like fabric banner. It hung across the far wall of the tasting room—just a piece of tartan, or so it seemed to him. Mounted in front of it was a decorative cast iron sculpture of a briar and a rose.

He looked from Gracie to the decoration on the wall and back. Was there more to what she was looking at?

"What is it?" he said quietly into her ear.

"It's my clan's tartan. The Buchanan tartan," she whispered and nodded in the direction of the plaid tapestry.

"You're sure?" he asked. Though he already knew she was. He'd seen that fabric before—on the back of a chair, around her shoulders. Used, washed, worn thin. But unmistakably hers. Unmistakably Buchanan. The bright yellow, dark green, and red of the design was familiar and unmistakable.

Gracie nodded. A wrinkle formed in the middle of her forehead. She was deep in thought, no doubt wondering what her family's heritage could possibly have to do with a random distillery she'd never heard of in Inverness. Fletcher, too, was curious. Was the past reaching out to Gracie here—or was this all just coincidence, dressed in symbolism? Many clans had different branches and sects. Surely, one of them could've been behind the establishment of the distillery.

"Welcome to *GlenTrèigte*," a voice behind them chirped. The foursome jumped at the sudden appearance of an employee but recovered enough to offer her a bewildered smile. "What brings ye in?"

"My name is Fletcher McCullough," he began. "These are my…friends."

*Friends? Sure, that's what we're calling it now? Do you kiss your friends like that, Fletcher?*

Friends. He almost winced at the word. But it was too late to take it back now. Gracie's cheeks were flush, and he couldn't tell if it was from embarrassment or disappointment.

"What can I do for ye, Mr. McCullough?" the woman behind the bar asked.

Fletcher froze. His eyes caught hers and held them. They were the same green as Gracie's. Like storm-tossed seaweed, flecked with light and shadow. Deep, fluid, and chaotic.

"Could we see a menu of your whiskies, please?" Tate answered. He shot Fletcher a confused look and shrugged.

"Certainly," replied the woman, whose nametag stated her name was Freya. She broke eye contact with Fletcher and looked vaguely bored despite her practiced cheer. It was obvious she'd seen livlier groups than theirs and wasn't going to waste her time trying to entertain them.

Gracie tugged on Fletcher's jacket. Her eyes showed concern and a hint of letdown. He was sure it was because he'd called her nothing more than a friend. But there wasn't a label on what they were outside of the hushed moments they spent together when he wanted nothing more than just to call her his.

*Mine.*

He tore his eyes from hers and tried to focus on the list of whiskey offerings in front of them. The list wasn't extensive, but it was thorough. One of the things he had admired about *GlenTrèigte* when he first started ordering from them was that their flavors were bold and mature but unique. He treasured each bottle he stocked, and the ones he took to his apartment when nights were tough.

**Caorann 15** – *The First Path* – Heather honey, wild pear, golden sultanas, toasted hazelnut, and woodland smoke.

**Dùthchas 18** – *The Heart of the Glen* – Dried fig, polished oak, burnt orange, toffeed date, charred heather, and cedarwood.

**Maireann 21** – *What Remains* – Baked spiced apple, bramble preserve, nougat, aged beeswax, cocoa nib, and a whisper of sea air.

**Sàradh 25** – *The Echo Beyond Time* – Stewed black cherry, spiced plum, dark chocolate truffle, sandalwood, aged tobacco leaf, and rain on old stone minerality.

*Sàradh 25* had been his favorite from the first taste. The initial sip was like a culmination. Everything he wished he would've said in his life and didn't. It was emotional. A reckoning. It lingered and endured.

He could feel Gracie's gaze on him as he pretended to study the tasting notes of each, but he didn't turn toward her. A pang of regret—over his clumsy words, and the unsettling echo in a stranger's eyes—kept him from it. Instead, he shoved his hands in his pockets and suggested they order one of each dram so each of them could sample them all.

"A full flight? Who's going to drive?" Keira asked, crossing her arms in front of her chest.

"I will," Fletcher replied. "I've had the opportunity to try their whiskies before, so I'll be the designated driver."

Gracie pressed her thumb hard into the underside of his forearm. It was all he could do not to yelp from the surprising amount of pain. Instead, though, he glanced down at where her hand was now clutching his wrist, tugging him to her side.

"Can we talk?"

It sounded more like an urgent demand than a question.

Fletcher pursed his lips and then let his shoulders fall. "Sure."

As Keira and Tate debated whether whiskey was better with your meal or on its own, Gracie pulled Fletcher toward the far end of the bar. There was no one else in the tasting room. The time of day and the lack of tourism during the winter guaranteed that they had the place to themselves. Still, Gracie's insistence made it clear—this wasn't a conversation for an audience. Even one of friends. And Fletcher knew better than to stand in the way of her determination. It was one of the things he liked most about her.

Gracie huffed out a breath. "Did I do something wrong?" she asked. "You barely looked at me on the drive here. I thought maybe you were upset. Then you called me your friend like I'm just… part of the group."

She seemed genuinely confused. The guilt landed quick and sharp. He hadn't meant to make her think she'd done something wrong. Nobody was perfect, but he'd never so much as seen Gracie swat at a fly. She shouldn't be standing here, now, wondering if she'd displeased him somehow. It wasn't the kind of relationship he wanted with anyone. Especially not her.

"You didn't do anything wrong," he sighed, lifting his glasses and rubbing the bridge of his nose.

"Then what is it? First, you included me in the group as your *friend.* And if that's all we are, that's fine. But I need to know if that's how you feel about me. And then ye just stood like a statue when that woman—Freya?—spoke to you. *Are ye alright?*" she asked. The last couple of sentences had poured out more frantically than Fletcher had expected.

"Gracie… I'm so sorry, but I… I'm not sure what to say. I don't think this is the time to talk about what *this*," he gestured back and forth between them, "is."

Her eyes widened and then the sparkle in them dimmed, ever so slightly. "Okay," she said softly, and smoothed down her dress, more to steady herself than to fix it. She looked nervously from Freya, who was nearly done pouring the drams, to her feet and back. "I guess, I'll just leave it be."

Fletcher's hand twitched and he reached out to brush her cheek, but she strategically took a step to his right to avoid contact. He flinched then tried to mask it by plucking a thread from his lapel as if that's all he'd meant to do.

*Back to square one.*

# 24

# Distilled Doubt

Gracie could see the four drams they'd ordered, lined up like sentinels, when she turned away from Fletcher. She'd been just in time to keep out of reach when he tried to bridge the strain between them. He'd tried to come across gently, she could tell. But the rejection still felt like glass cracking behind her ribcage.

Fletcher's face shifted into something almost unrecognizable—distant, closed off. Not like the charismatic, yet somber, person he was the day they met. And certainly, different than the magnetizing, albeit grumpy, man she'd come to know over the last month. His melancholy had always felt like depth, not despair. There was always a flicker of light breaking through his clouds. Until now.

What had seemed like four friends sharing a jovial drink now felt unfamiliar. Suddenly, Gracie felt out of place and exposed. She looked over to Freya, who was busying herself behind the bar with a screen, punching buttons on it in a robotic fashion. Then, her gaze fell on Keira and Tate, snickering over the shape of some guy's nose in a portrait hanging on the wall. If she didn't know any better, she might've begun to think they had more than friendly feelings for each other. But Keira, in her fierce independence, probably wouldn't notice someone doting on her even if they headbutted her in the forehead.

Gracie watched in silence as Fletcher retrieved the flight, then strode to a leather chair opposite the tartan banner. He sat with one hand on the arm of the chair and the other gripping his knee as it bounced up and down. His eyes focused intently on the cast iron briar and rose across from him.

Keira swiveled toward a wingback chair covered in Jacobean-inspired floral jacquard and ran her fingers over the luxurious fabric. Stopping short of sinking into it, she glanced at Gracie's face—growing redder with each tick of the clock. Gracie's eyes were bloodshot and watery. But when she met Keira's gaze, she only shook her head.

Keira didn't need to ask. The red in Gracie's cheeks said enough.

The room was built to hold beauty, but Gracie was quietly unraveling in it. The weight of the moment was steeping in the dense silence. Still, she was determined to hold herself together—even as the scaffolding of her emotions swayed, ready to collapse.

"Whoa, whoa, whoa… what just happened? Fletcher, what did you do?" Keira's eyes narrowed as she zeroed in on him. Her voice held the tone of someone willing to do anything to protect their best friend.

"Keira… Don't," Gracie began. She could feel the dam of her tears, terrifyingly close to breaking.

"No, Gracie. No," Keira held her hand up in protest. "You *always* defend the people who hurt you. And you brush off their bad actions, like pricking yer finger on a thorn. If you won't stand up for yerself, I will."

Tate, still standing on the sidelines, looked at Fletcher for an explanation. But Fletcher offered no answer. Even between brothers, the reason was unreadable. Fletcher pressed his thumb to his frown lines, closed his eyes, and sighed heavily. The quiet bewilderment rippled outward, landing with nothing but shared confusion.

Gracie shifted precariously close to Fletcher and reached for her own dram. She's chosen the *Maireann 21* and, immediately, her nostrils were filled with the smell of spiced apple, hazelnut, and dried lavender. Even before it touched her tongue, or settled in her chest, it calmed her nerves.

She took a swift swig and straightened her shoulders. "I think… I think we should just have a drink."

*Healing by immersion. An olive branch.*

"Okay…" Keira replied cautiously, wrapping her fingers around the glass on the small table between her chair and Fletcher's.

"I'm not sure what's going on, but I'll take the bait. Bottom's up, mates!" Tate saluted as he took a long draw from the last cup.

The moments that followed felt like trying to breathe through a plastic bag.

"I can't explain it," Fletcher said. He didn't look up from the spot on the floor he'd chosen to stare at for the last five minutes. Gracie grasped her glass a bit tighter, and her brows pinched together. She waited impatiently for his next words.

"There's something about being here that feels…strange and spooky," he added.

"Of course it does," Gracie began. "Ye didn't expect this project to lead to family drama—retracing my roots—"

"It's not that," Fletcher cut her off. "It's being *here*. Specifically. At GlenTrèigte. Since we walked in the door, it's been gnawing at me."

"But *you* brought us here? Now it's weird?" Keira asked, unconvinced.

Fletcher nodded emphatically. "Yeah. I can't put my finger on it. The Buchanan tartan hanging beside a sculpture symbolizing unrequited love and death? It seems coincidental, yes. And creepy." His eyes roved over the décor on the far wall again and he shuddered almost imperceptibly. "Then, there's Freya…"

"Freya? What's she got to do with anything? She just works here." Gracie's words landed with uncertainty even as she spoke them. Was there something about Freya she'd missed when they walked in? She was unfriendly, maybe. But exhaustion could explain that. Couldn't it? It was Friday evening, after all. She would probably rather be out with her friends than stuck here witnessing whatever drama was unfolding.

"I'm not sure if she's got anything to do with anything. But those eyes—same shade as Gracie's—feel like a thread tied to something bigger than coincidence."

*You mean they're fatally gorgeous? And had you under their spell?*

"It's like I recognized them," he finished.

"Gracie's got a secret twin wandering the countryside?!" Tate exclaimed, as if he'd just laid down the final piece of a puzzle.

Fletcher's expression remained serious. "I think I'm losing my mind," he said, disbelief softening his voice. A cynical laugh barely covered the flicker of fear.

Just then, his phone chimed.

He was spiraling. Gracie could sense it. Though he masked it well, Gracie could see the edges fraying and felt a flutter of sympathy. Surely his self-deprecation and attempt to explain the irony he was seeing around him stemmed from the overwhelming information he had received since he'd arrived in the Highlands. Could he be seeing something in Freya that wasn't actually there? Did he wish he'd never gotten involved with a girl who had ghosts in her past?

# 25

# Cracking the Vault

As he dug his phone out from his pocket, the lines in his face diminished. He slid his finger upward on the screen and it unlocked, revealing a text from his contact, Corbin, in London. Fletcher and Corbin had gone to university together, the same as he and Tate, but had never had the same bond. He was, reliable, though, when it came to research. And, right now, that's all that mattered.

The message contained two PDF documents. The first was the deed to the home Arthur Windsor had occupied in Mayfair, at the time of purchase. The other was a marriage certificate: Miss

Audrey Windsor to Mr. Harrison Browning. Fletcher let his gaze linger on the name Audrey Windsor. Was it really possible that things were falling into place?

After a moment, his phone chimed again. This time with a note from Corbin. It read:

*Looks like your hunch was right, McCullough. You always were a great sleuth. Cheers*

Gracie was standing behind him now, and he knew her well enough to guess she was probably reading over his shoulder. He could feel her peering straight through his back collar, and into his soul. Still, he refused to turn around and make eye contact. He'd wounded her, he was sure. If not her heart, then her pride. Neither of which was what he intended.

Fletcher wasn't a confrontational person. He didn't like fighting, or fussing, or overthinking—even if it was a reflex at this point. He hated melodrama and usually avoided anything that brought him into a relationship close enough that these things needed to be dealt with. Writing the note to Gracie after the museum incident had been an exception, but Gracie had been different. Gracie *was* different. So much so, in fact, that he wasn't sure he had earned his place, basking in her warmth.

The emotions running through him were feral. Gnashing, growling. But he couldn't bring himself to acknowledge their existence. Not considering all that was coiled in the quiet of *GlenTrèigte*. And definitely not with Tate and Keira within earshot.

"Well…?" Tate ventured, leaning forward from where he was posted against the doorframe. "Was it Mr. Green with a candlestick in the billiard room, or wasn't it?"

"What are ye talking about?" Keira rolled her eyes.

"Has the mystery been solved? Arthur Windsor, remember?' Tate grinned. "Do try to keep up, Keira, darling."

"We were right. Audrey Browning is his granddaughter. And, since she owns and lives in the house, I think she is the next person to talk to," Fletcher stated flatly. Only then did he finally look at Gracie. "I think *you* should be the one to reach out."

"Me? Why me?" Gracie's voice barely rose above a whisper. "If she doesn't know we're family, won't it feel strange?"

"Then, we can call her together. But I think that at least having another woman on the phone would go a long way with her. People tend to bristle at the idea of a historian digging up their dirt."

"It's not just theirs. It's mine," she insisted.

Fletcher blinked up at her from his chair. She was calling her own bluff. Not hiding behind detachment or packaging her emotions as part of someone else's story. She was gentle, but persistent. Her point was made, and it was necessary. *She* was necessary.

He needed her. How long would it take before she knew just how much?

His fingers twitched slightly against the armrest, like they wanted to reach for something he wasn't sure he was allowed to touch.

He'd told her already that he was as good as at home with her. And yet, he had backtracked and named their relationship as a friendship. In public. Amongst others. It was too late to take it back and now she surely thought all that had transpired between them was nothing but a fire born to fizzle out.

"I'll let you think about it," was all he could manage to say. He briefly placed his hand over hers before she slipped away to perch on the arm of Keira's chair.

His eyes wandered to the bar and settled on Freya. The mundane tasks she was performing had a pleasant, if mechanical, rhythm. She didn't appear thrilled by the group's arrival so near closing time. Her rehearsed cheer held a distinct tinge of weariness.

It was when she looked up from wiping a glass clean that he felt it again. The jolt of wonder and the realization that if he left without investigating the quiet pull of familiarity surrounding her, he would regret it. It wasn't a physical attraction. Rather, he was drawn to what lay behind the veil of secrets *GlenTrèigte* seemed to hold and Freya might be the only one who could lift it.

"What's on your mind, mate?" Tate asked, observing the path of Fletcher's longing look. He placed a hand on Fletcher's shoulder and gently shook him back into the moment.

"Oh…nothing," Fletcher dragged a hand over his face, trying to wipe away what he couldn't quite name. "There's just something I need to take care of." With that, he stood and, taking the fourth dram with him, marched with purpose over to the bar.

"Can I help ye?" Freya asked, without looking up from her mission to scrub the bar until it gleamed. She was focused on the task at hand. Obviously, she hadn't felt the earth shake the way he had when they met each other's gaze earlier. Fletcher wondered now if approaching her at all had been a mistake. But he was standing awkwardly at a crossroads, and it seemed turning back was no longer an option.

The burning stare of the others and the curiosity they no doubt had about what he was doing seared into him. Small droplets of sweat formed on his forehead—accusing reminders of how far from calm he felt. He wouldn't have described himself as the nervous type, but this territory was unexplored. And if his inkling was wrong, he would look like a paranoid fool.

"Doesn't look like ye need a refill yet. Would ye like to change out the pour?" Freya suggested. She said the words as if she was choking on arid desert air. No one in their right mind would criticize a *GlenTrèigte* whiskey. Her eyebrows were raised nearly to her hairline, awaiting his answer. A challenge.

He hadn't expected judgment wrapped in a black apron, but here it was: polite, pointed, and personal. A beat of glass-blown silence passed. It hummed with invitation and interrogation.

"I was actually just coming over to ask about the establishment of *GlenTrèigte*. The distillery already holds a special place for me," he replied, collecting himself into a refined professional. The charming, vague version he wore every morning at the office.

"A special place, eh? And what exactly do ya want to know?" Freya seemed skeptical. At any moment, if Fletcher didn't play this right, the rocky ground would give way to a landslide.

"I own one of the businesses *GlenTrèigte* allocates inventory to, in Edinburgh. It's my first visit to the distillery itself though, and I'd be delighted to meet the owner if I could. Is he in, by chance?" Fletcher cooed. "I was hoping to pick his brain."

Freya plastered on a diplomatic smile and put her hand on her hip. "He's not here right now. Rarely is, to tell ye the truth. My father is a very busy man."

"I'm sorry, did you say your father?" Fletcher sputtered.

"Aye. Kenneth Windsor. Shouldn't you already know that?"

"Wait, so your name is Freya *Windsor?*"

"Yes… Am I missing something?" she replied warily. She no longer had her hand on her hip, but her face was a mixture of concern and irritation. Logically, Fletcher knew that she had every right to be territorial and to think that he might be some sort of affected eccentric-type. Still, the weight of it pressed too close—more than he could bear.

"Ah, of course," he stated, trying to sound composed. "Mr. Windsor is a pillar, as far as I'm concerned. I just wasn't aware he had any children involved in the business."

"I wouldn't say I'm *involved*. More like, between options," she explained with a shrug. "Anyway, *Mr. Windsor* is usually private about family life. I'm not surprised he didn't mention me in the press."

"I can't fault him for being a vault for these secrets," Fletcher chuckled, pointing to his full glass. "I was just wanting to ask him about the inspiration behind… all this," he said as he gestured to the surroundings.

"Not my story to tell," she replied. "Besides, yer girlfriend doesn't look too pleased that yer over here talkin' tae me." She nodded slightly toward Gracie.

Fletcher's stomach sank, even as his face held its polite polish. He hadn't meant for it to look like anything but curiosity. But Gracie's presence—her warmth, her silence—pressed at the back of his throat. Unfortunately, this conversation needed to conclude quickly, and he was determined to get answers before that happened.

"Um, yeah…" Fletcher scratched at his scruff, as was his habit. "She's not my girlfriend. Or maybe she is? I'm not really sure right now, to be honest."

"Shame. Ye'd make a cute couple."

Fletcher couldn't detect any sarcasm in her comment, so he mumbled a quick thanks under his breath. "Before I go, is there a way I could contact your father directly to ask my questions? I hate to go through the manager here, if I don't have to."

"Ha. My father hates phones. Texting, email, social media. It's the bane of his existence. But, if yer lucky, ye might find him at his cabin in Tomintoul. It's the only one on Lochan Dùil," she sighed.

"Thank you," Fletcher said softly and patted the top of the bar a couple of times. "I have a feeling we'll see each other again."

Freya didn't react. She carried on, picking up a checklist of duties to perform and marking the ones she'd already done. Fletcher's epiphany wasn't on her radar. But his elation was evident to the rest of the group. He practically floated over to them with a wide smile on his face. A far cry from the wary figure who'd approached the bar only moments ago.

GlenTrèigte hummed beneath the floorboards, its secrets steeped in peat and shadow. Behind him, the bar shone and whatever truth waited beyond Tomintoul, he suspected it had already begun surfacing from the bottom of his glass.

# 26

# The Curtain Rises

As Fletcher settled back into his seat, the eager faces of Gracie and their friends followed him. They watched as he relaxed into the supple leather and crossed his ankle over his knee. He took a long look into the glass, wishing for a sip, and managed to keep his eyes on the bottom instead of on their baffled expressions.

Keira swung the metal pendant on her necklace in slow arcs, fingers clutching it as if to still a thought. Tate tapped his glass in time with the na-na-nas of *Hey Jude,* with a crinkled brow. Across from them, Gracie ran her hand over the string of Aisla's pearls, now wound tight around her wrist.

The air in the room was thick with questions. The edges of their innocent curiosity were colored by the enigma of Fletcher's conversation with Freya. And what did he mean when he said he'd recognized her eyes?

Jealousy prickled Gracie's skin as she scooted closer to Keira and tried to act as unaffected by Fletcher's words and actions as possible. It took all her strength not to be the first to break the silence, but she refused to dilute herself in his opinion any further. He'd made the call. They were friends, by all accounts that mattered, and she was resolved to prove how little this altered her self-worth.

Except his carelessness had landed with all the weight of *Excalibur*—clean, swift, and entirely unforgettable. He'd run her through with a lack of action and intention. And now, he was icing her out by not being forthcoming with whatever information he'd just exchanged with the dragon-riding princess with powder blue eyes.

Freya looked downright Viking. Her hair was the color of cranberries ready for harvest, her lips were painted a sepia brown, and there was a very distinct Norse compass tattoo on her forearm. All she was missing was a shield and hammer.

"So...," Keira spoke first. "Are you gonna fill us in on what in the world is happening here?!"

"That depends," Fletcher replied. "Are *you* going to keep your voice down?"

"Tell me why I should!" she exclaimed.

"Aye, aye aye. This is *not* my day with women," Fletcher muttered.

"Well, it sure didn't look that way when you were talking to little miss medieval over there."

"Look, Ther, you do kind of owe us an explanation. You can't stonewall us after you stalked off to have a friendly chat with Freya in this—what was the word?—spooky distillery," Tate added.

The argument crackled like a campfire.

"I'm not trying to make enemies," Fletcher assured them. It was clear he was drained, but there would be no rest until they had an answer. Gracie empathized, yet her face didn't betray her. She remained quiet, spine straight, lips sealed around the storm swirling inside her.

"The only reason I went over to talk to her was because I had this feeling…A suspicion that there was more to this place than just my connection with the spirits lining their shelves," he tacked on.

"And?" Keira asked. She didn't blink. Her tone was blasé and arrogant. Another perk of having a feisty best friend? They have your back when the man you're swooning over is suddenly less swoon-worthy.

"And, I was right," he said in a low voice. Stealing a glance at Gracie, his cheeks glowed crimson. "When I said I saw something in her eyes… It was like I saw someone I'd met before. It gave me the heebie jeebies because I've never seen that Viking girl before in my life. But her eyes and Gracie's are eerily similar," he explained.

Gracie guffawed loudly into the pause. It was sharp and sudden, like a secret she'd let slip. The corner of Fletcher's mouth turned upward. But, as quickly as she'd broken her stoicism, she stitched back up it.

"So, you went over there and said, 'Hi, I'm Fletcher and I see the girl I came with in your eyes'?" Tate scoffed. "Highly unlikely."

"No, dimwit. I went over there to find out if there was more to the story. Of GlenTrèigte and the guy who owns it."

Fletcher's eyes flicked to Gracie again. She blinked back, unreadable—though she listened with a hopeful heart.

"Again… the point is?" Keira was getting impatient and with her dwindling calm, more sass surfaced—more obstinance.

Gracie was grateful for her defensiveness, since the walls she'd put up in the last half-hour were close to crumbling as it was. Even so, she gave Keira a nudge in the side. *Lay off a little.*

Fletcher clenched his jaw. It seemed his tolerance for Keira was waning too. He'd never admit it though. Especially not when the tether that held him to Gracie was currently worn thin.

"It turns out," he began, glancing between them, "that she's the daughter of the owner." He paused. "And you'll never guess what his name is! I've known it all this time, but didn't connect the dots until now," he revealed.

"For heaven's sake! Who is it?" Tate scream-whispered.

"The Earl of Sutherland? No! The Duke of Argyll?" Keira guessed. She was a fangirl for celebrities and titled nobility, and Gracie knew that the possibility of someone prominent—not only owning *GlenTrèigte* but being connected to her best friend—would defrost her cool exterior sooner than later.

"Close, but no cigar," Fletcher laughed. It wasn't the full-fledged, deep rumble that Gracie knew she could conjure from him. It was quickly becoming her favorite sound and daily goal. She thrived on his levity—chased it, even. But watching him smile now? It still left her insides a melty mess, barely holding shape beneath her skin.

"His name is—drumroll please—" he held his hands out to the side, ready to announce what they'd all been waiting to hear. "Kenneth Windsor. Emphasis on the Windsor."

No one moved. The name hovered around them. Windsor wasn't a Scottish surname. And was Fletcher suggesting that this distillery owner had something to do with Audrey Windsor? Maybe they were related or hailed from the same place?

Recognition hung in the air like vapor from the stills.

"Wait—you're saying he's tied to Aisla's adopted son?" Tate uttered in disbelief.

"I don't think he's connected, I think he's the *key*," Fletcher replied. "His daughter says he's holed up in a cabin in Tomintoul. Between talking to Audrey and going to see him, I figure we'll be able to piece together a pretty good picture of things."

"Seems like ye already know where you're headed from here," Gracie said, standing and collecting her things. Her glass sat on the side table, empty. "Don't let us hold ye back," she continued.

Gracie was drawing a clear line—and daring Fletcher to cross it, or not.

"Gracie, I—" Fletcher started. But she slung her purse over her shoulder and took a step toward the door.

"It's getting late. We should go," she cut in.

The ache between Gracie and Fletcher was palpable on the walk back to the car. Keira fell into step with Gracie and wrapped her arm around her shoulders, drawing her to her side. Tate and Fletcher trod, side-by-side, hands in their pockets, sharing knowing glances. The ground crunched beneath their shoes, but no one spoke.

Tate's silence very clearly said, *You messed up, mate.* Fletcher though, was more ambiguous. And because Gracie didn't know how to reconcile the evening's events with where she stood with Fletcher, she slid into the backseat, next to Keira, without explanation.

Resting her head on Keira's shoulder, she let the engine's quiet murmur thread through her bones, not sleep—but stillness. The ride back to Glenrinnes was crushingly quiet. Even when the radio played the bridge to *Lover*, she didn't sing along. The words felt too soft for the ache in her chest—an ache no melody could mend.

# 27

# White Flag

*4:03 AM.*

The red digital numbers on the clock across the loft mocked Fletcher as he tossed the blankets back and let out the breath he'd been holding since leaving Inverness. Each time he closed his eyes, they came in flashes—his parents, Freya's gaze, Gracie turning away, and Aisla's necklace winking against pale skin. He was falling—down a rabbit-hole where nothing stayed still long enough to hold.

Sitting up, he placed his socked feet on the floor. Seemingly the only stable thing in the room. His head pounded and the room was slanting to the right. He shook his head and blinked his eyes a few times, willing the tilt-a-whirl sensation away.

For a moment, he was right back at the county fair in Shearvale—the hometown he'd spent his life trying to outrun. He could smell the manure and fried food in the air, the autumn hay, and metallic smoke of the evening fireworks. Dizzy from the series of rides he'd gone on with June Carrigan, his fourth-grade crush. On the verge of either retching in the bushes or going for another corndog. It was the edge of euphoria and disaster.

*Fresh air. Fresh air will fix this.*

When they had arrived back at the farm, Gracie had disappeared into the house without so much as a glare in his direction. Even feeling her anger would've been better than nothing. She had sauntered inside without a word, and he hadn't even changed out of his jeans before sulking beneath the blankets on the cot.

Tying up his shoelaces, he pictured her back to him as she trudged up the stairs to the house. Strands of her paprika hair fluttering against the darkened sky. The things unsaid felt like a kick to his spleen. He was bursting inside—debilitated and breathless. His body wasn't cooperating. Lungs tight, heart faltering, something in his ribcage caving in. He needed oxygen. He needed her.

Outside the moonlight was silvery white and impossibly romantic. It diffused through the trees as Fletcher stepped outside and started off in the direction of the shadowy woods behind the barn. The starless sky was a blank canvas, ready for an artist's strokes to paint the sunrise in just a few hours. But even the promise of a new day ahead couldn't lift Fletcher's mood.

He kicked a few rocks out of the way with the toe of his boot and climbed over a few logs. The scent of moss filled the air and the damp earth sunk under his footsteps. Chantilly followed close behind.

Fletcher was a few hundred feet into the tree line, and far off the well-trodden path, when he spotted a narrow dock looming out over the edge of a small, shimmering pond. He paused at the edge, watching the way the moonlight floated across the water like silk.

As he crept closer, twigs snapped under his weight and branches swayed as they brushed his shoulders. But Fletcher kept his eyes fixed on the weathered wood of the little pier. Hidden by several thick bushes, but bobbing behind them, was a rowboat built for two. It looked as if it was practically antique at this point, though the oars were laid neatly between the two bench seats. As if it was waiting especially for him.

There was no dust. No leaves in the boat. Just water lapping softly beneath it.

Maybe it was Lach's and he spent some of the sunnier days out on the water with a fishing pole. Or maybe the farm manager used it to escape when duties got heavy. Whatever it was, Fletcher was glad he'd stumbled upon it. There was nothing like pumping up your heartrate and your muscles when you were working through a problem.

He tore off his thick outer layer and placed it in the boat, lifted Chantilly off the shore to a place near the bow, and then reached for the wooden oars. They were cool to the touch, but smooth where hands had gripped them hundreds of times before. He shoved off the bank, stepped inside, and let the hush of the pond swallow his thoughts.

The systematic tempo of dipping the oars into the water and pulling back, finding momentum, was all-consuming. Ripples in the water, the hoot of a nearby owl, and the speckled wings of a treecreeper in the soft early morning glow—it was a world within a world. One of complete serenity. Fletcher wondered what it might be like to stay here, in the ecosystem of instinct and foliage, and to morph into a rock at the edge of a pond. Steady and observant.

Tilly's ears perked up at the sound of the gentle breeze and the soft call of a doe to her fawn. But it seemed like even she knew that disturbing the peace and balance of this haven was something unholy. She rested her head on the edge of the boat and twitched her whiskers.

They stayed that way, on the water, for over an hour. Sunrise was still a couple of hours off and Fletcher relished in the fact that there was nowhere to be. He remembered another time in his life when a similar rowboat had sailed him away from his troubles. When he was twelve and he'd fixed up the heap of junk his dad called Bonny Linn and taken her out on the calm river that ran next to their property. Once he discovered the solitude of that escape, he went back to it again and again.

Between the river and his history books, Fletcher had seen plenty of days pass without ever crossing paths with his largely intoxicated father. And, by the time his mom called him in for bedtime, he was streaked with dirt from head to toe and carrying soggy notes from studying ancient cultures. Those days had been the ones to get him through. The ones that lead to Cambridge, to Tate, and ultimately, to this moment.

Mend what's broken, row away, survive. That had always been his pattern. But what if something broke beyond repair? What if where was nowhere to run, and you didn't want to survive without what you'd shattered? Maybe this time he was trying to row *toward* something instead.

Eventually, Fletcher stopped rowing. Oars up, boat slowly rotating in place, and glow worms illuminating in the nearby grass. And, in the distance, he saw a white flag waving on the dock.

Squinting, Fletcher leaned forward trying to get a better look. Had the fabric, now billowing in the wind, been there when he'd struck out onto the pond? Surely, he would've heard the rustling of it or seen the way it whipped back and forth in the darkness.

Its starkness was jarring, even haunting. Yet, he was inexplicably drawn to it. Had it only unfurled when he was *ready* to see it?

Slowly, he gripped the oars again and began his journey back across the pond. The dock was probably only seventy feet in front of him, but it was hard to tell in the distorted grey-green light of the woods. Clouds had begun to clutter the sky, and the moon was hidden behind their long, outstretched arms.

Growing closer with each push and pull, the vision became clearer. The white fabric wasn't a flag at all. But the nightgown of a young woman standing on the dock. Barefoot and wrapped in a shawl, Gracie looked out over the water, through the trees, and to the contour of the hills beyond.

She appeared as if she was levitating. Like the ghost of a memory; of a good thing he once held. A treasure he wanted to possess again. One look from her and he'd fall all over himself, he knew.

They say a year can do a lot to a person. But three weeks with the *right* person could do even more. It could delight you and devastate you, heal you and make you run and hide. The right person could draw you like water from a well and pour you out just as easy. Gracie had done all that and more. A lifetime of it wouldn't be enough.

He pulled up to the far bank, behind the same bushes where he'd found the boat, and tied it off. His shirt was soaking with sweat, despite the chill in the air. Drenched in the effort of rowing coupled with raw nerves, Fletcher knotted his fingers in his hair and took a handful of steps in the direction of the dock but stopped short. What if Gracie wouldn't hear him out?

Taking a tentative step onto the aged planks of the dock, he felt the structure wobble lightly under his weight. He moved with stealth and grace, one foot in front of the other. Each time his boot landed on the timber beneath it, it felt like a game of chicken he was playing against himself. Every foot that brought him closer made him want to turn tail and camouflage into the woodland.

It wasn't that Fletcher feared rejection. He feared erasure; becoming part of the background again, unseen. The way he'd lived his days, from dawn to dusk, for the better part of fifteen years, wasn't enough anymore. Gracie had shown a flashlight into his cave of existence and didn't allow him to hide. He was done hiding.

"I know yer there," Gracie interrupted his thoughts. "You're about as subtle as an ox."

"I couldn't sleep," Fletcher said, the only explanation he could offer for his appearance.

"Neither could I," she replied. She sounded defeated, but her voice was burnished with gold at the edges. Her words were, as always, laced with the enchantment of pixie dust.

*If only I were Peter Pan…*

Her nightgown was carried once again by the wind, then wound around her legs and tightened around her ankles. She stood, a tower of strength, in the chaotic motion. Just like she did in life. A warm flare in the chill of winter's farewell.

"Gracie…" Fletcher breathed.

"Fletcher," she said flatly.

"I want you know that—"

"That's the thing wi' you, isn't it?" she broke in. "You always have to make yer point."

Fletcher blinked back confusion. What did she mean? Of course, he was trying to make his point! And do anything he could to make up with her. Didn't she see that?

"It's not about the point, Fletcher. It's about how you make me feel like I'm part of a thesis," she continued. "You kissed me, told me I was like home to you, and then…" She sighed and her hands fell to her sides.

"I overthought. I always do. It's one of my worst faults," he admitted. "But that's not an excuse. I know that."

"No, it isn't." A sinister laugh rose from her chest and into the night sky. "McCullough, don't you understand? We're all bruised and broken. The difference between you and me, is that I don't want to die alone."

He sucked in a sharp breath, counted to three, and let it out. "You won't die alone, Gracie."

"And why is that?" She was looking at him now. Even in the charcoal morning, he could tell that her nose was red and eyes swollen from crying.

"Because…" He took a cautious step closer to her. "I'm not allowing it. If you go, I go too."

"You don't mean that." She shook her head, and a tear slid down her cheek. A shimmering moonstone on her dapple skin.

"Don't I?" He crossed the expanse between them, stopping with the toe of his boots resting at the top of her petite bare feet. "I'm here, Gracie. And not as a friend. Just, as me. Someone who's going mad with how in love with you he is."

A tiny smile played on her lips but worry lingered in her eyes. "And you're sure ye don't want me to get a Vegvisir tattoo, like Freya's? We could get matching ones," she teased.

Fletcher snorted, caught off guard. "Oh, I don't know," he poked. Daring to wrap his hands around her waist and draw her close, he whispered near her temple. "I'm already marked, by you." He pulled back to look at her, her agitation now vanishing.

"I'm sorry," she said softly. "My words shoot to kill when I'm cross."

"I've noticed," he chuckled. "But, Gracie, you're wrong about one thing. You're not broken. You're a mosaic. And I want every piece of you."

She swatted him on the arm. "You say things like that, so I'll forget why I'm mad at you."

"Does it work?"

"Dangerously well." She smiled widely now. "Don't think this means you're forgiven. It just means I missed your stupid metaphors."

"I didn't come here to be forgiven. I came here because you're the only place I want to be."

The way she nuzzled herself into the space between his neck and collarbone after that was all the response he needed. They stayed like that, rocking back and forth in an indefinite slow dance, until Chantilly began pawing Fletcher's pant leg and whining. Golden streaks were beginning to find their way into the sky by the time they headed back to the house, sleepy and dazed.

## 28

# Reaching and Rooted

"I know I've asked before but, who's Sophia again?" Gracie asked quietly, soaking her feet in a pot of hot water. Walking in the woods barefoot before March had even arrived? She'd have liked to know what had gotten into her.

*Fletcher McCullough. That's what's gotten into me.*

"Are we really going to do this again?" Fletcher asked. His eyes pleaded for her to say no, but hers silently confirmed that they were officially pursuing the conversation. He sounded exasperated, the way he did when Tate had shown up at The Caledonian Cuppa, blubbering about Sophia missing Fletcher and wishing he'd call her. Gracie hadn't forgotten the irritated look Fletcher had when Sophia's name was mentioned and her imagination ran wild with possibilities.

Though it didn't take long for Fletcher to confirm her suspicions, but he had left the conversation without any closure, and she found that it bothered her more now than before.

"I already told you. She's just someone I was seeing for a while. It was nothing serious," he grumbled.

A flash of insecurity ran down Gracie's spine.

"What was she like? Seems like she would've been special to catch your eye."

"Argh. I think it was more like I caught hers and she laid claim to me. I was a distraction. But it didn't last long. We didn't have anything in common. In fact, we had *nothing* in common," he assured her.

She could tell that talking about her made Fletcher uncomfortable. The last thing she wanted to do was ruin the golden glimmer of dawn, spent in the quiet kitchen with him. But, knowing about Sophia, especially after the confrontation between Daniel and Fletcher, grounded her trust in him. In his confidence that he wanted her, and no one else.

Gracie watched as he grabbed a towel off the rack and gently tugged at the hem of her dress to signal it was time to take her foot out of the water. He delicately dried and massaged them, and placed her warm knit socks over them, like it was his daily ritual.

"How did being with her make ye feel?" she prodded.

Fletcher gripped her ankles and looked deep in thought. He gnawed on his bottom lip and wrinkled his forehead. "It made me feel used. Small. Lonely. It was the kind of relationship that was a tourniquet for a bigger wound. For a while I thought it could be enough. But eventually, I bled out."

"I'm sorry," she said. Her voice was low and her eyes brimming with feeling.

He shook his head and angled himself into her space. "Don't be. She didn't want to be with me for who I was and didn't support where I was headed. I'm grateful, because it was just a bump in the road on my journey to what was meant for me."

"And are ye ready for what comes next?" she asked. "With Audrey and Kenneth, I mean," she stuttered.

Fletcher chuckled lightly and put his hand on her knee. "If you are, I am," he said. "Not trying to get your hopes up. But I feel like we're being pushed toward…something."

"I love that look," Gracie said, tracing his face with her index finger. Trying to commit each curve of his bones to her memory. "The one you get when it's clear you hear space and time whisperin' in yer ear."

"You make me sound like a prophet," he smiled. "It's more like the past, tapping on my shoulder and saying, 'Help her figure out where she belongs.'"

"Maybe it's not tapping you on the shoulder. More like leading you by the hand," she suggested and held onto his hand, gently pulling him closer.

The moment landed, at first, like a feather and then like an anvil. Fletcher's gaze dropped, then lifted again as fingers grazed the edge of his sweater, nervous but steady.

He smelled of lye and cedar. Metallic and woody. Welded copper in a freshly cut forest.

She'd never thought about how someone could smell like both memory and machinery. But that was Fletcher—remade and aching. Tempered by loss, shaped by choice. She wasn't sure if she was drawn to the weight he'd carried, or the way he made space for others to lay theirs down.

"When should we make the call to Audrey, do you think? If you're still up for it," he ventured.

"Probably as soon as ya think she'll be awake. D'ya have her number already?"

"Yeah, it was pretty easy to find. I guess we should get her take on everything before we go looking for Kenneth."

Fletcher leaned into the quiet space between them, lifting the kettle and refilling Gracie's teacup. The dampness from her wandering to the dock had soaked under her skin and she shivered, even now, as she stirred the milk up from the bottom of the cup. She tugged the cardigan she'd replaced the shawl with tighter around her.

"I always forget how raw March can feel," she said, taking a sip of the steaming liquid. "Eh, and it's not even the first, until tomorrow."

"Would you ever want to live anywhere else though?" Fletcher wondered aloud.

"Other than Scotland? Nah," she replied confidently. "Though my heart is often torn between the Highlands and the cozy life I could have here. Compared to the more modern one I have in Edinburgh."

"Are you thinking seriously about *ever* moving back here?"

"I've thought about it, yeah. But, truly, I'm not sure it would do much good. I'd want something of my own. Not just a life braided into Da's," she gestured to the walls around them. "Nah. If I ever moved back to the Highlands, it'd have to be on me own terms."

Fletcher walked over to the window and peered out over the illuminated glen. Gracie watched as he surveyed the land and the animals, the life both hedged in by low stone walls and the one beyond.

"Edinburgh is the only place I have felt like I could really make something of myself, for the longest time. I always felt like it was where I needed to be, to stay tough, focused—"

"Surly?" she offered.

"Maybe," he teased. He wrang his hands and shifted his weight from one foot to the other. "I guess, with the roots that have been exposed to me, the last few days especially, I've started to wonder where I should set down my own."

"Well, if yer thinkin' of planting yourself somewhere, don't forget you'll need soft soil," she reminded him.

"Or maybe just a generous crack in the cobblestones," he replied.

"It's true. The larkspur that grows outside Thistle and Tulip is proof enough."

"Ah," he mused. "It knows how to bloom where it shouldn't. Just like me."

Gracie smiled softly, her eyes never leaving his. "Then maybe you've already found where you belong after all."

Keira meandered into the room, wearing a long sweatshirt with the words *Probably Caffeinated* embroidered on the front. Wrinkled boxer shorts peeked out from the hemline and tube socks nearly reached her knees. She looked every bit like the chronic over sleeper she was.

"Don't you two ever get tired of staring at each other?" she quipped.

"I don't know what yer talkin' about," Gracie giggled.

"Oh sure. Like the moony faces and wide sparkly eyes aren't a dead giveaway," Keira rolled her eyes. Though her posture was more light-hearted ridicule than malice. Gracie knew her friend could never truly hold it against her that she was happy. They were like sisters and Keira would've gladly both kissed and killed for her.

"I can't help if my rugged good looks are being appreciated," Fletcher remarked with a wink at Gracie.

Keira grabbed a scone from the counter and took a dramatic bite. "Well, just know that if you two start composing sonnets by the fireplace, I'm calling for backup."

Gracie snorted into her teacup, nearly spilling. "Backup? What, like Tate?"

Keira pointed at her with the half-eaten scone. "I'm not above it."

Fletcher chuckled and held up his hands. "Hey now, I've worked hard to be emotionally available. It's now one of my top three skills."

Keira gave him a mock salute. "Well done. What are the other ones? Finding the Dead Sea scrolls and baking creme brûlée."

Gracie shook her head, smiling at both of them—her heart warm, her tea warmer. The kind of morning that felt stitched together by laughter, love, and the tiniest crackle of commotion.

Keira's eyes narrowed slightly, playful tone fading. "Anyway, all this wooing's adorable, but have you figured out what yer sayin' to Audrey yet?"

Gracie and Fletcher exchanged a glance. The quiet warmth in the kitchen shifted with awareness.

"Not really, but I guess we're out of excuses now," Gracie murmured.

But Fletcher was already pulling his phone from his pocket. "Time to make the call."

# 29

# Odyssey

Her voice was smooth, almost fragile. Like a fine china vase cradled in tea towels and bubble wrap for safe keeping. Audrey Browning seemed like someone made for grace—until the pressure came close enough to crack it. And this phone call was testing her brittleness. Especially at her age.

"And how did you get my telephone number again?" she asked. Her elderly tone was testy.

Fletcher was pinching his bottom lip between his thumb and index finger, squirming with nerves.

"Ma'am, your phone number is in the public database. I understand this might feel sudden, but I promise I'm legitimate.

I can share references, if you'd like," he said. He was trying to sound poised enough to pacify her doubt, but his tone carried an edge of frustration.

"I suppose that won't be necessary. For now, anyway. But I'm not sure why my grandfather's estate is of interest to a Scottish historian. My grandfather was a wealthy man, yes—but to my knowledge, our family has no historical ties to Scotland.," she insisted.

"That depends on what yer definition of significant is, Mrs. Browning," Gracie piped up.

"What do you mean?"

"The ties you have to Scotland may not be tethers in the traditional sense," Fletcher continued. "I'm acting on behalf of Historic Environment Scotland but, to be honest, I represent Grace Buchanan too."

"We're looking for a man… or, the family of a man we believe was related to you," Gracie followed.

"Oh?" Audrey was clearly skeptical.

"Yes, ma'am," Fletcher said, struggling to keep his voice even. "We don't have his first name available to us. But we do know that he was adopted by your grandfather during a time of famine in the Highlands. We were hoping you could help us connect the dots."

"If there's anything you remember—or have access to—we're hoping ye can help us understand what got lost," Gracie pleaded.

Audrey was silent for a beat on the line. For a moment, Fletcher thought that perhaps she'd hung up. But he could hear her breathing steadily on the other end of the call.

"I believe you're referring to my uncle, Andrew Windsor," she exhaled.

She paused again, dropping the name like a stone into deep water.

"Andrew…" Gracie repeated, barely audible. "And he was adopted from the Edinburgh Orphan Hospital?" Her voice was stronger now.

Audrey didn't answer immediately. Her breath hitched—just slightly—but the silence behind it felt thick with recognition. When she spoke again, it was with renewed resolve. Though not the kind that Fletcher was hoping for.

"I don't see why that's any of your business," she responded.

"Well, for the sake of full transparency, we are pretty sure that Mr. Andrew Windsor is Grace Buchanan's cousin. A few times removed, that is," Fletcher said with a nervous laugh.

"Be that as it may, my uncle died four Decembers ago. And I don't wish to discuss what I know of his affairs with anyone. Lost little girl or not," Audrey concluded.

"I'm truly sorry for yer loss, Mrs. Browning," Gracie acknowledged. "We're not trying to invade anything. Just trying to reconnect what's been severed."

"I understand," Audrey said. Her weariness seeped through the receiver. "Still, it's not something I'm willing to wade through with you. Now, if you'll excuse me—"

"Just one more question!" Fletcher said, sounding desperate now. "Do you know a Kenneth Windsor? He lives here in Scotland. Or his daughter, Freya?"

Audrey sighed heavily and let out a bone-chilling laugh. "My brother and I don't speak. And, as for his daughter? Last I heard she joined a cult." She hesitated and then continued. "I'd be careful digging up this grave Mr. McCullough. Some things should stay dead." Then, with a click, she was gone.

The silence in her wake was glacial and grieving. Fletcher lowered the phone slowly, as if unspoken truths were still echoing through the speaker. Audrey's jagged laughter still sliced through his mind. She was afraid and filled with regret. That much was obvious. But question marks as to why bounced around the inside of Fletcher's eyes when he closed them.

One thing stood out though. Kenneth Windsor and Audrey Browning were siblings. Freya was her niece. And none of them got along. Would Kenneth be more forthcoming with information about his uncle, Andrew, than the women of his family? There was only one way to find out.

Gracie reached across the table, her fingers brushing his knuckles. No words escaped her. She simply sat in resolute silence. Fletcher gripped the edges of his chair.

"I need to find Kenneth. Now. Today," Gracie said finally. She glanced at Fletcher and there was no mistaking her urgency.

"*What* are we doing today?" Tate asked, casually strolling into the kitchen.

"Going to find Kenneth Windsor," Fletcher said with conviction. "You don't have to tag along. This is something Gracie needs to do though. And I can't leave tomorrow knowing I missed my chance to help."

Gracie nodded slowly, her fingers still resting on his. "Let's go, then."

"Gracie, are you sure you want to? You don't know what we're walking into."

"That's exactly why I want to," she assured him. "What are we waiting for?" She released his hand and stood.

"Are you afraid of *anything?*" he asked.

"Not when I'm with you."

Fletcher looked at her then—really looked. The kind of gaze that stirred like wind through thistles. It was her that wrapped around him like sunlight on stone. Warm and welcome, like a July day spent on a pebble beach.

He wished he could bathe in it. Finding her was more than most people found in a lifetime. Was it his estimation based on perfection, or wit, or that her laughter was a melody? It was all of those things and none of them. She was the end of June and blooming foxgloves in a cottage garden.

She deserved honeysuckles in her hair and endless summers. But here she was, hair the color of persimmons, blowing in the breath of the glen. Ready to embark, hand-in-hand, on a twisted and time warped pilgrimage to Lochan Dùil. The moment felt mythic.

*Is this how Homer felt when he wrote the Odyssey?*

The hills beyond the farm waited like old souls. The impending afternoon spilled over them and something ancient stirred. It was as if Lochan Dùil was calling to them; calling Gracie home. Fletcher didn't speak. He didn't need to. The path ahead wasn't mapped, but they would somehow find a way. Something out there was waiting to be remembered.

# 30

# Elemental

Reaching Tomintoul was almost too easy. Less than thirty minutes from the Buchanan farm. But then there was the business of finding Lochan Dùil, the lonely cabin, and Kenneth Windsor himself.

Gracie had put on a brave and unwavering face in front of Fletcher, as she headed to the car and held hope close to heart that today would be the day they finally got to the summit of what they'd been climbing towards. She also knew though, that Lochan Dùil wasn't exactly a place of childlike wonder and sunflower fields. And despite never having seen it with her own eyes, it was well known to be cradled in the Highlands like something forbidden.

Some said it was like black glass—still, without even a ripple. Its surface held a mirror to the sky, and made you question which side you were on. Mist always threaded low along the water's edge and concealed whatever watched from the reeds. No bluebirds called. No insects stirred. The land held its breath. The trees that ringed the loch were said to be frozen mid-reach, their branches gnarled and bone-like where they met the water.

What warning could she give Fletcher, though? She needed someone to stick by her through the unanswered questions and uncertified past. Even if that meant walking along the shore of days gone by and kicking in the door of the cabin.

She couldn't offer Fletcher assurances, so she resolved to keep hold of her bravery. It might come in handy if things didn't turn out the way they intended. Of course, Fletcher didn't need protection from his determination to help, but she couldn't keep from thinking it was unfair to ask him to provide relief from the ache if Kenneth wasn't who she expected. Or perhaps even if he was.

Sometimes, the past didn't just hurt when it disappeared—it hurt more when it showed up exactly as feared.

As they followed the narrow dirt road, crowded with brush, the sun-kissed canopy above turned shadowy and shaded the car grey. The view from the windows gave them little but ash green and saddle brown—no glimmer, no umber pool in sight.

"This is a warm welcome if I've ever seen one," Fletcher smirked.

"I'd say Mr. Windsor doesn't get many visitors," Gracie replied.

"What do you mean? There's practically a welcome mat in front of us," he laughed in response.

"Hmm, seems to be blending in well with the murder mystery surroundings. I guess I missed it," she smiled nervously.

Then, suddenly, the car halted involuntarily. It was as if a hand had reached out and stopped it from moving. No matter how hard Gracie's foot pressed on the accelerator, it wouldn't budge. She attempted to switch the transmission into reverse and go back the way they'd come, but that didn't work either. Not to mention the loud snap and odd grinding sound that accompanied her efforts.

Gracie's knuckles whitened on the wheel. The snap echoed— not just outside the car, but somewhere deep inside her. She could sense Fletcher was also uneasy. It seemed, though, that there was no way out but through.

The door lock clicked, and Fletcher reached for the handle.

"Where are ya going?!" Gracie exclaimed.

"Gracie, I've gotta check out what's wrong with the car," he said. It was practical, but his eyes were compassionate. "I'll be right back, I promise. Just going to take a quick look," he softened.

As Fletcher pulled the handle, the air outside felt colder, denser. Gracie watched the tree line beyond the hood, as if expecting something—or someone—to shift.

When he rounded the front of the car, Fletcher made a face that was somewhere between a scowl and pout.

*That can't be good*, Gracie thought. She was sure that at any moment Kenneth Windsor would appear with an ax or some other weapon and make sure she and Fletcher served as a warning to anyone else who tried to arrive at his cabin uninvited.

She tightened her grip on the seatbelt. Maybe she should've brought pepper spray.

Fletcher bent to look under the chassis and then straightened with his hands on his hips. The metal buckle of his belt flashed under the glary sky and Gracie wondered if they could use it to signal for help. Now, she couldn't think of anything she wanted more than to get out of these woods.

The cabin no longer felt like a destination—it felt like a dare. Gracie was strategizing, rationalizing the dread coursing through her. The surrounding forest that had, at first, felt reverent now felt predatory.

With trembling fingers, she pressed the switch to roll down the window. She didn't let it descend more than an inch.

"What's going on out there? Can we get going?" she said in a loud, urgent whisper. The intensity was more alarming than comforting.

The car felt like a waiting room for something unwelcome. She needed movement and sound, but not like this. Keira's laughter, maybe? Tate's terrible jokes? Yes, those would suffice. But being stranded on an unknown road outside of a place most Scots avoid due to folklore was barely tolerable.

Fletcher looked up and then walked to the driver's side of the vehicle, resting his hand on the roof and leaning into the door frame—though he was shielded from getting too close by the window. Gracie refused to increase the size of the small slit, letting in fresh air and visceral daytime nightmares.

"We're going to have to walk from here," Fletcher said pointedly. "We're in a muddy crater-sized pothole and a branch has snapped off in the axle. The car won't be going anywhere until we can get someone to come and tow it."

"Tow it?!" Gracie screeched. Even she was surprised that her voice was so high. The last five minutes had done wonders on her imagination and she was a more vocal victim than some.

She didn't want to be the dramatic one. In fact, she hated that she was unraveling. But the thought of walking through this ghostly wildwood, even with Fletcher beside her, was far from ideal.


"Can't we just push from behind and see if it moves? Maybe the branch will fall loose," she offered. But Fletcher just shook his head and pointed to the handle of the door.

When she hesitated, he raised his brows and knocked gently on the glass. "C'mon sunshine. You don't think I'd let you get hauled off by a monster, do you?" He chuckled and threw his head back. "Nothing is gonna happen."

She searched his face for doubt—but found only confidence and strength. It was hard to argue with someone so invested and loyal. Both to her and to whatever lay on the other side of the twisted tree line. Surely Winsdor's cabin had to be close.

Heaving a heavy sigh, Gracie rolled up the window, shut down the car, and very slowly opened the door. First, a few inches. Then, a foot. She squeezed herself through the small opening, keys jingling in her hand. Slamming the door shut and pressing the button on the key fob, the horn honked, and Gracie jumped behind Fletcher. Her heartbeat echoed in her ears—sharp and fast.

Fletcher glanced over his shoulder, offering a half-smile that didn't reach his eyes. "You good?"

Gracie nodded, but her grip on the keys said otherwise. Some of them stuck out jaggedly between her fingers, and she wore the key ring around them like knuckle knives. The rest of the spikey teeth rubbed her sweaty palm.

They stepped forward in unison, pebbles shifting and crunching under their soles. Every branch and leaf seemed to lean inward as if bearing witness—waiting for their demise. Though Gracie noticed that it looked as if there was a small clearing around the next bend. If they could only make it that far.

She didn't trust the stillness that had fallen over the foliage despite the clouds churning in the sky above. Instead, Gracie tried to focus on the sound of Fletcher's footsteps beside her. One foot in front of the other, easing their way toward the opening ahead.

The curve in the road, mostly overgrown, shimmered like a mirage in the distance. Trees on either side stood guard, as if they weren't sure whether to allow passage or close the way for good. Wishing they'd brought Chantilly for protection, Gracie caught herself smirking. Tilly was no fiercer than a bunny rabbit. She'd have probably taken a nap in the thick ferns growing along the roadside or sprinted into Kenneth's arms, even if he was probably some sort of cleaver-wielding serial killer.

Gracie shook her head, the smirk fading. Even make-believe was starting to feel fragile out here.

Then she heard it. A loud *clop*, like someone was playing cricket with a coconut. It was only a few moments before she heard it again. Only, this time, it was more like a *thwack*. What was it? Where was it coming from?

As they edged closer to the gap in the brush, the sound grew louder. Somewhere beyond the brush, something was working. Splitting. Sharpening. Perhaps it was Kenneth in the process of dismembering his most recent victim. Gracie's teeth chattered.

Fletcher didn't flinch. If he heard it, he wasn't letting on.

*Unless… was that his jaw clenching?*

His eyes were fixed ahead and, following his stare, she noticed that the trail was coming to an end at the boarder of a small, coarse beach that encircled the entirety of what she now saw was, what could only be, Lochan Dùil. The water was nearly motionless and a deep peacock green.

The loch was nothing like she imagined. And exactly what she feared. It was iridescent and unsettling, deep and layered.

*It certainly would be easy to get rid of bodies out here*, Gracie thought. Her lips trembled.

*Clop!...Thwack!...* The pattern continued.

Without speaking, Fletcher took her hand in his and gripped it tightly. They were about to round the corner and a large, knotted tree trunk. The bark split into strange patterns—veins of age, or warnings. Gracie's breath hitched. The unidentified sound was steadily growing closer. It echoed through the air like a slayer's lullaby. She could only pray that whatever was making the noise wasn't as homicidal as she'd made it out to be in her imagination.

Their footfall was silent, softened by the sand beneath, though the tenor of their heavy breathing felt hot and ominous. Fletcher's hold on her was the only thing propelling her forward. Every bone below her waist had gone rogue and her legs begged to fold under her.

Beside her, Fletcher strode like someone born to face myth and memory. Gracie wasn't so sure.

Just when she thought her psyche couldn't take it anymore though, the noise stopped. No more claps, no more cracking. Only the sound of the shore whispering beside them.

"Hello?" Fletcher called out. "Hello there?"

"Fletcher, what are you doing?! Yer gonna get us killed. If not for trespassing, then for interrupting Poe before he stuffs his friend under the floorboards!" Gracie whispered. Her breath stilled, but her heart didn't. It pounded like it wanted out.

"You read Poe?" Fletcher blinked.

"Not the point right now!" Gracie rasped.

"Are ye two lost?" came a deep voice. But, looking around, she couldn't see where it was coming from.

Gracie's eyes darted between the trees. The loch was silent, but something had spoken. She swallowed hard.

"We aren't lost…exactly. Our car broke down on the road," Fletcher replied to the omniscient presence.

"It's not *exactly* a road well-traveled. Especially not by Americans," the voice answered. It was a mature voice, carved from hearty pine and seasoned with char. It wasn't intrinsically angry, but that didn't mean that whatever it was was pleased to have their company either.

Fletcher's hand relaxed around hers, but only slightly. "I understand you might be curious as to why we're here. If you come out from hiding, maybe I could explain." The sentence came out more like a question and Gracie could sense Fletcher's hesitation.

"Hiding? You call being stalked, by two strangers, around my own cabin, hiding?" the voice asked. The inquiry was laced with sincerity, but the figure that appeared from the woodland was mysterious and otherworldly.

*Perhaps Merlin has a long lost relative too.*

His eyes were bright, but unreadable—like he'd seen too much to be surprised anymore. He had a long, wiry gray beard and his forehead was a map of lines and caverns. His eyebrows seemed permanently creased, as if he wore a perpetual frown.

The man's clothing was loose and practical. His shirt looked like it was dyed with graphite powder and his pants, the color of flint and covered in bits of moss and splinters, hung, rumpled, from his stout frame.

Around his neck, on a leather cord, was a large Ogham Stone, covered in Gaelic symbols and images. His waist was cinched tight and dangling from his belt were pouches and various tools. The most peculiar thing, though, was that he wore a long wool cloak. The cowl was pulled over his head and tendrils of ashen hair spilled over his collar.

"Where did ye come from?" Gracie wondered aloud.

"I was choppin' firewood, yon," he nodded to where he'd just come from. "But there was no mistakin' it. I was bein' watched."

"But we couldn't even see you!" Gracie exclaimed, finding her voice.

"Aye, but I could see *you*. Lookin' fer somethin'?" He gripped his walking staff a bit tighter.

*Definitely related to Merlin*, Gracie noted.

"We are actually, sir," Fletcher cut in, giving Gracie a confused glance. "We're looking for some*one* to be more specific."

"No one's here but me," the man shrugged. "That's usually the case," he added and eyed them warily.

"We don't mean to intrude," Fletcher rushed on. "It's just that we were told that a man named Kenneth Windsor might be here."

"Hmm," he nodded. "Ol' Kenny, eh? What'd ye want wi' him?"

"We believe he holds the key to a very important door," Fletcher said honestly.

The man's mouth curved but didn't smile. The Ogham stone glinted faintly against his chest. He stamped his staffed against the ground a couple times and looked into the distance.

"Do ye happen to know Kenneth?" Gracie pleaded. She was tired of the guessing games, and if they were ever going to get home before dark—before something wild and ferocious left

them to die on the beach—they needed to find out if being here
was even worth their time.

She didn't care if he was a guardian, a hermit, or Merlin's
brother-in-law—she just needed him to say yes.

"Yeah… or I did once upon a time," he growled at the lake. "I
*am* Kenneth Windsor, but I'm not sure I'm who yer looking
for."

"What does that mean?" Gracie prodded.

"It means…" he sighed. "Ye'd better come wi' me." Then he
turned, the hem of his cloak floating above the green-glass of
the loch and walked toward the trees.

# 31

# Unwritten

Fletcher and Kenneth were about the same height and walked with a similar air of easy tenacity. As Kenneth's cloak floated around him in an otherworldly way, Fletcher plodded along beside him. Gracie hovered in the background, clearly unsure whether Kenneth was someone they could trust. It was as if she couldn't tell whether Kenneth's ease with Fletcher was a good sign, or something they should be watchful of.

Every few seconds Fletcher would turn and motion her along, but she was apprehensive. It wasn't just Kenneth's unearthly presence making her tense, he knew. It was the strange surroundings and the way he spoke about himself—as if he had been on a journey and never quite returned. The narrow, densely covered path to his cabin looked as if it was hardly used. And the cabin itself, as they approached, was disguised by a thick blanket of ivy and winding clematis. Delicate bell-shaped flowers in creamy white and pale yellow dotted the carpeted exterior of the unassuming home, made from sturdy logs and sealant between them.

If it hadn't been for Kenneth's abrupt stop at the stairs, to stomp the dirt from his boots before ascending them, Fletcher might've never noticed there was a house there at all. It wore the forest like a heavy coat and concealed itself enough to be missed by the untrained eye. Clearly, Kenneth didn't have a lot of guests.

The moss-covered roof had seen better days, but the place breathed enchanted seclusion. It was evident, in the way the lush olive and lime tones overlapped, over and around the cabin, that Kenneth and this land were largely undisturbed. The smell of sap and the unmistakable renewal of the earth crept into Fletcher's nostrils.

"It's peaceful here," Fletcher noted as he climbed the stairs behind Kenneth.

"Aye, 'tis that," he nodded.

"It must be lovely, livin' in such beauty all the time," Gracie added, glancing around the large, wrap-around porch. Coils of winter jasmine hung from the eaves, creating a curtain around the railing. She looked lovely—a silhouette against a veil of solitude. The light was dim, like the damp underside of a thistle, but her milky skin shone through the velvet murk.

Fletcher smiled to himself, smothering it with his fist. He could tell she was fighting against her good nature. Her gentle feeling and soft heart clashed with the doubts she had about Kenneth; about coming to Lochan Dùil.

"I'm just somethin' the forest hasn't chosen tae reject. I respect her an' she lets me remain in her abundance," Kenneth snorted.

"So, Kenneth, listen…," Fletcher began.

"Kenny, please. Kenneth is so formal," he interrupted. Then mumbled something like *aristocratic wannabe name* under his breath.

 "Okay… Kenny. We really need to ask you some questions, if that's okay. We don't have a lot of time to finish what we started. Tomorrow we're heading back home," Fletcher finished.

"Where's home?"

"Edinburgh," Gracie and Fletcher said in unison.

"City folks, huh? That shouldn't surprise me," Kenny stated.

"I was raised just up the road, in Glenrinnes," Gracie's voice sharpened, touched with pride. "Highlander, same as you." She crossed her arms over her chest and projected as much toughness as she could. Her face, though, looked as innocent as a fox cub inciting a romp with its litter mate.

"How'd ye end up so far south, lass?"

Gracie's face faltered at the invitation to open up. Nevertheless, she cleared her throat and began to speak. Softly at first, then firmer. "Me mam always loved flowers," she started. "In fact, she'd have loved a cottage as covered with vines and plants as this. I s'pose I got her green thumb, an' when she passed on it seemed like time to put it tae use." Her mouth twitched and a sad grin spread across her face. "I have a flower shop in Edinburgh. When I look in the shop window, sometimes I can picture me mam standing behind the counter arranging bluebells and avens—tellin' customers it's the perfect bouquet of gratitude an' grace…" her voice trailed off.

She flushed and Fletcher let her words settle.

Kenny's eyes twinkled at the petal of truth. "Yer mam sounds like my late wife, Mona. A good woman, that one. I think ye'd have both taken to her a sight better than a stubborn ol' man like me."

"So sorry for your loss," Fletcher soothed.

There was a reflective beat between the three of them, as questions gathered at the back of Fletcher's throat. His restraint was agonizing. But letting the world of conifers and lichens settle around them seemed crucial.

An understanding seemed to pass between Gracie and Kenny as they waited in the purgatory of wordless recognition. They blinked at each other and a quiet thrum drifted through the trees. Relief rose in Fletcher's chest. Maybe, just maybe, if they could find common ground with Kenny, he would be willing to give them some information about his uncle.

Breaking eye contact, Kenny began adjusting the wooden rocking chairs on the porch, without any more mention of Mona or his past, and offered one to each of them.

"Sorry I don't have much to offer ye. I get by on oatcakes an' tea most o' the time," he said regretfully.

"Don't worry about that," Fletcher replied. "We know you weren't expecting us. In fact, I apologize for not giving you fair warning. But Freya didn't give me a lot to go on."

"Ye know Freya?" Kenny squinted. His gaze lingered on Fletcher now, less friendly. "She sent ye, then?"

"Eh, no… she just mentioned where you might be," Fletcher admitted. "We ran into her when we were in Inverness the other day. At *GlenTrèigte*."

"*GlenTrèigte*," Kenny repeated wistfully. His expression was vague and the tone with which he spoke was flavored with yearning.

"We were there having a dram and I asked about who owned the place. I stock a few bottles of *GlenTrèigte* whiskey at my shop in Edinburgh and was hoping to meet you in person," Fletcher explained.

"Ah, so these are business questions ye've got for me?"

"Not exactly—"

"Good," Kenny butted in. "Because I'm not much o' a businessman," he chuckled. "The whole reason I left that place for Freya to take care of. Deal with the manager, the people…I realized quickly that I wasn't the kind of master distiller my uncle hoped I'd be."

Gracie and Fletcher exchanged a knowing look.

"Your uncle is the reason we're here," Gracie clarified.

"Then I think ye wasted yer time. He died a few years back."

"We know," Fletcher replied. "We talked to your sister, Audrey. Though she wouldn't give us much information either."

"So, you've talked to me daughter and sister, then came stalking me in the woods… Seems to me I'm the one who should have questions," Kenny said warily.

Fletcher didn't blame him. They'd come with questions, but the depth of the mistrust and family discord was unknown. Kenny had every right to be skeptical. He never expected two strangers to show up on his doorstep, prying into his personal life. And Fletcher could only imagine it felt unnerving. The likelihood that Kenny felt betrayed by his own family so that he would be found and interrogated in his peaceful woods was high.

Fletcher rubbed his thumb along the edge of the chair's armrest, grounding himself in the moment. He didn't know whether he should lead with insight into his profession, enthusiasm for helping Gracie find Andrew Windsor, or preface his next words by explaining their meeting with Freya more fully. But it was Gracie who spoke first, while his thoughts wrapped around his neck—the quiet strangle of indecision.

"Mr. Windsor, I know ye weren't expectin' anyone to come out here looking for you and meddling in your family affairs," she began. "But Fletcher is a historian whose work life and personal life are suddenly intertwined. And we think you could be the person to help with the final puzzle piece." She nodded, noting that she'd said her piece, and then looked at Fletcher to pick up where she'd left off.

"I am a historian, whose alter ego dabbles in pouring whiskey," Fletcher laughed nervously. "Starting out, sir, I was just trying to gain access to a behind-the-scenes look at the Highland Clearances and the people of the area. Long story short, it turned out that those people are my people. Ones I never knew about—because I didn't have a close family."

Kenny didn't say anything. Just stared at the porch railing, like the grain of wood might offer a sign.

"In our research, we found out that Gracie has, or had, a long lost relative. A man who, when he was young, was adopted by a family in England. As it turns out, that man was Andrew Windsor. Your uncle," Fletcher concluded.

Kenny's fingers curled around the armrest. Not tight—just deliberate. The screen of jasmine swayed gently in a fresh breeze and the trees listened as he gathered his thoughts. Finally, he turned and faced Fletcher.

"What'd you say yer last name was, lass?" Kenny asked.

"Buchanan. But I've seen old records where it was spelled Buchannan or Buchan. I've seen so many documents now, it's all a blur."

"Aye, I know the name. It's just never come knockin' on me door."

"Have ye known some Buchanans in your time then?" Gracie hoped aloud.

"I haven't but, I think I know the reason ye came to find me. How you got anything out of Audrey, though, is beyond me. She and I haven't talked in ages. Got her walls build pretty high, that one," Kenny responded.

"Forgive me for noticing, but you both have very different accents. She was very… British on the phone. But you sound like you were planted in Scottish soil from birth," Fletcher mused.

"Audrey was raised in England. Mam and Da thought it'd be better for me to be with my uncle. He loved the wilderness and the possibility here. But Audrey took to London like ivy climbs stone—faster than ye expect, harder to pull free. We never saw eye to eye."

"What was it yer uncle saw in Scotland?" Gracie pried.

"A better life. Oh, not one of riches and luxury, but of freedom. And somethin' more than that… A chance to rewrite his story. Reclaim what had been lost to him," Kenny said, not meeting her eyes.

Fletcher felt it then—the way Kenny's uncle hadn't come to Scotland just to disappear, but to be remembered on his own terms. Or perhaps he was groping for the past, and he was the one remembering. The thought clung to him—not just who Andrew Windsor had been, but who he'd tried to become.

"So, you knew he was adopted," Fletcher remarked. His voice was quiet with disbelief.

"Mhm. It was never a secret. He talked about finding his birth mam and how her family had cast him off, even as a man his in own right. They wanted nothin' to do with him. But I always knew he had fondness for her, even though she'd died," Kenny swallowed. "He knew she wouldn't have given him up if it hadn't been for them."

Fletcher felt the words land in his chest—grief shaped by loyalty, truth softened by belief.

"I wish this story hadn't been kept secret in my family," Gracie offered. "Aisla, Andrew's mam, was my great-great-great aunt. And I never knew about her until a couple of days ago. It breaks my heart."

Kenny didn't speak for a moment. Just let the names settle like dust on old timbers—weightless, but impossible to ignore.

"You have the Buchanan tartan hanging in the tasting room at *GlenTrèigte*," she went on. "It is because of her?"

He nodded slowly. "Me uncle put it there, along with the sculpture. A symbol of two worlds torn apart. With his own da havin' passed there wasn't a lot left. But he knew enough that his mam had been separated from him by circumstance an' plotting."

*Loss, yes. But also, injustice.*

The tartan wasn't just history, it was absolution.

"Did he ever mention a Finlay McCullough?" Gracie asked.

Kenny scratched his jaw, eyes softening into the kind of memory passed down more in feeling than fact.

"Aye," he said. "He did mention Finlay McCullough. It was bits and pieces. From things whispered by my grandad when he thought no one was listenin'."

Gracie didn't breathe.

"Said it was love, once. Deep and difficult. But true. Stolen from his mam by expectation," he concluded.

"Yeah. From the evidence we found, Aisla and Finlay were very much in love," Fletcher inserted. "We found letters… not many, but enough to know they planned a life together. Before everything fractured."

"It's strange, feeling grief for someone you never met. But I do," Kenny revealed.

Fletcher let the word grief hover between them, unexpected in Kenny's mouth, but not undeserved. It echoed with loss wrapped in lineage, threaded through time.

A jay called out, its notes rising and falling like a thought abandoned mid-sentence. The wind, fragrant with jasmine, drifted toward the chairs, and Fletcher felt reluctant to return to reality the next day. What they'd just unwrapped with Kenny felt like a gift and he wanted Gracie to be able to hold onto it as long as possible.

Kenneth broke the silence by speaking again. "Ye came looking for a man you never knew. I reckon he'd have wanted you to find him here. In the quiet," he sighed. "Andrew always wanted to be working with his hands. Either at the distillery or in the dirt. Once he passed, I picked one of those passions and stuck to it. My name might be on the paperwork for *GlenTrèigte*, but it was his dream. Not mine."

"If someone had told me last week that I'd feel tethered to two people I've never met... I'd have laughed. But now they feel so real. It's strange and sacred and heavy," Gracie murmured.

"Something strange about the way those who are in our past find their way into our future," Kenny replied. "I've got one of Andrew's notebooks inside," Kenny said finally. "Mostly scribbles about barrels and yeast. But it might be worth a look." He stood and nudged open the door. "Come in, if ye like."

Fletcher watched as the sky softened to lavender. Gracie rose slowly, as the smell of woodsmoke and juniper wafted out to them. Through the screen door, Kenny moved with purpose.

He crossed the floor to a wooden hutch in the corner and withdrew a small leather-bound notebook and placed it on the worn kitchen table.

*Some things should stay dead.*

Audrey's words echoed in Fletcher's head. What had she meant? Were they about to find out?

# 32

# Shattered Silence

"He was always more of an English an' Scottish crossbreed. I understood that more as the years went on," Kenny said as Gracie and Fletcher stepped over the threshold. "You can't truly move on from a place that's in your blood. Especially when you plant roots there."

He was standing over the stove, fussing with the knob, trying to ignite the burner under his kettle. There was something ethereal about his movements. The way he carefully held a dainty teacup in his thick fingers, or the smoothness with which he glided from one side of the open concept kitchen to the other. It was a graceful kind of masculinity.

"How long have you stayed in Tomintoul?" Gracie ventured. Now that she was sure he wasn't a threat, at least not the murderous kind, she was growing more curious about him. She could imagine him as a child, kicking rocks down a dirt lane, reading by a babbling brook, always by his father's side.

"Oh, I couldn't say for sure. This cabin used to be where my uncle an' I would come for holidays. He worked himself to the bone at the distillery mostly, but I've got good memories of the two o' us here," he replied.

"Why did Andrew want to start a distillery?" Fletcher's pondering came in the form of a question. He walked around the small space as if it were a museum or an antique store and he was a boy told not to touch anything inside. His hands were deep in his pockets and his steps were light. Even as he passed the small china cabinet, nothing rattled. The two large men in what was the equivalent of a studio apartment amused Gracie, and she stifled a smile.

"I think he just wanted something, somewhere, to feel like home. And it was a nod to his mam. *GlenTrèigte* means 'forgotten hollow'. Not havin' her in his life, being cast away by the Buchanan clan, an' never havin' his real father or Finlay… It left a hole in him. He tried to fill it with somethin' that honored that we never had."

Kenny said the words honestly, as if he'd said them a million times. Casually, rinsed his hands and dried them on a threadbare towel, then tossed it over his shoulder. Gracie realized that it was less that he didn't like strangers and more about who the strangers were. She knew all too well that not just anyone could walk onto someone's property searching for answers and be given them. This kind of interaction was unheard of in Glenrinnes without being met with the nose of someone's shotgun and a few harsh words.

Fletcher observed Gracie, taking in Kenny's reply like she was drinking ice cold lemonade—each word a sip, sharp with truth and strangely sweet. As if every word refreshed him. He had tried to understand what these revelations would mean for her but, until the idea of meeting Kenny had turned into a reality, he hadn't fully grasped the weight of his existence. It was more than just a friendly encounter. It was a rendezvous with heritage itself.

"Did he ever look for Finlay?" Gracie asked. Urging the conversation forward was taking time, since Kenny seemed reminiscent. But finding the full truth behind who Andrew Windsor really was would probably take a lifetime. Making the most of this conversation was just the start and, if it meant direct questioning, she wasn't above it. She hadn't meant the question to sound sharp. But legacy didn't always wait for the right tone.

Kenny didn't answer right away. His fingers brushed the kettle handle again, as if to make sure he was still in reality. Or perhaps he was contemplating how much information he could trust them with. When he finally opened his mouth to speak, his voice came out low and rough. Gracie could see he was like a dam, moments from breaking.

The kettle hissed softly. "There are things Andrew never said outright," Kenny began. "An' things I'll never understand. Lord, knows I'd have searched high and low, if it'd been me." He unfastened his cloak and hung it on the back of the storm door. "But I think… I think not knowin' hurt him less than knowin'. Or hurtin' Finlay by being the son of the woman he loved, but not his own flesh and blood."

Fletcher circled back to the table and he could sense Gracie was impatient to dig into the journal Andrew had left behind. Even if it was only notes about his work and whiskey formulas, it was an artifact that he was real. It was odd how the absence of evidence that someone lived seemed to make their entire existence questionable. Just saying they were here isn't enough. Yet, once an artifact was found it was irrefutable.

Maybe Gracie was reflecting on what kind of memory she would leave behind. What kind of things would be found in her wake? A few fossilized asters and a scarf scented of lemon verbena? Would there be children to carry on in her stead?

Would Fletcher, or someone else, be there to eloquently grieve her the way Kenny was still mourning his uncle?

He watched as she tucked her hair behind her ear and glanced at the teapot beginning to whistle.

"You said this was his notebook, right?" Fletcher said, gesturing to the leather booklet. He didn't reach for it, but the longing look in Gracie's eyes and the twitch of her shoulder under her sweater was a tell. He knew her well enough now to perceive her restlessness. He wanted to open the book, the door to the past, and let her walk through.

Intuitively, he stepped up beside her and placed a caring hand on her shoulder. If he could've transported her back in time or into the pages of the journal itself, he would've. But the only thing he had to offer was himself as an emotional prop.

Kenny watched the two of them with soft eyes and a knowing grin. It wasn't smug, but respectful. Bashful even. Fletcher wondered if his lack of physicality and the earlier reminder of Mona had tugged his mind to a tender place of bittersweet heartbreak.

The whistle of the kettle grew sharper, curling through the room like a call. Kenny turned away first, reaching for the tea, but something in his posture had changed—less host, more son.

"Aye, it was. He was always scribbling something in there," he answered. He poured three cups of tea, even though he hadn't confirmed they wanted any and searched the counter for a spoon. "Do ye take sugar?"

Gracie and Fletcher nodded mutely, and, within moments, they accepted the porcelain cup without looking at its contents. He wasn't sure he wanted tea, but she accepted it the way you accept a peace treaty. Only this one was signed in steam and silence that wound around him like a whisper.

Fletcher sat, elbows on the table, eyes trained on the leather journal as if proximity alone might unlock its secrets. His thumb grazed the edge, and he jumped back, as if it'd bitten him. Like he could feel the sting of the unuttered scrawl through the binding.

Kenny stood quietly at the stove, sipping his own cup, shoulders relaxed in a way that suggested the past hadn't stopped hurting—but had stopped demanding to be the loudest thing in the room. Outside, a breeze pressed against the screen door, gentle and persistent. A storm was blowing in. It hadn't started raining yet, but legacy had begun to pour.

"Go ahead and look inside. I know yer dyin' tae," Kenny cocked his head.

Fletcher rubbed his hands together, warming his palms and blowing gently on his fingers, as if the diary would crack under his touch. Delicately he lifted it from its place on the table and unwound the suede lace from the smooth binding. A silky bookmark ribbon marked a page three quarters of the way to the back cover and he carefully turned the leaves to find the one it indicated was last read.

Next to him, Gracie exhaled slowly. She seemed unsure if she was ready, but maybe readiness didn't matter anymore. Perhaps all that did was embracing the truth.

The ribbon, frayed at its edges, looked like it had been pulled through a lifetime and small, almost illegible, writing and accompanying doodles were on each page. The paper was tinged yellow with age and the ink was faint in places where it looked like a hand had smudged the words. It was obvious that Andrew Windsor had spent a lot of time spilling his disquieting thoughts onto the blank space the book offered.

"Have you read all of this?" Fletcher asked Kenny. "You must know his mind inside and out. Nearly every page is filled!" He handed the book to Gracie.

"Nah, I've never had the patience for reading straight through. Just skimmed it enough to know—he had scattered thoughts and big dreams," he replied, patting down stray hairs at the crown of his head and shaking the loose silver waves that lay atop his shoulders.

Gracie's eyes flickered over the ink and his mouth moved with the shape of the words; as if each one carried a magic spell. History folded between lines she had been waiting her whole life to read. Beside him, she scanned the scribbles and, he imagined, it was as much for emotion as for meaning.

Suddenly, though, she turned the page and stopped echoing the words with her own voice. She was wide-eyed and one of her hands was clenched into a fist, resting on her knee. Under the table Fletcher could see her leg bouncing wildly up and down. He could make out the lines around her mouth, usually deeper when she smiled, casting shadows on her silky skin. Something was wrong.

Kenny had his back turned to them now, searching for oatcakes in the cupboard.

"What is it? What's wrong?" Fletcher murmured. Gracie's breathing was quicker but she ignored his questions, and Fletcher figured she was busy worrying that Kenny had seen them as easy prey for some kind of poison or other. Maybe any family secrets about Andrew were going to die with them there that night.

Gracie finally looked at Fletcher, her pupils sharp with panic. But when she spoke, it was directed at Kenny.

"What about you and Audrey? You said you two haven't spoken in some time… family feud of some sort?" she tried.

"Feud's one word for it," Kenny's voice was flat. He placed the tin of oatcakes on the counter and turned around. "When I was a lad, I asked a lot of questions. I was curious—always getting into what I shouldn't. One day, I stumbled into something personal…and we haven't spoken since. That was more than twenty-five years ago."

"She must be awfully private," Gracie said, fiddling nervously with her earring.

"Agh, I prob'ly pushed too hard," he replied. "There was tension long before I knew what to call it," Kenny muttered. "Audrey was different after that one summer. Disappeared for months, came back quieter. No one talked about it, but everyone knew something had shifted."

Fletcher felt the change immediately—the kind of discomfort that hummed low, like tension in the walls before a thunderstorm. He gripped the edge of the journal, as if it could absorb the restlessness crawling over his skin.

Unexpectedly, Gracie turned the page of the journal toward him and tapped a group of lines near the bottom of an entry dated November 19th. No year.

*They sent Audrey away this summer. Poor child, she's only fifteen—some convent near the coast. She came back alone, quieter, angrier. I never saw the baby, but I heard she left him with relatives near Brighton. No surname, no claim.*

The sound of the cracker tin popping open brought Gracie back to reality, with misty eyes.

Fletcher's gaze slipped to Gracie, who was staring at the journal as if it might rewrite itself. There was grief there—not just for Audrey, but for every woman who'd been boxed in by expectation and erased by protocol.

He reached for her hand, anchoring them both.

Kenny snapped one oatcake in two, slowly. If he noticed the uncomfortable silence, it didn't show. Surely, if he had known he wouldn't have shown them the notebook in the first place.

"Do you think he knows?" Gracie mimed to Fletcher.

"If he does, he is a vault," he whispered back.

Gracie looked toward Kenny's shoulder blades, broad and still. There wasn't a tremble or flicker. The journal was still open in front of Fletcher, but his eyes weren't on it anymore. He was listening—determining if Kenny was guarding the untold.

Kenny twisted the lid back onto the tin. "Oatcakes've gone stale," he muttered.

"Kenny, we aren't trying to overstep any boundaries," Fletcher prefaced. Then, he paused before continuing in a low voice. "The journal, though, says—"

"I know what it says," Kenny interrupted. He squared his shoulders and let his eyes rest on the wall, like he could see through to the forest beyond it. "I don't think she ever forgave them," he said. "Or herself."

"Ye knew about Audrey?" Gracie confirmed.

Kenny's body tensed from the weight of the question. "Aye. Found out when I was a younger man. T'was an accident."

"You didn't say anything. But you still let us read the journal… knowing that entry was there?" Fletcher probed.

"S'pose I don't see the point in guarding skeletons of the past sneaking up to lay their bony fingers on ya," Kenny sighed. "Audrey begged me not to say a word, and I haven't, until now. She said I'd undo everything mam did to keep it from getting out."

"That's why you stopped speaking?" Gracie added.

Kenny nodded, just once. "She thought silence was safer. Only reason I even knew was that I found an envelope with a picture stuffed inside. Audrey with a wee babe, and a date. No names, but I pieced it together."

Gracie stood, crossed the kitchen and wrapped him in a hug. At first, he resisted. But, after a moment, he gave into the caress of a young woman who had more empathy in her funny bone than most people did in their entire being.

Fletcher didn't know if the hug healed anything, but it made space for something else.

# 33

# Lamplit Truth

Kenny didn't move at first. Her arms around him felt foreign, like warmth he'd forgotten how to receive. He hadn't spoken of Audrey in decades—not even to Mona, or to himself in the quiet hours. Keeping her secret had felt like loyalty. But over time, it had turned into loneliness. And now, with Gracie's arms around him and Fletcher watching like he understood, Kenny realized he hadn't just lost a sister. He'd let the silence speak for him, and it had said nothing at all.

Gradually, Gracie released Kenny from her embrace and stepped back, fumbling for her teacup. Instead, Fletcher caught her hand and squeezed it. Reassurance that she had done the right thing to keep the moment from unraveling.

Kenny was quiet and stared into the hearth in the corner of the room. It was glowing with embers—orange and stubborn—of what had once been a raging flame. Fletcher wondered if maybe Kenny felt like those embers. As if he were the leftover spark from a once brightly burning fire.

After a long pause, Fletcher, daring to lift the heavy blanket of burden that hung over them, uttered the nagging question that was in his mind. "What exactly happened…between you and Audrey?"

Suddenly, Kenny didn't look like the magnetic force he had when they arrived. He seemed like he was just a man trying to find contentment. It took him a few beats but, finally he found his voice.

"I reckon I knew before I asked her," he began.

## 25 Years Earlier

Audrey's den was the coziest place you could be on a winter evening. Dim lamplight. Flickering candles. Whispered conversation. Her boys, Titus and Sydney, on either end of the sofa—one reading and the other engrossed in a game of solitaire. Audrey had raised her children with all the attributes a mother ought to have. Patience and grace, among others. The boys were turning out to be smart and sophisticated, despite their young age.

Everyone thinks that men grow up to be strong and clever because of their father. But a mother's presence left deeper marks. Kenny knew this from living without his own mother for so long. Living in the hills of Scotland was beautiful, if not a bit lonely, and he sometimes wondered if Audrey had more advantages by staying in London. And the advantages of bonding with their mother, Helen.

He had always wondered what it would've been like to grow up in London instead of the Scottish hills. To share inside jokes and childhood memories with Audrey. He could've played the role of endearing nuisance. In fact, he would've welcomed it.

He quickly shook off the thought. It was too late for any of that. Audrey was already thirty-three years old and living a vibrant life in London seemed like what she was born to do.

When she'd met her husband, Harrison Browning, she was an accomplished young lady and more than ready to settle down and have a family. Kenny envied it. The way life seemed to come easy to her. How much more grown up she was than him. It was like hugging a cactus. Affection that came with prickles—reminders that things were different for him.

Out of the corner of his eye he watched as Audrey and Titus laughed together about one of the lines in his book, and his heart ached. He'd had plenty of moments with his uncle that mimicked the exchange, but none that could be compared to having the same relationship with his mother. Or any woman, for that matter.

Kenny wasn't well acquainted with the ways of the world. Even grown up, Kenny was shy—still awkward, still learning how to move through the world with intent. He'd been working to push those things into the background, though. Sometimes it worked but, mostly, he was still floundering.

The scent of rosemary drifted from the kitchen, and Kenny realized Audrey had slipped away—again. He didn't get to visit often and, when he did, it somehow always seemed like she was trying to distance herself from him. Physically and emotionally. Often, he wondered why, despite them both being adults, they couldn't seem to have a normal conversation. Not even one as elementary as the ones she had with Titus and Sydney.

He quietly walked to the doorway. Audrey stood at the counter slicing oranges for the simmer pot. Kenny watched her hands— deliberate, practiced, graceful. Everything about her was composed. Elegant. Detached. It only made Kenny feel less real.

He leaned against the doorframe, suddenly aware of how foreign the warmth of the room felt.

"Did ye ever think about what it would've been like?" he asked, voice low. "If things had gone differently. If we'd really grown up together,"

Audrey didn't look up. She pressed the blade through the citrus, then reached for the cinnamon.

"Not this again, Kenneth. Things could never have been the way you wanted," she replied cooly.

Like a ghost in his own skin, Kenny turned pale, and his mouth formed a tight line. She was shutting him down again. Like she always did. Her life was picture perfect and neatly wrapped and, just once, Kenny wanted to see what was under all the fancy trimmings.

"Sometimes I wish things were so perfectly stitched," he said. "For once, that we could just say what we mean."

"Careful, Kenneth," she said. "You're poking at things better left forgotten."

"Maybe," he replied. "But forgotten things have a way of calling out. Especially when they're part of someone's story."

She finally turned, eyes wary. "This again? You don't understand what you're asking."

"I'm asking to understand why ye treat me like an outcast. I'm in yer home and I feel like I need tae be invisible. When Harrison said I could stay, he didn't say I was goin' tae be treated thus by my own sister."

"Well, believe it or not, Harrison doesn't know *everything*. And if he had asked me, I would've told him not to send for you!" she exclaimed. Her left hand perched on her hip, and she wiped a droplet of orange juice from her cheek with the back of her right wrist. "There are chapters in our family that weren't meant to be reread. I don't avoid you, Kenneth." Her voice cracked slightly, and her eyes burned a hole in the butcher block below.

"He frowned, trying to keep his breath even. "That sounds like guilt. Or fear," Kenny admitted.

"Well, they're one in the same. And trust me, you didn't miss much," she answered, exasperated.

*One in the same?*

"Seems I did, that one summer," Kenny replied.

"They sent me to a convent. I came back without a child! I was told to forget. To move on. To build a life clean enough that no one would ask questions. And I did." She swallowed hard. "Until now."

"The babe from the picture," he sighed. "Audrey…"

"Kenneth," she soothed. "I was scared of being a mother. Of being less. I knew I could have a full life but, I messed up and got pregnant. Everyone viewed me as ruined. You won't tell anyone, will you?"

"So, keeping a child, would've made your life emptier? Ye would've been less of a person?? I think I've got the picture," Kenny said through gritted teeth. "There's nothing to tell."

"I was terrified. I didn't know how to be a mother," she pleaded. Audrey reached for the cinnamon again, but her fingers trembled.

"Even now, ye care more about oranges and spices than about family. I know it's not what ye wanted. But maybe think about what you left behind one day." He turned on his heel and strode toward the door. One he knew he would never walk through again.

He stepped out into the streets of Mayfair. Soft rain falling and distance piano music from a neighboring home. He let the air bite him awake; let the raindrops soak him through.

London blurred around him, but he didn't look back. There was nothing behind him but silence and orange peels and the kind of truth that makes you walk faster just to keep it from catching up.

# 34

# Ashes and Inheritance

"And you never spoke again?" Gracie whispered.

Kenny shook his head, taking a seat at the table. "Life has a way of breaking and burning bridges. Until, somehow, it begins again."

Fletcher watched the way Gracie leaned in, her eyes still shining from Kenny's story. There was a softness in her expression—a kind of listening that felt gracious, and it caught him off guard. "I know about that, all too well," he said, voice low. His gaze drifted toward the fire, then back to her. "I haven't spoken to my parents in over a decade. And honestly... I was dead inside before I met you." The words landed heavier than he expected.

He gave her a smile—small, unsure, the kind that used to feel impossible but now stirred something easier in him. A chuckle hovered in his chest, not quite formed, but full of light.

"Ye didn't find out some dark family secret too, did ye?" Kenny pressed.

"No, no. Nothing like that," Fletcher laughed. "My parents…just didn't know how to love. Each other, or me."

"Seems to have been a problem with a lot of people. Maybe we are the exceptions. The ones meant to hold on to what's good."

"But ye already lost Andrew an' your Mona. Are you an' Freya close?" Gracie asked openly.

"Aye… we are, I suppose. Not in every way, but in the ones that count. The years without her mother have been hard on us both. But I try my best to see after her," Kenny blinked hard, then looked toward the window, as if tracking a memory only he could see. "She's got a rough shell, but she's also all the best parts of Mona and me."

Gracie brushed her hand over Kenny's. The gesture spoke more than any words could've. Kenny's admission had risen like the sun on a dreary morning. Barely visible behind the clouds but bringing life with it regardless.

"I don't think I got anything from either of my parents. Besides my red hair and freckles," Fletcher mused.

"They gave ye life," Kenny said. "One it looks like you've put tae good use."

"I just always wished they could've been there for me the way I needed them to be. Especially when I was young. Maybe things would've turned out differently."

Fletcher, slipped away into his thoughts, imagining—for the billionth time—what his life might've been if he had grown up with parents who didn't spend all their time drunk, or arguing, or working. Parents who, instead, went to town picnics, had snacks ready for him after school, and spent time with his friend's parents playing cards and laughing. Maybe he would've stayed in Shearvale, or nearby. By now, maybe he would've been married to a girl like June Carrigan and had a kid or two to tote around. Perhaps that wouldn't have been so bad.

*What am I thinking?!*

Fletcher cast the images of what safe could've looked like for him, thousands of miles away, in another lifetime.

"Are ya alright, lad?" Kenny asked. He had been waving his hand in front of Fletcher's face, to get his attention.

"Uh…yeah," Fletcher mumbled, running a hand through his hair. "Actually, I'm better than alright, sir. You've helped me see clearly for the first time in a long time."

Kenny smiled faintly, like the compliment had landed somewhere deeper than it showed. "I don't know what I've done, but… I'm glad."

"You've made me realize," Fletcher explained, "that I don't need anything more than what I've got. If it hadn't been for the path my parents set me on, I wouldn't have my best friend, Tate. I wouldn't have met the amazing woman sitting next to me right now, and I wouldn't be sitting here with you." He looked down for a moment, the firelight flickering across his face. "We *were* meant to hold on to the good things, Mr. Windsor. Only I've been blind to most of those things until recently."

Gracie's smile held quiet pride. "Scotland isn't just you're home now, McCullough. It's who you are."

"It's who *we* are," he replied. "I've changed so much since setting out to learn about Aisla, Finlay, the Windsors," he motioned to Kenny. "And I think there's more to come."

Kenny didn't respond with words—just raised his cup in a silent toast, and Fletcher felt the weight of every story that had led them here. It wasn't just history. It was his inheritance.

Holding up the thick notebook, inspiration touched his core. "I have an idea. But, first, sir, I have to ask you—can I borrow this journal?"

"Of course, but whatever for?" Kenny asked, surprised.

"I haven't figured out all the details yet, but I think I want to include some of the contents in my report on the Highland Clearances. I'll be sure not to include Audrey, or even you, if you object. But now… it feels like more than just a project. It feels like I've stepped onto holy ground that should be roped off for conservation. This story, the people of the past, need to be preserved."

Kenny leaned back in his chair, studying Fletcher for a long moment. The fire crackled, low and steady. "Aye," he said finally, "you've got a heart for history—but it's the people you really see. Not just facts and years... ye catch the truth that lingers. That's rare." He raised his mug again, this time with a grin. "So if you're asking me whether to follow the thread—go on and tug it. You might just unravel something the world's forgotten it needed." Kenny nodded toward the notebook. "That journal's a good start. But I think your real report's written in how *you* and Gracie see the world."

Fletcher didn't know how to say thank you for something like that, so he didn't try. Instead, he let the warmth settle in his chest.

With a small stretch and a wide yawn, Gracie's eyes flick to Fletcher's. "We need to get home," she insisted. "It's been a long day. But," patting Kenny's arm, "we'd love to come back and visit wi' ye again, if that's okay?"

Kenny smiled, the kind that lived in the corners of his eyes more than his mouth. "Of course, Miss Gracie. This old cottage's been waitin' years for company like yours. And I'd like to think Mona would've invited ye back."

"Next time we'll bring treacle tart," she promised.

"Ye do that, and I'll tell ye every story that's *not* written down in that book," he winked.

Fletcher glanced out the window and frowned. "Speaking of… the car is still stuck. I don't know what kind of horror stories they'll come up with if we don't make it back tonight."

Kenny walked them out to the car with an ancient flashlight, tugging his coat tighter against the chill that had settled in. He crouched beside the car with Fletcher, and they squinted together at the branch wedged like a splinter in the axle.

"I thought it'd snapped clean. Looks like it's just jammed in tight," Fletcher said.

"Aye. She'll be stubborn, but the job's not impossible," Kenny resolved.

They worked in silence for a moment—Kenny wedging a crowbar beneath the branch, Fletcher steadying the flashlight and bracing the wheel. The wood groaned, then cracked. Gracie stood nearby holding her breath.

"Hold her steady," Kenny muttered, giving the crowbar one final twist. The branch popped loose with a thud, rolling into the ditch.

Fletcher exhaled. "That felt like something from a folktale."

Kenny chuckled. "Well, if ye write it that way, make me taller and younger."

Fletcher grinned, brushing dirt from his hands. "She won't drive smooth, but I think she'll get us home."

Kenny stood, brushing off his knees. "Then go. And come back when the road's less dramatic."

Gracie stepped forward, wrapping Kenny in another hug. One that smelled faintly of hearth and tea leaves. "I don't know how to say thank you for today," she said, pulling back just enough to meet his gaze. She wiped a tear with the edge of her coat sleeve. "You're officially family now."

Kenny blinked, startled by her brightness but visibly moved.

"And next time," she added, tapping the car door with flourish, "we're arriving with better tires."

The headlights illuminated and the engine roared. Kenny grew smaller and finally disappeared into the darkness as they reversed the way they'd come. Only their retreat was unburdened, in contrast to their arrival. The visit with Kennth Windsor had lit a match and ignited the wick of Fletcher's determination to preserve what history forgot and protect the truths still flickering beneath its ashes.

The trees bent softly in the wind as they pulled the car onto the main road, and began rolling forward, carrying his resolve into the night.

# 35

# Bathed In Oxford Blue

Settling into the stillness of the drive back to Glenrinnes, the journal tucked safely into the glove compartment, Gracie watched Fletcher. He stared out of the windshield with tousled hair and sleepy eyes. Her breath hitched with quiet longing and admiration. She thought about the way he had moved around Kenny's kitchen—absently, tenderly—and a gentle throbbing rose in her chest. It was the kind of ache that whispered, *You're safe here.*

Finding love was last on the agenda when she had met Fletcher at The Caledonian Cuppa. But their chemistry had been undeniable. It would've been pointless to try and ignore it.

She hadn't thought of much else halfway through the drive when he reached out and placed a hand on her knee. It seemed more like a way to ground himself through whatever was on his mind than anything else. But it felt like a hush before the sunrise to Graice. It was enough that he touched her like she'd always been chosen—and not for anything she had to prove.

"What are you thinking about?" he asked. His voice was deep and gruff, betraying his exhaustion. But, still, the question was earnest.

Gracie turned her head slightly, catching the edge of his profile in the glow of a streetlight. "I'm thinking about how quiet it feels right now," she said after a beat. "Not just outside, but in me." She placed her hand over his.

"I didn't know I could feel this way around someone," she continued, voice low. "Like maybe I don't have to be different. That I could just be myself."

"Why would you want to be any different?" His fingers flexed slightly beneath hers. "You're pretty great just the way you are."

The compliment was uncomplicated. Undiluted, in a way most praise isn't given. Gracie blinked, her throat tightening.

"I guess, since me mam died, I've had feelings of…not knowing where I belong. Feeling like I should blend in with everyone else, so I don't make a fool of myself. In Edinburgh that was easy, until I met you," she murmured.

"Why would you want to blend in? Not that you ever could," he teased. "Gracie, you're too bright to blend into the background. Your mom would've wanted you to be yourself. The way you are around me, Keira…she wouldn't want you to hide who you really are."

"On the outside, I'm always tryin' to project light. But there are times when I've had some dark thoughts. It makes me wonder if the rosy way me mam saw the world—the way I try to see it—is just a way of escaping reality."

"Joy isn't an escape," Fletcher replied. There was no wavering in his voice. "It's brave."

"You think so?" Gracie asked.

"I *know* it," he grinned. She could see the outline of it, even in the dark. "Sunshine, being happy isn't fake just because it's hard. It's a choice. One you've taught me is more courageous than carrying your misery with you." His fingers flexed under hers and his hand tightened, just slightly.

She thought back to the way he had awkwardly introduced himself at the Cuppa. The way he cared for Chantilly without fail or expectation, and how he'd really listened when she needed it most. Those things might've seemed small from the outside, but maybe that's where love lived—in the small things.

The tires hummed beneath them and the light outside was shifting from midnight to oxford blue. It was a deep and solemn color. Muted and cozy. The feeling of dark academia rising.

She used to think dramatic gestures, grand confessions, big endings were the hallmarks of devotion. But this? A sleepy smile. A hand on her knee. A quiet ride through bruised blue light. This was the kind of bond that lasted.

Gracie leaned her head onto his shoulder and let out a soft sigh. "It feels like we were always headed here. Not just to the Highlands, but to each other." Her confession was like an affirming echo around them. It said *I trust you* as much as it clarified what their relationship truly looked like on the inside.

Her words didn't just drift—they nestled, like warmth in winter bones. Like proof that two people could choose each other without fanfare, and still make it feel like magic.

# 36

# Bring It On Home

Fletcher watched from the car, Sunday morning, as Gracie hugged her father in front of the house. No tears today. Just two people handing each other the peace they needed to move forward.

The morning was grey. Silver streaks brushed across the sky. Even a pale amber glazed the underside of the clouds as the sun rose slowly behind the mist-laced hills. A low fog clung to the meadows. It blurred the edges of the stone walls and sheep dotted fields.

The crisp air stirred with the songs of robins and curlews calling out, and, in the distance, peat smoke rose from distant cottages.

The breeze rustled the fir trees, and the bleat of newborn lambs was carried on it. Meanwhile, daffodils and crocuses pushed through the thawed earth.

Lach had given Fletcher a small speech about his gratitude for the clarity he brought with the visit and, as any father would, made sure to give him a good dose of *Take care of my daughter, or else*. Now, Fletcher could hear them muttering goodbyes to each other outside the window. Lach wasn't just saying farewell to his daughter, but to someone who had stepped into her own emotional truth.

"Ye take care, lass. And don't let anythin' change ya. You're one in a million, Gracie girl," Lach said, voice shaking.

Fletcher could hear the confidence in Gracie as she murmured something about the strength she inherited from him. Then, more directly, she gave him the words Fletcher imagined she had wanted to say for a long time. It's not an emotional collapse. Instead, it's mature and calm.

"Da, my home is forever with you and this land. And I'll always return to it. But I've learned lately that the path I'm on, in Edinburgh, with Thistle and Tulip, and my friends who are like family. It's where I belong, at least for now. I haven't felt that way in a long time, and I want to soak it in while I can."

Lach stroked his heavy beard and glanced at the car. At Fletcher, Keira, and Tate waiting, and to Chantilly, with her lopsided tongue, hanging out of the window. Then, he turned back to Gracie and took her hand in his, as if asking for permission.

"This life isn't always kind to us, love. When you find something, or someone," he nodded towards the car, "that makes you happy, ye've got tae hold on tight. That's the way I've always felt. On this farm, with your mother… with you. And now, it's time to find yer own way of doin' that. I'll be here when ye need me."

Watching them, Fletcher felt something stir in his chest—not envy, not intrusion, but the quiet hope that love, when given room, could look just like this.

Gracie kissed Lach on the cheek and headed to the car, sliding into the back seat with Keira and resting her arm on the windowsill. Fletcher instinctively wanted to comfort her. To let her know that, if she wanted, he would come back with her and that she had the right to enjoy life in both places. In fact, he wanted that for himself as well.

The hills rolled like worn velvet outside the windows and the sleepy morning clung to the damp earth. The road curved gently past distilleries and stone houses and the pewter sky felt close enough to touch. Speyside wasn't just a place, it was a feeling.

Selfishly, Fletcher also knew that, if he got the chance to return to Glenrinnes, it would likely be because he and Gracie had let their relationship lead them back there. Gracie didn't make him feel the way people like Sofia had. Like a caged animal being stared at and prodded. High anxiety with no reward.

Everything with her was a reward. A gift to be put on the highest shelf and cherished and shown off to others. She made him feel new and untainted for the first time in his life.

He looked in the rearview mirror. Chantilly contentedly lay in the middle of Keira and Gracie with her head in Gracie's lap and her paws neatly under her chin. Gracie was looking out the window, observing the wide valleys and pine forests. They passed lochs and through small towns that felt like they were built for reflection.

The farther they drove from Glenrinnes, the more Fletcher realized that Gracie, the land, the clarity, and all he'd found waiting for him had been stitched into the fabric of who he was. They'd become part of the map he would carry forward. Perhaps they were even the key to holding joy without clutching too hard. Maybe it didn't have to be all or nothing.

Soon the city's silhouette—Arthur's Seat, the castle, the spires—greeted them like an old friend. The cobbled street and the stone-fronted terraces weren't just a destination but an exhale. Not merely markers of arrival, but an invitation to settle into stillness. It had been a restless week, and the soft landing back in Edinburgh gave way to a new beginning. One rooted in grace and remembrance.

As they pulled up to Gracie's flat, the low rumble of the engine slowed. Thankfully, Lach had had the tools to fix the axle on the car properly, so that it hummed softly over the stone streets. The wrought-iron railings were in sight and Gracie's building stood with dignity against the washed-out sky.

Opening the doors, they could hear the distant call of hulls and the rustle of leaves. The faint aroma of roasted coffee and mulch greeted them. The city didn't ask for admiration, it simply offered presence.

Fletcher rubbed the back of his neck as they unloaded the bags from the car. "I know we're all running on fumes," he said with a weary smile, "but maybe we can meet at Thistle and Tulip tomorrow? Around lunch?"

Keira gave a mock salute. "Only if there's caffeine involved." Tate stretched and nodded. "And sugar. Lots of sugar."

Fletcher glanced at Gracie, who met his gaze with soft agreement. "We've got things to talk about." He smiled wide. "And I need your help," directed at Gracie. "I think it's time we talk legacy."

# 37

# New Traditions

The next afternoon, Thistle & Tulip smelled like cappuccinos, damp stems, and memories you could touch with your fingertips. Fletcher stood behind the bouquet-making table, palms resting on the wood grain, as Keira passed out the coffees in mismatched mugs that looked like they'd been collected during every chapter of someone's life.

Gracie was already there, sleeves rolled and hair twisted into a loose knot, sorting through buckets of flowers Tate had carried in a few minutes earlier. She looked wildly delighted to see the camellia heads tilted open like little confessions. Sprigs of rosemary waited in bundles near the center, and eucalyptus spilled over the edge of the table without restraint.

"Okay," Keira said, flopping onto a stool, cradling her mug. "We survived the Highlands. Is this the part where Fletcher gives a speech?"

Fletcher gave a small laugh, then pressed his lips together and tapped his temple.

"Not a speech," he said. "Not really. Just something I've been processing."

"Sounds dangerous," Tate chuckled.

Fletcher didn't react. Instead, he reached into his satchel and laid Andrew Windsor's journal down on the table. Its worn leather cover creaked faintly, and the corners had been softened by time. He let it sit there for a moment, surrounded by petals and humidity.

"You all know that this entire research project started as work," Fletcher said quietly. "Cross-referencing land records, family trees, the usual rhythm. But then… I started seeing things differently. Because of what we found." Then, he locked eyes with Gracie with honor. "Because of you."

"Kenny's story opened something for me," he continued. "Not just about loss. About how people choose to go on. About joy—not as escape, but as commitment. And Andrew

Windsor's words—his grief, his longing, his strength—they're not just historical. They're human."

Gracie's hands had stilled, holding a long, budding stem. Fletcher reached out and plucked a sprig from the bunch of rosemary and twirled it lightly between his fingers.

"Your voice belongs in this, Gracie" he added. "You helped me find my way. That has to be part of the story because without you there wouldn't be one at all."

There was a hush. The kind that settles when something real enters the room. Gracie blinked once, slowly. Then she smiled.

"I didn't think I'd ever be part of anything like this," she said, her voice gentle. "Something so… important."

Fletcher's voice dropped to something steady, low.

"I didn't think I'd meet someone who would teach me what legacy really means."

Keira made a quiet sound—somewhere between a sigh and a smile. "Emotional accuracy," she said matter-of-factly. "That's what history's been missing. This? This is the record."

Tate nodded and leaned in. "Gracie, he needs your perspective. We all do."

Gracie looked down at the journal. The initials in the corner. The stains across the paper from years of hands and weather and memory. "So, what are you asking me to do?" she said.

"Help me present it," Fletcher replied. "Not just the findings. Not just the facts. Help me share the heart of it."

"It's not traditional," Gracie murmured. "And I'm not a coffin-office kind o' girl." A laugh escaped her lips.

"No, it's not traditional" Fletcher said. "But neither was Andrew Windsor. Neither is Kenny. And neither are we."

She took a breath."Then I guess we tell it like it's ours," she said. "Because it kind of is."

Over the following days, they worked together in quiet tandem—Gracie pacing between the counter and the window seat as Fletcher sorted notes and citations with his usual precision. He'd offer her snippets from the journal, and she'd respond with reflections that turned facts into something felt. They built the presentation like a bouquet: careful layering, distinct voices, and blooms of emotional truth tucked between.

Late one evening, with printed drafts scattered and tea gone cold, Fletcher leaned back in his chair and looked at her—truly looked. She was sitting cross-legged on the floor, a pencil behind one ear and a notebook full of margin scribbles in her lap.

"You've made this better than I ever imagined," he said softly. It was true

Gracie stood, stretching, then stepped between his knees. "We're not just telling the story," she murmured, fingers brushing his jaw. "We're becoming part of it."

Fletcher exhaled as her lips met his—light, certain, like a ribbon tied not for decoration, but for keeping. And in that moment, it felt like history had made room for them.

# 38

# All That Endures

The library smelled faintly of beeswax, old books, and the damp hush that followed a morning drizzle. It wasn't grand—not cathedral-tall or oak-paneled—but it had charm: high arched windows, poufs and ottomans next to upholstered armchairs, and a floor that creaked when you walked as if history were shifting beneath your feet.

Gracie stood at the front of the room, heart knocking against her ribs. The rhythm was too fast to be justified by the constant proximity to Fletcher since they'd gotten back from Glenrinnes. They had been working around the clock to make sure the presentation was ready. Highland conservation efforts and heritage funding were hinging on it being a success.

She'd chosen a teal wrap dress—muted but intentional—and her boots made soft thuds against the flagstone floor as she paced between the lectern and the front table. Fletcher was across from her, seated and sorting through a stack of notecards, his brow furrowed like he was negotiating with himself.

"Fletcher," she whispered. "Are you sure ye want me up there? Am I ready?"

He looked up, met her gaze, and nodded. "You're probably more ready than I am," he laughed. "Relax. If anything, I'll forget all my parts. I wasn't made for public speaking. Sometimes it just comes with the territory."

Gracie stepped closer. "Then let's just tell the truth. And if words fail, hopefully the visuals won't."

The audience was large and included some intimidating looking men and women. Historic Environment Scotland representatives, government officials, professors, students, members of the press, and more that Gracie couldn't name. She scanned the serious faces, unsure whether she was welcome or was just being watched.

Andrew's journal lay open on the table, alongside a display of scanned letters and photos. Beside it, Gracie had arranged a small bowl of rosemary sprigs and camellias, tucked just so. She had made the arrangement herself, choosing the blooms deliberately—memory, resilience, love unspoken but not erased.

A hush settled as the clock ticked toward eleven.

Fletcher stood. His jacket creased slightly at the waist and he cleared his throat—once, lightly—before speaking.

"What we're about to share is the culmination of months of research. However, the most important research was done over the course of the last few weeks. Journals, letters, land records, and oral history have been compiled for consideration. But, more than that, we've brought with us a story about legacy," he stated.

He glanced at Gracie, and she nodded—a quiet cue that she was with him, that the story belonged to both of them.

"Through the help of a local and her family, facts and fragments were turned into memories and hope. A quiet kind of rebellion against the events that tried to shape them," he paused briefly. "It wasn't just archival. It was emotional."

With that, Gracie stepped forward.

"I'm not a historian," she began, her voice clear and low. "But I know what it means to look at something and feel it tug at your bones. This research brought me closer to my own family than I thought possible. I came into this with curiosity. What I found was connection."

She lifted one of the scanned letters.

"We thought we'd be presenting lineage. Instead, we're presenting resilience," she added.

"It's a generational arc that started with Aisla Buchanan. Her name was barely legible in parish records, but she's more than a footnote. She was fire and stillness, and she loved a man named Finlay McCullough. Who, surprisingly, was my great-great uncle," Fletcher said, shrugging his shoulders. One eyebrow raised. "Their letters suggest devotion. Their separation— forced by circumstance and pride."

Gracie held a photograph aloft. "This is Andrew," she said confidently. "Aisla's son. He became steward of GlenTrèigte. But, in truth, he should've been a poet. Through his writing, you feel the fracture—that he knew about the love that came before him and didn't survive. He wrote of grief, not to dwell on it, but to preserve what others tried to forget."

"This research doesn't just chart bloodlines. It follows emotional geography—land removed, language forgotten, stories half-erased. Aisla's fortitude was the beginning. Andrew preserved it," Fletcher went on. "Andrew also raised his nephew, Kenneth Windsor," Fletcher continued. "But what's remarkable is how that choice—one man's decision—set the stage for something restorative."

Gracie nodded in agreement. "Kenny didn't inherit land or lineage in the traditional sense. He inherited memory. He was entrusted with history, even when the truth was painful. By preserving Andrew's journal and giving us insight into what both tethered and tore apart the Buchanan/Windsor family, he helped shape this entire presentation."

Fletcher's gaze warmed. "And that's where Gracie enters. Her journey wasn't just curiosity—modest as she may be. It was reclamation. She, as the great-great-great niece of Ailsa Buchanan, is here, not to polish facts. But to speak to the heart of them."

"We used to think truth was best handled with gloves," she said. "Now I know it's meant to be felt without barriers. And that's why you're here."

The screen behind them faded from old photographs to a sepia-toned map with a slim dotted line marking the site of the former Buchanan home. Gracie could almost feel the weight of her great-great-great aunt's footsteps along that trail—flattening moss, pushing through heather.

Fletcher concluded the presentation with a soft inhale. "The Highlands were reshaped by violence and silence. The Clearances didn't just take land—they scattered memory. But the echo lives on. In journals. In love letters. In who survives to tell the story."

Gracie reached up instinctively, fingers brushing the edge of the pearl necklace resting against her collarbone. She hadn't planned to wear it, not until that morning when she found herself standing at the edge of the sink. That day, she needed Aisla's strength to show her own.

They stepped back together. A moment passed. Then applause, soft at first, then growing, and Gracie blinked against the rise of sound like it was something sacred. Not praise. Permission.

Fletcher didn't smile—he pressed one hand over his heart like he wasn't sure how else to hold it. The other pressed to the small of Gracie's back.

Later, after the audience had dispersed and the archival materials had been gently repacked, Gracie wandered to the back of the room. The pearls still rested cool against her skin. She peered out the window to the dreary street below.

Fletcher approached quietly. Only the sound of his boots echoed across the now empty room.

"You glowed," he whispered. "Like… if stories had their own north star."

Gracie laughed, but a tear slipped down her cheek. Not sorrow. A release.

"I wore Aisla's pearls," she said.

"I know," he replied. "She would've been proud of you."

Suddenly, Tate and Keira appeared with two paper cups of tea.

"We snagged the good kind before the professors swept it. Rooibos and something floral," Tate said. "We were waiting in the lobby to see how it went but got a bit antsy. Pins and needles and all that."

Gracie took a cup and curled her fingers around it, letting the warmth bloom into her palms.

"I know this started with the past," she said slowly. "But I don't want it to end there."

"Are you saying you want to chart new geography?" Fletcher asked, voice half-teasing.

"I'm saying there's room for a new chapter," she replied. "And I want to write it with you. All of you."

"So do I."

His hand found hers. The library lights flickered. Keira and Tate exchanged smirks.

History had rethreaded itself and chosen them to carry forward what had once been left unfinished. To stitch their names into the quiet seams of a tapestry that had frayed at the edges, now mended with intention.

Outside, the skies wept soft rain and Gracie was sure that, back in the Highlands, the glens leaned in to listen—but inside, where light stayed, Gracie let lineage rest and love begin.

# Epilogue

## 12 Years Later

Gracie's fingers worked nimbly as she braided vibrant cosmos into Amelia Mae's long, copper brown, wavy hair. It was soothing, the way the thick strands slipped in and out of her grasp as the plait grew longer and smoother. Amelia, Millie to her mam, and her little brother, Clark, had begged for a field picnic and the day was too gorgeous to ignore their pleas.

Millie was seven years old, but had the maturity of someone many years wiser. She spent every summer day, first light to last, gathering wildflowers, frolicking with the lambs, and wading in the shallow part of the creek. Sometimes she let Clark bring Winter, their Irish Setter pup, along on the adventures. Other days, she curled up under a tree with a picture book and marmalade sandwich. Gracie was sure she was related to *Paddington Bear.*

"Okay, little lady," Gracie said softly, tying a small elastic around the bottom of the braid. "You're all done."

"How does it look, Mommy? Do I look like a princess?" Millie asked with bright eyes. They were Tiffany blue and eager, just like Gracie's mother, Lileas, had been. But a mischievous storm brewed behind them. She got that from her father.

"Not just any princess. The prettiest one," Fletcher said from behind her. She spun around, into his arms, and he threw her into the air as if she was light as a handful of glitter. Her smile sure was that sparkly though.

Clark clapped enthusiastically from his patch of dandelions, cheeks smudged with jam and dirt. "My turn! My turn!"

Fletcher scooped him up too, spinning twice before pretending to stumble. "Whoa! You're heavier than a whole basket of turnips!"

Clark giggled so hard he snorted, which made Millie laugh harder.

Gracie sat back on the blanket they'd spread across the tall grass, lifting a thermos of hibiscus tea to her lips and letting herself exhale. The hill just beyond their picnic sloped toward the old boundary fence—the one Fletcher had restored last spring with Kenny's help. It was still crooked in places, but Fletcher said crooked things held charm. Gracie believed him. After all, it was true about his grin whenever he looked at her.

She reached for the small locket nestled beneath Aisla's pearls, fingers grazing the edges. Inside was a faded photo of Da with her and Fletcher on their wedding day, standing outside of *GlenTrèigte*.
And here, with her children tumbling through the meadow and Fletcher mouthing "I love you" over Clark's bouncing curls, she knew the truth:

The past had made room for them. And they had filled it with a future worthy of light.

Da had passed a couple years before. A heart attack in the barn, right after he finished squabbling with Ailene. Millie was only five then, but she held the family together as much as any adult could've. Kept the memory of her grandad alive—drawing pictures of what his daily routine was with her colored pencils.

It was because of her, and baby Clark, that Gracie and Fletcher knew they had to take over the farm. Not even a week went by before Fletcher went remote for Historic Environment Scotland, and Gracie turned over the shop to Keira. It was past time for her to be more than a partner anyway.

Since then, Keira had hired two other women to rotate with her on the schedule. With a growing baby bump herself now, it was getting harder for her to stand for long periods making bouquets. Two years of trying to have a baby, after three years of begging Tate to marry her, made it all that much sweeter.

Fletcher had even spoken with his mother a few times—each conversation brittle, but real. With his father, reconciliation still hung in the air—unsaid, unfinished. And somewhere between the long days and the colder nights, Fletcher had begun to dabble in whiskey making—a patient craft that let him shape the echoes into something warm.

Sometimes, in the cool hour between breakfast and chores, Gracie would walk the border of the farm just for the quiet. The chickens clucked with the rhythm of routine, the sheep grazed like clockwork, and Clark—now four—was usually trailing behind her with a wooden stick and a head full of questions.

"Mommy," he'd said that morning, "do ye think the baby will like frogs? When uncle Tate and auntie Keira come visit?"

"Depends," she'd replied. "Will ye teach her the good ones from the cranky ones?"

He'd nodded solemnly, like it was a very serious calling. His half-Scottish, half-American accent was as adorable as his dimples.

Gracie smiled to herself as they reached the row of blackberry bushes near the east paddock—her favorite spot to think. The berries weren't ripe yet, but the promise was there, just like everything else that spring seemed to offer.

"Can the baby have a name with a bug in it?" Clark asked, skipping sideways. "Like Lady? Or Cricket?"

Gracie laughed, smoothing his wild curls. "We'll keep it on the list."

Gracie watched her son crouch to inspect an ant trail, narrating their progress like a wildlife reporter in corduroy overalls.

This—this was the new rhythm.

Da's boots still sat by the barn, worn and waiting. T+K was still carved into the oak bench behind the shop, the one that was sunbleached and rickety. Keira had nearly toppled it by pouncing on Tate the day they finally said yes to forever. And inside the house, decorating the refrigerator, were pictures of the farm with every season she could imagine—snowy fields beside sunflowers, pumpkins growing next to lambs.

Gracie sometimes played a quiet game with herself as they walked. She called it *The Three Things*. A gentle challenge to herself each day: name three things that endured from the day before.

1. Millie's laugh when Fletcher tickled her, tucking her in at night

2. The curve of Aisla's pearls in the mirror before tea

3. Fletcher's voice, quietly singing a lullaby to Clark in the nursery

Sometimes the list was short, sometimes it went longer than the walk itself. They were mostly simple things that made her wonder, *What would Aisla say if she saw all this?*

As Millie darted across the field with Winter trailing in delight, and Clark debated worm-naming protocol from his throne of dandelions, Gracie tilted her face toward the sun. The breeze teased the edge of the blanket, and the pear in her palm had gone warm. Fletcher was sketching something into his notebook—not notes for work, but the outline of a cradle base he swore would be finished by Keira's due date.

Gracie took a slow breath. The sky had looked almost too blue, as she watched Clark loop his little belt around a stick and proclaim it a bug harness.

Their life had lapsed into something small and honest. There was nothing grand and majestic, but there were awe-inspiring moments every day. Little bits of magic sprinkled throughout their time together.

It reminded Gracie a lot of how things were when she was just a girl. It hadn't been hard to adjust back to that. Even for Fletcher, who had always said Edinburgh was the place he pictured himself living; where he pictured himself dying.

Now, sitting in the tall grass, the pearl necklace resting like a tether to every woman who'd loved and lost and dared to build again, Gracie added today's final thing to the list. Not written. Just felt.

This—this blanket, this sky, this moment where joy didn't feel borrowed.

Fletcher leaned over and kissed her temple. "Everything alright?" he asked softly, pencil paused mid-curve.

Gracie smiled. "I was just adding."

"To the list?"

"To the life."

# Acknowledgements

For those of you who weren't around when I was beating my brains out trying to finish this novel, please know that it didn't come fast. It didn't come easy. But the time I spent with these characters was something so special and, when I got to chapter twenty-nine, I realized that I never wanted this story to end. Alas, Fletcher and Gracie were always meant to have an HEA, and I was obligated to give it to them no matter how many more chapters I could've written.

I have to thank my entire family for this one, especially my husband. As always. Thank you, my love, for listening to my crazy ideas and bending to my wanderlust even when it's not always the most convenient. Without our trip to Scotland, this novel wouldn't exist and that would be tragic. There is no doubt in my mind that it's one of those places that can never be explored enough, and I can't wait for us to go back one day.

My oldest daughter, Charlie, you're such a creative storyteller in your own right and I am always so grateful when we have our chats about what I should name people in my books or what they should look like. You keep me laughing and that's something I treasure. Don't grow up too fast.

Thank you to literally everyone who has said something nice about *When Tides Meet*, my debut and the first book in this series of standalones. I never meant to start a series, but here we are, and I wouldn't trade it.

Huge hugs to Romancelandia (Centreville, MD), The Spice Cabinet by Em and Bee (Wallingford, CT), and Pages & Peonies (Grand Rapids, MI) for being the first ever bookstores to take a chance on me and giving me the opportunity to be sold in stores. You have my gratitude forever. Indie bookstores deserve all the love.

To the Bentonville Arkansas Public Library, and Tara specifically, thanks for fostering my love of research and letting me geek out every time I walk through your doors. The fact that I actually went into the genealogy room for this project made me feel extra nostalgic. Grandpa Leslie, you and all the searching you've done over the years for long lost family members definitely inspired some of this story. Now, somehow all those times we went for drives to random cemeteries don't seem so silly.

To my mother-in-law, Jeanette, who passed away during the dark times of Covid-19. I think she would've loved this book, especially with Scotch-Irish heritage and her binders full of info from Ancestry.com—oh, how I'd have loved to pick your brain for this one. Love you.

Kudos to @bookclubcaines for the idea to write a man with a cloak into the story line. Kenneth was always going to be a loner in the woods and that element totally leveled him up.

To my beta readers—each of you is my hero! So much of the depth and clarity in this story is there because it passed through you. Reading your reactions and suggestions was a delight. Let's do it again!

I'm thankful to everyone who has picked up, read, reviewed, and recommended my work. Can't wait to keep sharing stories with all of you. There's more where this came from!

# Fletcher's Chantilly Cream

<u>Equipment:</u>
- electric beaters
- a deep bowl

<u>Ingredients:</u>
- 1 cup cold heavy cream
- 2 Tbsp powdered sugar
- 1 tsp vanilla extract or paste

<u>Instructions:</u>
1. Put the cold cream, powdered sugar, and vanilla into a deep bowl.
2. Start beating on a medium speed, a medium speed will allow you to have more control over the process.
3. Continue beating on a medium setting until you see the beaters leaving trailing marks in the cream. This can take 2-3 minutes or so.
4. Lower the speed of your beaters and carefully continue beating, checking the cream every 5 seconds or so. Lift the beaters to see if the cream stands in 'stiff' peaks. Once you see that, stop beating.
5. Your Chantilly cream is ready to pipe or 'plop' onto your dessert. You can also refrigerate it, tightly covered, for up to 2 days. Note that it is a better choice to whip the cream the day you want to use it.

Quintana McConnell writes emotionally resonant fiction. Her stories are rooted in slow-burn intimacy and layered character journeys, often told with restraint and poetic clarity. She invites readers into spaces where emotional truth takes center stage.

A self-proclaimed mood reader and avid traveler, she draws inspiration from life's journeys—whether on a scenic hiking trail or enjoying new foods. Quintana values building genuine connections with her readers, often sharing her personal insights and inspirations along her writing journey via social media @quintanamcconnellauthor.

Her passion lies in creating stories that feel like safe harbors —places where readers can linger, reflect, and feel seen.